D0464586

SWIM THE FLY

SWIM THE FLY

★ ★ ★

DON CALAME

CANDLEWICK PRESS

First edition 2009

Library of Congress Cataloging-in-Publication Data is available.

Library of Congress Catalog Card Number 2009920818

ISBN 978-0-7636-4157-3

2 4 6 8 10 9 7 5 3 1

Printed in the United States of America

This book was typeset in Melior.

Candlewick Press
99 Dover Street
Somerville, Massachusetts 02144

visit us at www.candlewick.com

To my wife, "bossy boots"—
thank you for insisting I write this book.

CHAPTER ONE

SWIM TEAM

Movies don't count," Cooper says. "The Internet doesn't count. Magazines don't count. A real, live naked girl. That's the deal. That's our goal for this summer."

"Been there, done that," Sean says.

"Taking baths with your sister doesn't count, either, Sean." Cooper snorts.

"Screw you, meat stain. I haven't done that since I was, like, two, okay. And that's not what I was talking about," Sean says.

We're walking up to the pool. Cooper, Sean, and me. Bare feet tucked into untied sneakers, ragged towels draped around our necks. It's our first day of swim practice, which means that summer's really started. We've been friends since kindergarten. We've been on swim team since third grade. The Rockville Swimming Association. Six years as Lower Rockville Razorbacks.

"He's talking about Tina Everstone's left boob," I say as we turn onto Maple Drive and walk along the curb.

"Oh, please. Not that again." Cooper rolls his eyes.

"It's true. I saw the whole thing when she was taking off her sweatshirt during gym. Her T-shirt came up just enough—"

"And she wasn't wearing a bra and her left one popped out and you saw the entire thing, nipple and all, and even if I didn't think you were lying to us, it still wouldn't count," Cooper says. "I'm talking *totally* naked. Not a quick flash, okay?"

"Whatever." Sean shrugs and looks off at the run-down ranch houses like he doesn't care what we think.

"How are we supposed to see a live naked girl?" I say. "Maybe we better set a more realistic goal for the summer. Like finding Atlantis."

"Matt, Matt, Matt." Cooper puts his arm around me like he's my wise uncle. "That kind of attitude will get you nowhere in life. Don't you get it? You have to follow the natural way of things. It's like that picture in our bio textbook. First there's the monkey. Then there's the caveman. Then there's the human. It's the same with sex. First there's Internet porn, then there's seeing your first *real* naked girl, and finally it's the dirty deed. You do want to have sex someday, don't you, Matt?"

Every summer there is a goal. It's tradition. I don't remember when it started or why. But as long as I can remember, we've always come up with something we had to accomplish before the start of the new school year. When we were ten, it was riding our bikes fifteen miles away to Perry Lake and skinny-dipping. When we were twelve, it was going to the Fern Creek Golf Course every day until we collected a thousand golf balls. Over the past few years, the goals have become more centered around girls and sex. Two years ago, each of us had to get our hands on a *Playboy* and show it to the others. Last year the ante was upped to finding an illegal password for a porn site. And now, Cooper's challenge for this summer. Which I can't see ever happening.

Maybe if we were even a little bit cool, or had any chance of getting girlfriends. But that's just not the case. By the time you're fifteen, you've either had a girlfriend — maybe even had sex — or, like Coop, Sean, and me, you haven't even mustered the courage to ask a girl out. There's also a third group, I guess. Guys who say they've had girlfriends but who nobody really believes. Which just means they're liars who fit into the second category.

We make it to Rockville Avenue Pool just in time to hear Ms. Luntz, our swim coach, calling the team over for a meeting. Ms. Luntz is a gourd-shaped woman who wears her blue-and-white Speedo stretched to capacity underneath denim short-pants overalls. Her legs are thick and pockmarked, and purple worm veins bubble up beneath the see-through skin on her thighs. She doesn't make things much better for herself with her Campbell's Soup Kid haircut and gigantic pink-tinted glasses. You could almost feel sorry for her, if she wasn't so nasty to everyone.

"Hurry up, people," Ms. Luntz squawks. "Let's go, let's go. Before winter comes. We've got important business to discuss."

Cooper, Sean, and me make our way around "the toilet"—a shallow, oval kiddie pool that's always suspiciously body-temperature warm. My mom says it's warm because there's less water in there and the sun can heat it up faster, but nobody's buying that. Last year, Cooper bet Sean ten bucks he wouldn't bob for a Life Saver over the painted picture of Elmo, which is where most of the little kids hang out, and Sean did it without blinking an eye. It was pretty sick. Sean kept saying how they put chemicals in the pool for a reason, but there's no way I could have done that. I feel my stomach lurch now just thinking about it.

We walk along the edge of the adult pool toward the deep end where the diving boards are. I breathe in the sharp chlorine smell and watch the swimmers stringing the swim lane dividers, and it's like "Yeah, I know this" mixed with "Oh, God, not this again."

We hang back at the edge of the crowd that forms around Ms. Luntz. It's all the same people from last year. A sea of blue and white Lycra. Guys and girls from seven to seventeen. All of them serious about swim team.

It's different for Coop, Sean, and me. We do swim team because we've always done swim team. Between the three of us, I bet that we have the largest collection of green fifth-place ribbons in the entire league. It's not like we try to lose. It's just that we happen to be the three least athletic kids on the team. Maybe even in all of Rockville.

"Okay, so, welcome back and all that crap," Ms. Luntz says, tapping her pen on her clipboard. "It's another summer, which means another chance to make a run for gold. Our first meet is in three weeks. I want us to set the bar high right away. I want us to take first in this year's relay challenge."

Coop leans over to me and whispers, "Yeah, and I want to take a whipped-cream bath with Miss October. Which will happen way sooner than us placing first."

"I thought you had the hots for Webcam Pam."

"You've got me confused with Sean," Coop says. "He likes the chunky girls."

"Hey, she's not fat," Sean says. "That's the wide-angle lens on the webcam."

"Right." Coop smirks. "Besides, I've got enough plump stuff for me and Miss October both." Coop puffs out his soft belly, making it large and round. He puts his two hands on either side and jiggles it. "Ho, ho, ho," he says.

"That's sick, dude." I look away, back toward Ms. Luntz.

"We've got most of our team back this year," Ms. Luntz says. "Just one addition, which we are very excited about. Kelly West from the Dowling Dolphins will be joining us this summer."

I look over and see a girl standing in between Reena Higgins and Gordon Burrows. I don't know how I missed her before. She rolls a Tootsie Pop around in her mouth and waves at everyone. She is beyond hot. Short brown hair, bright green eyes, small round breasts. I feel my tongue and throat go dry.

"Kelly's family just moved to Lower Rockville last month," Ms. Luntz says. "She's a gold-medal-winning backstroker, so we are very lucky to have her swimming for us."

"That's not the only reason we're lucky to have her." Sean stifles a laugh.

I can't wrap my mind around this. I remember Kelly West from last summer's swim meets. She's a skinny girl with freckles and greasy hair and braces, not this hottie who's standing by Reena and Gordon.

"From Slim Jim to goddess in under a year," Coop says. "That's why you shouldn't slag the ugly ones. You never know when one of them will spring from her cocoon looking like a supermodel."

I haven't blinked since I spotted her. My head feels funny. My chest feels heavy. It's hard to breathe.

All of a sudden, everything's changed.

CHAPTER TWO

ADRIFT

EARTH TO MATT. HELLO? Is anyone home?" Cooper snaps his wet fingers in front of my face.

"What?" I say, yanked back to reality.

We're resting after our third set of laps, hanging on the wall in the far swim lane. Coop was saying something to me, but I zoned out. My mind keeps skipping back, playing the same thing over and over again. Kelly, Kelly, Kelly. All week long it's been the same. I keep trying to find her in the pool. Swimming breaststroke, swimming backstroke, drying off by the fence, shaking the water out of her ears, padding off to the bathroom.

"I asked you a question," Coop says.

"I didn't hear you."

"I know. I asked you three times."

"Sorry, I was spacing," I say.

"Well, focus, man," Coop insists. "This is serious stuff. I'm talking about our plans for this summer. You have any ideas who we could get to see naked?"

"I want to see Kelly. But alone. You guys don't get to join in."

Coop rolls his eyes. "Look," Coop says. "Whatever you're thinking about Kelly West, you might as well bring it home to the privacy of your bathroom because you don't have a chance."

"Why not?"

"Because she's dating Tony Grillo."

"Oh." I suddenly feel like a five-day-old balloon. "How do you know?"

"Sean heard from Cathy, who heard from Reena, who knows a guy on the Dolphins."

"Huh," I say. "Well, maybe they broke up when she moved."

"You're hilarious, dude." Coop pats out a drumbeat on the pool ledge. "If she dates guys like Tony the Gorilla, then she dates jocks, which means she doesn't date guys like us."

Kelly run-walks from the bathroom. She shivers, her lips blue and trembling, her arms and hands tucked up close to her body. She makes her way to the pool and slides back into the water.

"That's too bad," I say.

"Think of it as a blessing, dawg." Coop claps me on the shoulder. "Now you don't have to torture yourself about not having the guts to ask her out." He laughs. "Hey, Sean and I were talking about seeing a movie later. You in?"

I shake my head. "I've got to go to a funeral for my neighbor Mr. Hoogenboom."

"Bummer," Coop says. "Have you ever been to a funeral before?"

"No."

"Is it open casket?"

"I don't know. Why?"

"If it is, you should try to touch his face."

"Ew, dude, that's disgusting."

"It's not like it's actually him. It's just his dead body."

"Exactly."

"Just pretend that you miss him and you're saying good-bye. I'm telling you, dude, it's freaky. It's like waxy or something."

"I'm not touching him," I say. "What's wrong with you?"

"I'm a curious person."

"You're a disturbed person."

"Suit yourself," Coop says, shrugging. "But you're going to want to feel his skin when you see him. Don't ask me why. But you will. Trust me." With that, Coop turns and starts his next set of laps.

I don't move yet. I try to get Coop's gross idea out of my head.

I look across the pool and watch Kelly doing a perfect backstroke. Slicing through the water. Arms windmilling, breasts in the air, long legs kicking.

Man, oh, man. I take a deep breath and let it out. I push off the wall and do the only thing I can do right now: keep facedown and swim.

CHAPTER THREE

THE FUNERAL

I BROUGHT KLEENEX," Mom says. "In case anyone needs them."

My older brother, Peter, laughs and punches me in the leg. "Did you hear that, Sir Whacks-a-lot? She's got tissues for you if you get choked up. *Not* if you want to choke the chancellor."

"Look who's talking," I say. "They could decorate a parade float with all the tissues *you* use."

We're on our way to Mr. Hoogenboom's funeral. Mr. Hoogenboom lived across the street from us, but I didn't know him more than being kind of angry all the time. He never said "Hi" or anything like that. He'd just yell at you to keep your street hockey ball off his lawn, and he'd shut off all his lights on Halloween and pretend not to be home. That sort of thing.

Mom's at the wheel of our rust-bucket Buick. Grandpa Arlo's in the passenger seat, and me and Peter are in the back. All of us wearing dark suits that don't fit us anymore.

My sleeves and pants are too short. Peter's two-sizes-too-small jacket gives him a permanent shrug. Grandpa Arlo looks like a kid playing dress up, and Mom's buttons are one deep breath from being launched all over the car.

"I find a spanky hanky works well," Grandpa Arlo chimes in. "Saves on paper and you can rinse it and hang it out to dry."

"Whoa, TMI, Grandpa!" Peter crows.

"What's a spanky hanky?" Mom says.

"Nothing," I say. "Let's just drop it."

"No, you don't want to drop it," Grandpa Arlo says. "Not before you've washed it."

"Ixnay on the ankyspay ankyhay, Grandpa!"

Grandpa Arlo throws his hands up. "Ateverwhay ouyay aysay."

Mom just shakes her head.

I turn and stare out the window at the neighborhood passing by. I have to figure out what I should say to Mrs. Hoogenboom. "I'm sorry" sounds weird. It's not like it was my fault Mr. Hoogenboom died. "I'm sorry for your loss" sounds like I lifted it from a television show. Am I supposed to hug her or shake her hand or what? They should teach you these things in school. Practical things that you can use in your life. Like, how you're supposed to approach a hot girl. I mean, what are you supposed to say after "Hi"? And how do you hide the fact that you're not very interesting?

There I go again. My mind drifting over to Kelly like

a misaligned skateboard. Sometimes I feel like I'm not in charge of my own brain.

"You know who I feel bad for?" Grandpa Arlo says out of the blue. "Edith. Left all alone like that. She's a very special lady. She deserves happiness."

Mom shoots Grandpa a look that could melt plastic army men. "Don't *even*, Dad."

"Don't even what?"

"The woman's husband just died, for Christ's sake," Mom says. "We're going to pay our respects."

"I know." Grandpa sniffs. "All I'm saying is that Edith is an exceptional lady. And Ray Hoogenboom, however much of a grump, was a very lucky man."

"That's all you're saying?"

"You're very suspicious, Colleen. I don't know where you get that from. Your mother and I didn't raise you that way."

Mom gestures with her hand. "Okay, fine, whatever."

A hot quiet fills the car. Grandpa Arlo adjusts his glasses and strokes his white goatee.

"Of course, she won't be on the shelf very long," Grandpa says. "That's for sure."

"I knew it," Mom says, slapping the steering wheel. "You're going to hit on Mrs. Hoogenboom at her husband's funeral."

"That's preposterous," Grandpa scoffs.

"It doesn't take a genius," Mom says. "Everyone sees how you always flirt with her."

Grandpa shrugs. "I'm not going to lie and say I don't find Edith attractive. And you don't let a plump peach like that hang on the tree too long or someone else is going to come along and pick it."

I lean forward. This is getting good. "Are you going to ask Mrs. Hoogenboom out, like, right there in the funeral home, Grandpa?"

"Well, since you brought it up." Grandpa twists and looks over his shoulder. "I've been giving this a bit of thought and I decided it might be uncouth to ask her out on an actual date at her husband's wake."

"*Might* be uncouth?" Mom says.

Grandpa ignores this and works his tongue like he's got a tea leaf stuck to the roof of his mouth. He does that when he's rolling something around in his head. "What I *will* do, however, is wait until the end of the wake, then walk her to her car and ask if I might take her out for coffee tomorrow. As friends. To get her out of the house. To get her mind off things."

"That's pretty smooth, Grandpa," Peter says. "A date that's not a date. It puts her at ease. All the greatest pickup artists say you have to put them at ease before you can pounce."

"Pickup artists?" Mom looks in the rearview mirror at her oldest son. "What's happening to my family?"

"There it is." Grandpa points to the Park Hills Westside Funeral Home sign.

Mom makes the turn into the parking lot but misses the driveway by a few inches and the car thumps over the curb. She pulls into a space between two SUVs and shuts off the engine. Somehow she's got a cigarette out and she's lighting it before any of us have even unstrapped.

"Can we just agree to behave ourselves?" Mom asks, taking a puff.

She used to smoke Marlboro Lights, but she switched to these organic ones when she started her own NutraWorld Organics home business. She says the cigarettes taste like crap but they're much healthier for you and since they're so unpleasant she only has three or four a day. Mom works at the Lower Rockville Community Center most of the time, but she's been doing her home business now for over a year and she says that she has the potential to become a millionaire in five years. There's an entire closet in our house filled with organic products. Not just cigarettes, either. Vitamins and soup mixes and pasta sauces and shampoos.

"Can we agree on that?" Mom repeats, blowing a thick stream of organic smoke out the window.

We all mumble "Yes" and "Sure" and "Of course" as we get out of the car, but I can tell by the secret smile on Grandpa's face that he has every intention of following through with his plan.

The bottoms of my pant legs hover around my shins as we walk toward the funeral parlor. I'm glad that Kelly and her family only just moved to the neighborhood, because that means they won't know the Hoogenbooms and Kelly won't be here today to see me in last year's suit. I tug my pants a little lower and run my hand through my hair just in case.

"How did Mr. Hoogenboom die, anyway?" I ask.

"It was his feet," Grandpa says. "He kept telling everyone they were killing him but nobody believed him."

"Is that appropriate?" Mom says as she strides ahead.

We approach the funeral parlor and Grandpa Arlo holds the door for us. "Chop-chop. Look alive."

Peter and I laugh. Mom doesn't.

"I don't find that funny," she says, taking one last, long drag on her cigarette before flicking it onto the pavement and crushing it out with the toe of her scuffed black dress shoe. She blows the smoke out of the corner of her mouth as she enters. Peter, Grandpa, and I follow her inside.

The lobby is all gray and gray-blue and smells like sprayed pine and awkward silence. It's refrigerator cold in here and my body gives a quick shudder from the sudden shift in temperature.

A removable-letter sign in a pedestal stand greets us just inside the door. It reads: HOGENBOOM SERVICE — MOONFLOWER ROOM.

Grandpa squints at the sign. "*Hog*enboom?"

"They must have run out of *o*'s," Peter says.

"Maybe they thought nobody would notice," I say.

"Maybe they knew Ray's disposition." Grandpa laughs.

"Of all places." Mom shakes her head in disgust. "You'd think they'd have some respect here."

"Death is just another business," Grandpa says, then leads the way down the hall to the Moonflower Room.

The space is set out symmetrically: a square of seats on both sides with a row down the middle. This could just as easily be the setting for a small wedding if you replaced the coffin at the front with an altar. You could even leave all the bouquets.

There are probably two dozen people here, some sitting, others standing in clusters. All of them in Sunday church dress. Everyone speaks softly, like Mr. Hoogenboom is just sleeping and they don't want to wake him.

The first thing I do is scan the room for cute girls. You'd think that being in a room with a dead body might push those feelings down deep inside you. But no. It's like trying to force a kickboard to stay underwater; unless you give it your full, constant attention, it eventually explodes to the surface.

Mom strides right over to Mrs. Hoogenboom, who sits in the front row, surrounded by people with heavy eyes. Grandpa waits in the back. He stands up tall, smooths his hands over his jacket, and combs his fingers through his hair.

"Come on," Peter says to me, pulling on my coat sleeve.

We head straight to the front. I see immediately that it's an open casket, and that nearly-missed-hitting-a-parked-car-with-my-bike feeling rushes through my body. Cold, clammy fingers grasp the back of my neck.

Peter and I step up onto the raised platform where the coffin is laid out.

"There he is," Peter says.

At first glance, the body in the casket looks more peaceful than I'd imagined it would. Mr. Hoogenboom seems like he really could be asleep. Except for the fact that he's not breathing and is wearing a lot of makeup. The more I stare at him, the more I realize that the face only sort of resembles Mr. Hoogenboom. Like someone didn't get it quite right. Like in those wax-figure museums. Where you think maybe they used look-alikes for models instead of the actual famous people.

"You almost want to touch him, don't you?" Peter says.

I didn't believe Coop, but Pete's right. You do kind of want to touch Mr. Hoogenboom's face to see what it feels like. To make sure he's not there anymore. I remember when Sean and I found my cat Milkshake sprawled out under a bush. She'd been hit by a car and I had to feel her body to make sure she was dead and it felt cold but it also felt empty. Hollow. Like a piñata or something.

Mrs. Hoogenboom has placed a few things around Mr. Hoogenboom in the coffin. There's a dried, flattened white rose. There are two Buffalo Sabres hockey ticket stubs. There's a picture of Mr. and Mrs. Hoogenboom when they were teenagers, laughing and sharing a hot dog at a carnival.

"Can I ask you something, Pete?" I say.

"As long as it's not for money."

"How did you get Melissa to like you?"

"I don't know," Peter says. "She just liked me. Why?"

"Never mind."

"You've got the hots for someone?"

"No. I don't know," I say. "If I did, though, what would be a good way to get her to talk to me?"

"You do realize it's a little weird, you asking me this over Mr. Hoogenboom's dead body?"

"That's the thing," I say. "I can't stop thinking about her. She's like a pebble in my shoe. But in a good way."

"Does she know you exist?"

"I don't think so."

"I guess you have to get her to notice you somehow," Peter says. "The professional pickup artists all say you need to look like the ripest berry in the bunch. The most interesting. You should do something interesting."

"Like what?" I say.

"I don't know," Peter says. "But it has to be something big. *Really* big."

CHAPTER FOUR

SOMETHING BIG

Ms. LUNTZ BLOWS HER WHISTLE. The white whistle she wears on a black string around her neck like a talisman. The squeal of it screams in your ears. It's higher-pitched than most whistles. It's more grating. More piercing. There are rumors she had it specially made by Hungarian gypsies, whittled out of a human femur. And it's been said that each screech of her whistle is like a curse. I don't know who started the rumor, but I believe it.

"Let's go, people. Out of the pool," Ms. Luntz howls, her voice hoarse from all the yelling she's been doing during practice. She sounds her whistle again.

I hoist myself out of the pool and hurry over to my towel. Coop and Sean are close behind me.

"If she ever takes that whistle off, I'm going to steal it, tie it to an M-80, and blow it the hell up." Sean says this a little louder than he should, because his fingers are jammed in his ears.

My skin had adjusted to the temperature of the pool water and now the air feels icy. I wrap my dark-green towel tight around my hunched body. The towel is old and frayed. I catch one of the loose, wet threads in my mouth. I clamp down with my teeth and pull. The string doesn't snap, just unravels a bit more off the end.

"Over here, people. Come on, come on, come on," Ms. Luntz bellows, rapping her clipboard against the fence. "Before the next eclipse."

Kelly is only six people away. She pats her beautiful face, her smooth forehead, her little swooped nose, with her powder pink towel. I can't help but stare. It's like there's Kelly in crystal-clear focus and then there's the rest of the world, fuzzy and pointless.

I feel a smack on the back of my head. It's Cooper.

"Dude. Keep gawking like that and you'll be tenting your Speedo."

I shake myself out of the trance and follow Sean and Coop into the herd surrounding Ms. Luntz.

"Your effort today was pathetic," Ms. Luntz says. "Disgusting and completely unsatisfactory. Week one, I can excuse the apathy. But we're in week two, people. Continue on this way and we won't be able to beat a team of amputees."

Coop, Sean, and me share a look of disbelief.

"I expect everyone to step it up tomorrow," she says. "The workout I put on that board should not pose a problem." Ms. Luntz points to a chalkboard leaned up against the back wall, the words smeared and streaky. "You should be able to finish it with time to spare." Ms. Luntz fixes on us with her shark eyes. "I don't think three people got halfway through this morning."

I feel Kelly before I see her. Stepping up near me. Just behind my right shoulder. It's like she causes a wake in the air, warm and cool at the same time. My skin reacts. Tingling. Goose bumps. I have to catch my breath. It takes everything I have, every ounce of willpower, not to turn and look.

I can just see her out of the corner of my eye. She's right there. Wet hair tousled, cheeks rosy. I swallow the lump in my throat. I inhale, my lungs shaky, my head spinning.

"Now, to add insult to injury," Ms. Luntz says, "I just got a call from Mrs. Porter. Apparently, her brilliant son Steven chose to go dirt biking yesterday and broke both his legs and his right arm."

"Ouch," Sean says.

"Good thing Stevie's a lefty," Coop says as he mimes jerking off with his left hand.

Sean laughs but I pretend not to notice. I don't want Kelly thinking I find that kind of thing funny.

"I won't go into how idiotic it is to go dirt biking in the first place," Ms. Luntz says. "Or how selfish it was for him to do this during swim season. All I will say is that his moronic actions have left me with a big gaping hole."

Cooper is about to say something disgusting, but I surreptitiously whack him before he can get it out.

"The hell?" Coop says, giving me a look.

I shake my head quickly and motion furtively toward Kelly.

Coop cranes his neck and looks past me. He groans and rolls his eyes. "Traitor," he whispers.

I shoot him a death stare, but he just starts chuckling.

"So, then, I need to put this out to the team," Ms. Luntz says. "Who's going to step up and fill that hole?"

I clench my jaw and glare at Coop.

He bites his lip, trembling with stifled laughter. "Don't look at me, Fun Police." He holds his hands up in surrender.

I dart my eyes to the side. Kelly unwraps a grape Tootsie Pop and slides it into her mouth. The slick, sticky lollipop rolls around on her tongue.

I'll never look at a Tootsie Pop the same way again.

"We all know that over the past five seasons, Steven has finished second only to Tony Grillo in every butterfly event they've competed in," Ms. Luntz says. "And we're all aware that the boys' fifteen-and-over one-hundred-yard butterfly is the hardest event there is. But these are important points for our team to get. I know it's a lot to ask, but with the addition of Kelly to our team, I really think we have a shot at taking gold in championships this year."

Nobody moves. Nobody volunteers. A few guys shift

their weight from one leg to the other. A few clear their throats. Most just look away, not wanting Ms. Luntz to catch their eyes.

A one-legged crow lands on the fence and squawks loudly.

"Well?" Ms. Luntz says, machine-gunning her pen on her clipboard. "We don't need you to win. We just need you to place. Most of the teams don't bother entering a swimmer in the butterfly, so all it really amounts to is finishing. Otherwise we don't get a single point from the event."

I see Sean shaking his head. "It's a suicide mission," he mutters.

I stare down at the concrete. I need to cut my toenails. I curl my toes under my feet.

Without thinking, I look over at Kelly. She turns and our eyes connect. She pulls the lollipop from her mouth and smiles. I smile back. Her eyes are so clear, so green. They're the color of the water you see in those travel pictures. Where the man and woman are snorkeling and they're holding hands, and it's like they're the only two people in the world.

Kelly looks away, like she's shy or something. Still smiling. Her neck flushes slightly.

"Come on, people," Ms. Luntz says. "Who is the hero here? Who is going to challenge themselves? Who is going to swim the fly?"

And it's like some force outside of me suddenly grabs my right arm and thrusts my hand high into the air, and the words tumble out of my mouth before I know what's going on.

"I'll do it."

The entire team turns and looks at me. I feel my face get hot.

"Matt Gratton?" Ms. Luntz coughs like she's got a fleck of popcorn stuck in her throat. "Well. That's . . . unexpected. But I guess . . . we don't have any other option." She sighs, clicks her pen, and scratches something on her clipboard. Presumably my name.

I look over at Kelly, who nods and says, "Way to go," before she walks off.

Coop turns to me, blinking hard. "Holy crap, dude. Are you nuts?"

CHAPTER FIVE

MOMENTARY LAPSE OF REASON

YOU TOTALLY STEPPED IN IT," Sean says. "There's a reason most of the other teams don't enter swimmers in the fly. Because nobody can do it."

"It's his pants hamster." Coop nods. "It short-circuited his brain."

We're walking up to the mall. Sean wants to go to EB to check out the latest Ring of Light game. I can't remember if it's Ring of Light 3 or Ring of Light 4. I play video games but nothing on the scale of what Sean does. He came in fifth place in the Xbox Live Worldwide PsychoNinja Online Tournament. And fifth place in that is way different from fifth place in a swim meet where there are only five swimmers; there were thousands and thousands of people playing in the PsychoNinja tournament. Coop and I were pretty impressed. It's too bad you can't use a thing like that to pick up girls. Though don't think Sean didn't try.

"You don't honestly think that swimming the fly is going to get you anywhere with Kelly, do you?" Coop says.

"I don't know." I shrug. "I wasn't really thinking about it."

"Yeah, right." Coop laughs.

"Man, oh, man," Sean says. "You are up shit creek without a paddle, without a boat, without a kickboard, without water wings, without—"

"You can shut up now," I say.

"Yeah, Sean," Coop gibes. "Leave the poor guy alone. He already has it bad enough. You don't have to remind him how horrible it's going to be. How torturous four laps of butterfly are. Not to mention the fact that he can't even do *one.* You don't have to bring up the fact that he might drown. He already knows that. He knows how embarrassing it's going to be. Don't ya, Matt?"

"Thanks, Coop," I say. "You're a real pal."

Coop and Sean double over with laughter.

"You guys are feebs."

"Sorry, sorry." Coop can barely catch his breath. "Seriously, though. You're probably right. I'm sure Kelly finds the sight of a scrawny, pasty, white dude flopping around in the water like a spastic salmon very hot." Coop convulses his whole body, his arms flailing, his tongue waggling.

Sean nearly falls over in hysterics at Coop's

impersonation. And I can't help it—the whole thing is so ridiculous that I start to crack up, too.

We laugh ourselves to tears all the way up to the glass doors of the Rockville Mall. And I'm laughing, for sure, but there is also a drop of acid in my stomach that's eating away at my insides.

We spend about twenty minutes in EB, trying out the new games. Sean's Ring of Light game has been delayed, so he just buys a Demon's Basement strategy guide.

We make our way to the food court, flip a coin, and decide on Mr. Taco. I order a number four combo meal: a Burrito Excelente, chips, and a root beer. Coop gets the same. Sean gets the number two: three cheese enchiladas, refried beans, and a horchata shake. We find a table by the window and sit with our trays of food.

"That looks totally disgusting," I say to Sean, stifling a laugh.

"You don't know what you're missing." He scoops up a sporkful of cheesy brown goo and stuffs it into his mouth.

Coop unwraps his burrito. "Dude, didn't anyone ever tell you never to order the number two at a Mexican restaurant?"

"Screw you, okay?" Sean says. "It's not my fault they call it a number two."

"It's your fault you ordered it," Coop says, laughing.

"Yeah, well, it's your fault you're such a butt-wipe, so . . ."

Coop and I share a look. It's almost unfair, ragging on Sean when his arsenal of put-downs is so lame.

Coop clears his throat. "Okay, moving right along." He takes a sip of his root beer. "It's time to get down to business. We've got less than two months to figure out how to see a naked babe. In the flesh. Who has any ideas?"

We all think for a minute, eating and drinking in silence.

"Okay. I know," Sean says, sitting up tall. "We could get fake IDs and sneak into a strip club."

Coop teeter-totters his head. "That might work for me. Because I look mature. But Matt here's got a baby face." Coop scrunches up my cheeks with his free hand and I smack it away.

"And you're like, what, three feet tall, Sean?" Coop continues. "I guess you could sneak through the bouncer's legs, but where does that leave poor Matt?"

"Why do you always have to be such a load?" Sean slurps his shake.

"You should talk. You are what you eat." Coop points at Sean's plate of burnt sienna mush.

"That's like the *second* funniest thing ever. Right after your face," Sean says.

Coop laughs. "Dude, we're gonna have to work on your comebacks or you're never going to survive in this world."

"What about binoculars?" I say. "We could spy on Mandy Reagan's house."

"I don't know." Coop screws up his face.

"She's the hottest girl in school."

"True. But her dad's a gun freak. I heard he's a crack shot, too. Still, it might be worth it. Almost."

Sean wipes his hands on his napkin. "Mandy takes tae kwon do at the community center."

"That's great, Sean," Coop says. "What other interesting facts do you know about her?"

"I'm saying we could hide in the girls' locker room, douche."

"That's your brilliant idea?" Coop laughs. "And *I'm* the douche?"

I check my cell. It's three thirty. I need to get to the pool before dinner.

"I have to go." I stand and pick up my tray.

"Whoa. We're not done here yet," Coop says. "Sean's still working on his number two. And we have to finish formulating our plan."

I shrug. "I still have to go."

"What's more important than this?" Coop gestures toward the table.

"I'm gonna go practice my butterfly, okay? You happy?"

I walk over to the trash and empty my tray. Coop and Sean hoot with laughter just like I knew they would.

"Why bother, dude?" Coop says.

"Yeah, it's not like it's going to help." Sean grins.

I sigh. "I know it's a long shot, but I'm hoping that if

I practice hard enough over the next few weeks, maybe I won't make a total ass of myself by the time championships roll around."

"Okay, well . . ." Coop bites his lower lip to stop himself from cracking up. "You give us a call when you've rejoined us here on planet Earth."

This causes Sean to choke on his shake mid-sip.

I don't bother responding. I just turn and go.

CHAPTER SIX

DEAD ARM

I CATCH THE THICK SMELL of meat loaf as soon as I enter the house. It's only four o'clock. We never eat before six. Something's up.

I head into the kitchen, where Grandpa's in his usual position, hunched over the table, playing solitaire.

"Hi, Grandpa," I say.

"Don't talk to me. I'm on a roll." He counts out three cards and flips them over. "Goddamn it. You jinxed me."

"Ignore him. He's just grouchy," Mom says. She's in her peach-patterned apron, at the stove, adding milk to a pot of boiled potatoes. "Mrs. Hoogenboom decided she didn't feel like going for coffee today after all. Go figure."

"Sorry, Grandpa."

Grandpa Arlo waves this off. "Please. You think I'm discouraged? Nothing worth getting is easy." He shuffles the cards and starts dealing them out again.

"I'm glad you're home," Mom says, adding a few shakes of salt to the pot. "I forgot to tell you. I've got a

NutraWorld meeting tonight. They're introducing a new product. An organic laxative. Everyone's very excited."

"You don't want to get too excited where laxatives are concerned," Grandpa says, moving a red jack onto a black queen. "Trust me."

Mom ignores this. "We're having an early dinner."

"I just had a burrito at the mall," I say.

"That's fine." Mom grabs the masher and starts in on the potatoes. "You'll sit with us and you can have leftovers later."

"But I was gonna go to the pool."

Mom stops mid-mash and looks at me. "We eat dinner as a family. You know how I feel about that."

The thing about having a father who leaves your mother for a younger woman is that it's not only a cliché; it's also a pain in the ass. It makes you feel so bad for your mom that you can't argue any of her rules anymore. Especially the ones from after the divorce. Like this "we eat as a family" rule. What are you supposed to say to that?

Still, I have to get to the pool before it closes. I need to get in some practice before anyone on the swim team sees that I can't actually do the butterfly. Especially Kelly. I figure if I can work on my fly every afternoon for the next month or so, I'll eventually be able to do it well enough to try it at swim practice. And, hopefully, championships.

"When will it be ready?" I say, glancing at the rooster clock on the wall.

"Fifteen minutes."

I do the math. Eat at four fifteen. An hour for dinner and cleanup. Five fifteen. Ten minutes to the pool. Pool closes at six. That'll give me thirty-five minutes to practice if I get right to it.

"Would you tell your brother and Melissa dinner's almost ready?" Mom asks. "They're up in his room."

"Goddamn two of diamonds," Grandpa says, smacking his pile of discards.

I leave the kitchen and cross through the dining room. Climb the stairs and turn left down the hall. Pete's bedroom door is shut, so I lean in and listen to make sure I'm not interrupting anything. There are whispers coming from inside, and then Melissa laughs and there's the creak of the bed. I lean in a little closer and listen a little harder. Melissa laughs again and I'm imagining all kinds of things going on in there.

I hold my breath and get down on the floor, careful not to make any noise. I move my ear close to the open space between the door and the carpet. I feel a cool breeze on my cheek. They must have the window open. There's more movement in the bedroom, the squeak of the mattress, more whispers. I shift a little to try and hear better.

And that's when the lock snicks and the door opens and my heart leaps into my mouth. I scramble to my feet.

"Whatcha doing there, Matt?" Melissa asks. She steps out of the room and closes the door behind her.

"Oh. I thought I felt a, uh, wet spot on the carpet," I say. "I was checking to see if maybe Scratchy had gone there. Again. Sometimes she does. We haven't gotten her completely litter-trained yet."

Melissa is a tiny Italian mouse-girl with short straight black hair, a pinched pierced nose, and a whisper of a mustache and sideburns.

"A wet spot, huh?" Melissa asks. "From the cat?"

"Yeah," I say. "But I was wrong. I must have imagined it."

Melissa is wearing what she always wears: pink designer sweatpants and a tight white ribbed T-shirt, which hints at her dark nipples underneath. You'd think that nipples, being so small, would be as easy to ignore as almost anything else, but it's like they're eye magnets or something. I can look at her face if I'm really thinking about it but lose concentration for a split second and forget about it. I'm like a cat trying to ignore a piece of string.

"Up here, Matt." Melissa leans over to catch my eyes.

I blink hard and try to act cool. "Oh, sorry, I was just . . . thinking. I was trying to remember something."

"And you thought it was written on my chest? Let me give you a little clue here, Mattie," Melissa says. "Girls don't mind if you notice their breasts. Noticing can be flattering. Staring is creepy. You don't want to be creepy."

"No," I say, feeling my entire body burn. God, why does she have to wear stuff like that? "I wasn't . . . I was just . . . Dinner's going to be ready in fifteen minutes. That's what I was trying to remember . . . If you could let Pete know."

Melissa laughs. "Matt, you're such a geek." She spins on her heels and pads off down the hall to the bathroom. The word LUSCIOUS is stamped in Old English right there on the butt of her sweatpants, jiggling at me.

There's a familiar swell in my pants. I have to force myself to turn away. When the hell did I lose all control over my body?

I drop my head and trudge toward my room. Melissa's right. I have to focus. I don't want to finally get my chance to talk with Kelly and suddenly realize I'm asking her breasts out to a movie. Notice but don't stare. Remember that.

I enter my room and shut the door behind me. I have to step around piles of clothes and towels and CDs and food wrappers and computer cables and books and my guitar and the guitar amplifier and I don't know what else.

I started taking guitar last year because girls go for rock stars. Although, if you listen to Mom, they're the wrong kinds of girls. But I figure, if the wrong kinds of girls are the ones that toss their bras at you when you're onstage rocking out, then the wrong kinds of girls are right for me. Anyway, I'm not ready to perform in public just yet. I can strangle out "Stairway to Heaven," but so can everyone else, so it's not really a big deal. I have to practice more. I have to start taking lessons again. I have to learn more current songs.

Coop and Sean and me are going to start a band some-day. Me on guitar, Coop on drums, and Sean on trombone and, eventually, keyboards. Sean's really the only one who can play. He's been taking trombone lessons in school since he was five. But he needs to start learning keyboards because the trombone never sends girls into bra-throwing frenzies.

We already have a name but we don't tell anyone because it's probably the coolest band name ever and it took us a long time to come up with it. We're going to call ourselves Arnold Murphy's Bologna Dare. Coop was the one who finally thought it up. It's based on something that happened in grade school when Coop dared this dirty Oscar-the-Grouch kind of kid to eat a piece of baloney off the cafeteria floor. Which he did. Coop changed *baloney* to *bologna* because it sounds better. We won't ever tell anyone what it really means; they'll just have to wonder.

I find my Speedo wadded up on the floor, still damp from this morning. I figure if I get ready now, it'll save time later. I'm out of my clothes and wrestling the soggy bathing suit over my knees when my bedroom door flies open.

"Knock, knock," Peter says.

I drop to the floor like a felled tree. I scrunch up to try and hide as much of my junk as possible.

"Jesus Christ, Pete!"

"Hey, it's not my fault," Peter says. "If you're going to be using your spanky hanky, you ought to lock your door."

"I was putting on my swimsuit." I try to hoist my Speedo higher but it's impossible in this position. I just end up rocking back and forth.

"Sure, whatever," Peter says.

"What the hell do you want, anyway?"

"I *wanted* to know what you were doing listening at my bedroom door. But you've already answered my question."

"I wasn't listening at your door," I say, rolling over and tugging my bathing suit all the way up, giving Peter a nice view of my butt in the process. "I just came up to tell you we're eating in fifteen minutes."

"Just enough time to toss one off."

I get to my feet and find my team sweatpants draped over my desk chair. I step in leg by leg. "Not for me, but it's probably fourteen and half more minutes than you'd need."

Peter marches over to me and whales me in the arm with his fist. "There. Dead arm. How do you like that, smart mouth?"

"Ow! Crap! I don't like it, nut sack!" I clutch my now useless arm with my other hand.

"Now you know: you mess with the bull, you get the horns." Peter turns and walks out of my room.

I try to raise my arm, but it might as well weigh a thousand pounds. Sometimes I hate my brother. Like, real, deep down, wish-I-could-beat-the-snot-out-of-him hate. It'll pass. It always does. He'll do something out-of-the-blue nice and all will be forgiven. But right now I want to push him down the stairs.

CHAPTER SEVEN

THROW IN THE TOWEL

DINNER LASTED A DOG'S YEAR. I must have looked at the clock, like, every thirty seconds until everyone was done. I took some meat loaf and mashed potatoes even though I wasn't hungry. I thought it might help pass the time. I'm regretting it now as I ride my mountain bike, vurping onions and garlic and hard-boiled egg. I hop the curb and race toward the pool. I probably should have just bailed on the whole pool idea, but I got it into my mind that I was going to practice and I couldn't let it go. The good thing about dinner lasting so long is I've finally got feeling back in my arm.

I lock my bike to the fence, kick off my sneakers, and flash my pool tag at the lifeguard sitting by the gate. She barely looks up from her magazine. "We close in twenty," she mumbles.

It's chilly tonight. There are even fewer people at the pool than usual. Which is good. I chuck my sneakers, towel, sweats, and T-shirt in a heap on one of the concrete benches.

I walk over to the swim lane and dip my foot into the water. It's pretty warm. Warmer than the air, anyway. The smell of chlorine fills my nostrils. It's always stronger at the end of the day. I don't know why. Maybe the water evaporates during the day and the chlorine gets more concentrated.

There's no time to waste. I clutch my goggles in my fist and step off the ledge. I drop right down and dunk my head under the water. When I surface, I push my hair back and slide my goggles on. I look over at the clock on the wall by the bathrooms through the blue tint of my goggle lenses. Five forty-two. I've only got eighteen minutes now, which means I might have just enough time to finish four laps.

In case you don't know, eighteen minutes is not a great time for a hundred yards of butterfly. If it takes me eighteen minutes at championships, I'm pretty sure I'll be asked to stop. Tony Grillo's best time last year was fifty-six seconds. That's a record time for the Rockville Swimming Association. Ms. Luntz told me. I didn't ask.

The swimming lane is all mine. I take another quick survey of the pool to make sure nobody I know is around, suck in a deep breath, and plunge into the water. I push against the wall with my feet and I'm off.

The butterfly is the worst stroke there is. It's pure torture. It's all shoulders and legs. You need good upper-body strength and powerful thighs. Neither of which I possess. People worry about me. How thin I am. My brother calls me the broomstick in a bathing suit. Mom's friends tease her about me. "Are you feeding this boy?" they say. I eat plenty, for sure. I can even eat more than Coop, and that's saying something. We had a competition once. Who could eat the most slices of Napoliano's Meatza. That's their specialty. A pizza with every meat known to God or man piled on top. Sausage, bacon, ham, pepperoni, meatballs, chicken, lamb, and steak. It's pretty disgusting. Coop calls it the slaughterhouse. He ate eleven slices before he did the growling splash monkey all over the restaurant floor. I ate eleven and a half slices and kept it all down. Sean couldn't believe it. He had to stop after only five. So it's not for lack of trying that I can't gain weight. It's just my metabolism. That's what Mom tells everyone.

Which is why the butterfly is not my strongest stroke—not by a long shot. My body is much more suited to freestyle. That's when I can use my wicked thinness to my advantage. Piercing through the water like a dart. Okay, not really like a dart. But at least I can finish four laps before sundown.

It's up with the arms and head, suck in a breath, and back under again. A hard kick with feet together. Weaving in and out of the water. You're supposed to look like a dolphin. Smooth and graceful. You're *not* supposed to look like a palsied whippet struggling for its life. Which is exactly what I feel like. I am all splash and very little momentum.

I'm trying as hard as I can but I can't get any kind of rhythm going. I'm completely winded and I'm not even halfway across the pool yet. My arms feel like soggy jeans. I can barely lift them. Finally, I give up and free-style the rest of the way.

I hang on the edge of the pool. My head is pounding. My heart is doing a drumroll in my chest. My lungs hate me. They have shoved me aside and are sucking air in and out as fast as they can. The meat loaf and mashed potatoes are quicksand in my stomach. My body is in full revolution mode.

This whole thing is a joke. I don't know what I was thinking. Tomorrow morning I'll tell Ms. Luntz that I made a mistake. Coop was right. I'm sure Kelly doesn't give a crap if I swim the fly or not. She'd never be interested in someone like me in the first place. So she smiled at me. Big deal. I probably had snot hanging out of my nose and she was just embarrassed for me.

It'll be momentarily humiliating, and then it will all be over. Ms. Luntz will announce to the entire team that I am letting them down, but no one will really care. She'll try to get someone else to volunteer. And I'll be off the hook.

I swim freestyle back across the pool. I feel much lighter. It's the right thing to do.

I get to the pool's edge, pull off my goggles, and

smooth the hair out of my eyes. I boost myself out of the water. A light breeze sends a chill through my body. I hurry to my towel and start to dry off.

And that's when I see her. Kelly showing her pool pass to the lifeguard at the gate. She's with Valerie Devereaux. Valerie moved here from Montreal three years ago, and Sean has had a crush on her ever since. He loves her long, rust-red hair, her full lips, and most of all her French accent. Valerie's a pretty nice girl, but rumor has it she's not allowed to date until she's eighteen. Which works out great for Sean because it gives him a good excuse not to ask her out. It also gives him the satisfaction of knowing that no one else is going out with her, either. Sean plans on growing another eight inches in the next three years, and he thinks he'll have a shot by then.

Kelly and Valerie are both in their street clothes. Kelly gestures in my direction and says something to the lifeguard. Did they see me doing my imitation of a drowning man? Are they coming in to laugh at me? I should have gone to another pool to practice. I'm such an idiot.

The girls walk past the lifeguard and head right toward me. There's nowhere to run. I try to think of what to say. I was just having fun? I was trying to see what it felt like *not* to be able to swim the butterfly? It all sounds so stupid in my head.

"Hi, Matt," Valerie says.

I barely look up. "Hi."

"I'll be right back," Kelly says. She gives me a quick

smile and continues on toward the pool office. I do a fast wipe at my nose with my towel just in case.

"You here by yourself?" Valerie asks.

"Yeah." I nod and force myself to look her in the eyes.

"Where's Sean and Coop?"

"Dinner, I guess."

Valerie watches Kelly as she disappears into the office. "Kelly left her sweater here."

"Oh." I brighten. Maybe they didn't see me swimming.

Valerie looks back at me. "So. How's your summer going so far?"

I shrug. "Good, I guess. You?"

"I got a job," Valerie says, smiling.

"Cool."

"It's just some filing and typing and stuff. At Dr. Malkin's office."

"We go to him."

"Yeah, I know. I saw your family's file." Valerie's neck and cheeks flush. "But don't worry. I didn't look at it or anything. I just noticed it when I was filing something else."

I've been toweling off for the past however long Valerie's been talking to me. I only notice it now because my skin feels raw. It was something to do other than just stand here like a dork. "That's great you have a job. I should probably get one, but I'm too lazy."

"That's not what I hear," Valerie says.

"What do you mean?"

"Kelly told me you volunteered to swim the butter-fly race."

"She told you that?"

"She also said it's the hardest stroke ever. I wouldn't call that lazy."

"Maybe just insane." I drop my towel and start to put on my sweats. Something else to do.

Kelly comes out of the office carrying her green sweater. She walks over and smiles. "Hey."

"Hey." I give a quick lift of the chin.

Kelly shifts her weight and looks at me. "You come to the pool by yourself a lot?"

"Oh," I say, and shake my head. "No. I was just getting in some extra practice." I feel like I'm not in my body. Like I've stepped outside of myself and am being forced to observe just how much of a loser I am.

Kelly laughs. "I can't believe you volunteered to swim the fly."

"We were just talking about that," Valerie says.

I shrug. "It's no big deal. Someone had to do it."

"Well, it's pretty cool you stepped up," Kelly says.

I smile. "Thanks."

There is an awkward silence that balloons between us until Kelly pops it.

"Well . . . bye," she says, and waves.

"Bye." I give another quick lift of my chin. My smooth move.

Kelly and Valerie walk off. I try not to watch them, but I can't help it. They're talking to each other. I wish I knew what they were saying. They laugh. At me? I try to focus on putting on my shirt. I need to take my time. I want to wait until they are well out of sight before I leave. I don't want to have to walk with them, next to them, with absolutely nothing to say.

I stand and collect my towel, goggles, and sneakers. I walk slowly toward the gate.

So much for quitting.

Now I'm really screwed.

CHAPTER EIGHT

GONNA FLY NOW

I WASN'T LYING when I told Valerie I'm lazy. It's been three days since Kelly told me she thought it was cool I volunteered to swim the fly, and while she's made it impossible for me to back out now, I haven't exactly upped my exercise quotient.

If I'm really going to do this, I can't waste any more time. I have to get serious about training. And if I don't make myself work out for a couple of hours every day after swim practice, I'll just wind up watching my *South Park* DVDs for the umpteenth time and never get anything done.

It's got to be around three miles to Orchard Lane Elementary School from my house. I figure I'll jog up there to increase my endurance, then use the monkey bars and the ring trek and the chin-up bar to build my shoulder strength. I'll finish off with fifty push-ups and a hundred or so sit-ups on the grass. If I do this every single day, by the time championships roll around in five weeks, I should be in pretty good shape.

I'm in my blue sweatshirt and my cargo shorts, sitting on the slate floor of the vestibule. I've got Bleedingtoe on my iPod while I pull on my old Nikes. They're sort of trashed, the white leather cracking, the rubber separating from around the heel, but I don't care. I'll just pretend that I'm old school, that I have to get back to the hood. Back to my roots.

I'm out the front door and jogging down the driveway, the music blasting in my ears. I give a couple of air punches. A left and a right. I'm in the zone. This feels good. It's different from running around the gym, feet dragging on the hardwood floor, wishing you'd forged a note from your mom.

There's a reason for this. There's a goal to be achieved. And the music is like a jet engine strapped to my back, rocketing me forward. I've got the song on at full volume, and I feel like I could run all day. All week even.

I turn the corner, off my street and onto Old Rockville Road. My heart is pumping. I feel the blood coursing through my body. I take another couple of rabbit jabs at the air. It makes me smile. I don't care if anyone can see me. They have no idea what I'm about.

I bob and weave, pumping my arms hard, picking up my speed.

Which I figure out pretty quickly was a stupid thing to do.

After fifteen seconds, I'm completely out of gas and I've got a carving-knife stitch in my side. It's like I'm failing the President's Challenge Physical Fitness Test all over again.

I cut my speed by half and focus on my breathing. Try to get into a rhythm to keep my brain occupied. Once in through my nose and twice out through my mouth. Chugging, like a train. One breath in, two breaths out. One breath in, two breaths out. It keeps my mind off the pain.

There's something exciting about taking control of your life.

One breath in, two breaths out.

Setting your mind and then following through.

One breath in, two breaths out.

It makes you feel powerful. Like you can do anything you want.

One breath in and—

Gack! Fthew! Goddamn it!

A bug just flew up my nose. And it's buzzing like crazy. I exhale hard and a bee comes shooting out of my left nostril, flying off unsteadily.

I've lost my breathing pattern now, and the full force of how badly out of shape I am hits me. I'm doubled over at the curb. Dizzy. Nauseous.

There's no way I'm making it to my old elementary school. Not today. I may have overshot a little with my expectations; I should probably work up to three miles. I straighten up as best I can and start walking back home. I'll wait until this pain in my side eases and then do my push-ups and sit-ups in the comfort of my room.

When I get home, I head straight to the refrigerator. I grab the water jug, pour a full glass, and suck it down. I'm pouring seconds when Grandpa Arlo shuffles into the kitchen. He's got on a lavender dress shirt tucked into belted jeans.

"There you are," he says. "Christ, you look like hell. You just run a marathon or something?"

"Not exactly," I say.

"Well, collect yourself. I need your help." He's polishing his glasses with a handkerchief. Ever since the funeral, I see Grandpa's hankies in a whole different light.

"With what?"

"I need you to be Mrs. Hoogenboom for me."

I'm taking a sip of water when he says this, and it goes down the wrong tube. I hack and cough and finally clear my throat before I can speak. "I'm sorry, what?"

"I need you to be Mrs. Hoogenboom. You know. Pretend to be her."

"Pretend to be her? Why?"

Grandpa Arlo screws up his lips. "Don't look at me like that," he says. "I need you to role-play with me.

Obviously my tactic after the funeral didn't work out very well, so I need to refine my technique."

I move to the fridge and put the water jug away. "What do you want me to do?"

"You're going to be Mrs. Hoogenboom. I'm going to knock on your door and then I'm going to try to ask you out to dinner."

"What am I supposed to say?"

"Whatever comes to mind. Like you're Mrs. Hoogenboom."

I feel my insides clench up. "I don't know, Grandpa. I'm not really good at that sort of thing. Can't you just practice in a mirror?"

"No. I need feedback. Look, it'll be easy. You'll see." Grandpa Arlo grabs my shoulders and steers me out of the kitchen, through the den, and toward the entryway. "Now, I'm going to come up and knock. You'll answer and I'll try to get you to come out on a date with me. But I don't want you to just say yes. You need to be cagey. Noncommittal. Make me work for it."

"Like how?"

"You'll figure it out as we go. Just think about Mrs. Hoogenboom and act how you think she would act." Grandpa Arlo fixes me with his eyes. "You ready?"

I'll never be ready for this. But I nod.

Grandpa Arlo goes outside and shuts the door behind him.

I squeeze my eyes shut and try to get in the proper frame of mind. I'm a seventy-five-year-old woman. How do I feel?

I don't know.

Tired? Yeah, that's good. And maybe sore? Sure, old people are tired and sore.

I look around and see a throw blanket on the recliner in the den. I grab it and drape it over my shoulders like a shawl. I hunch over a bit.

Voilà! Mrs. Hoogenboom.

There's a gentle rapping on the door.

I pick a piece of fluff off the throw.

Another knock. This one a bit harder.

I rub my sore, "arthritic" fingers.

Grandpa Arlo opens the door and sticks his head inside. "What the hell are you doing? Answer the door."

"If I was really Mrs. Hoogenboom, I wouldn't be able to get to the door that fast."

"Oh, Christ." Grandpa Arlo runs his hand down his goatee. "Just pretend you were near the door already."

"Why would I be hanging around the door?"

"I don't know. You just are."

"That doesn't make any sense. It's not like I was expecting you."

Grandpa Arlo sighs loudly. "Just answer the door."

I think a moment. "Maybe I was going out to do some gardening."

"Fine. Whatever. Let's try this again." Grandpa Arlo steps back outside and closes the door. He knocks again.

I pad toward the door and open it. "Oh. Hello, Arlo."

Grandpa Arlo holds one hand inside the other. He can barely meet my eyes. "Hello, Edith."

"I was just going out to do some gardening. That's how come I answered the door so quickly."

Grandpa smiles shyly. "May I come in?"

"Oh, um, yes. Why don't you come in?" I move aside, and he steps into the house. I close the door behind him.

"So, uh . . . How are you?" I say.

"I'm very well, thank you. And yourself?"

"Me? Oh . . ." How am I? "I . . . uh . . . Well . . . I guess . . . My husband just died. As you know. So. I'm still kind of sad about that. But otherwise, I'm good. The gardening helps."

Grandpa Arlo rolls his eyes skyward. "I must say, you look positively radiant this morning, Edith."

"Oh, well, thank you." I pull the blanket tight around my shoulders. "This is just my old gardening shawl."

"All right. Enough with the gardening crap."

"But it's my motivation. You said—"

"I said be Mrs. Hoogenboom, not Robert De Niro."

"Okay. Sorry." I take a breath, resetting myself. "Oh, this old thing? I've had this shawl forever."

Grandpa Arlo smiles. "It suits you. It matches your eyes."

"That's, uh . . . very kind of you . . . I . . ." I have no idea what else to say. "That purple shirt . . . looks good on you, too. It matches . . . the blood vessels on your cheeks."

"Nice," Grandpa Arlo says.

"What?"

He pinches the bridge of his nose, scrunching up his eyes.

"I told you I was bad at this," I say.

Grandpa Arlo opens his eyes. "So, Edith," he says, "I was wondering if you might care to join me for dinner this evening?"

"Oh, yes," I say. "That sounds wonderful."

"No," Grandpa Arlo scolds. "I told you to be evasive."

"Oh," I say. "Right." I swallow. "I . . . Um . . . No, I don't think I can."

"I just thought it might be nice to get out of the house."

"I don't feel much like going out."

Grandpa Arlo nods. "Okay, well. Maybe I could come over and cook my world-famous beef bourguignonne for you."

"Mmm, that sounds delicious. I'd like that."

Grandpa Arlo scowls at me.

I wince. "But . . . I couldn't."

"It's my great-grandmother's recipe. You'd really enjoy it. The meat just melts in your mouth."

"I see. Well . . ." Grandpa Arlo slowly shakes his head at me. "To tell you the truth, beef gets stuck in my dentures. I'd spend the entire night picking it out of my teeth. So, I'm sorry but I'll have to say no."

"Can I at least invite you over to my house for some tea? I make a mean Darjeeling."

I look at my grandpa for some indication of how he wants me to answer, but he just stares at me all doe-eyed. I decide to continue along the same path. "No thank you," I say. "I'm just not up to it."

Grandpa Arlo glares over the top of his glasses.

"What?"

"It's *tea*. You're telling me she wouldn't even come over for a goddamn cup of tea. What am I, a leper?"

"I was just doing what you told me. I thought you were going to keep trying."

"What the hell is there to try after tea?"

"I don't know," I say.

"Exactly. Which is why you should have accepted the invitation."

"Well, I'm sorry. But it's not like you were very convincing. I mean, all you did was make the dates less and less interesting. Dinner out, a home-cooked meal, and then tea."

"I was trying to be nonthreatening." Grandpa waves at the air. "You know what? Forget it. This was a dumb idea." He storms by me and heads toward the kitchen.

"Grandpa, wait. I'm sorry. How would I know what

Mrs. Hoogenboom would say?" God, I feel terrible. "Grandpa?"

But he doesn't say anything more. He just turns the corner, and a moment later I hear his bedroom door slam.

Part of me thinks I should go talk to him, but the other part says I'll just make it worse. I have no choice but to leave it for now and get on with the rest of my workout routine.

I kick my sneakers off and fling them into the coat closet with my toes. There's a crash, and a bunch of canisters roll out onto the vestibule floor. It's Mom's latest NutraWorld containers, which she'd stacked at the bottom of the closet. I start collecting them up, when I notice that there are two different colored cans here, blue ones and red ones. The blue ones say NUTRAWORLD ORGANIC FIBER LAXATIVE and the red ones say NUTRAWORLD ORGANIC MUSCLE-BUILDING PROTEIN POWDER. Normally I don't pay too much attention to the products Mom brings home, but this protein powder catches my attention.

I grab a red can and read the back. It says how protein is essential to the building of muscle mass and that one NutraWorld shake a day provides all the protein you need. I'm sure Mom wouldn't mind if I took one of the cans. They can't be too expensive; I bet one week's allowance will take care of it.

I carry the canister with me to the kitchen; I might as well get started right away because, as my pathetic run this morning revealed, I need all the help I can get.

The directions call for two scoops of protein powder to be mixed with a glassful of skim milk. We don't have any skim milk, so I decide to just use water. I'm sure it won't taste much different; skim milk is pretty tasteless to begin with.

The label says that results should be seen in eight to ten weeks. I need results a lot sooner than that, so I dump maybe a quarter of the can into my glass of water.

It's a bit of a mess because the heaps of powder cause some of the mixture to seep over the sides and drip all over my hand. I stir and stir with a spoon but there are still big clumps floating around in the glass. I try to squish the lumps of wet powder against the sides of the glass but this just makes more of the drink spill. I can't afford to waste any of this, so I give up and just slug back the shake the way it is.

It's got the consistency of batter. I have to sort of chew it more than drink it. Also, it tastes pretty awful. Kind of orangey and chalky. Sort of like a baby aspirin.

It's impossible to get it all down without retching. I have to force myself to think about something else. I settle on Kelly, and how beautiful she is, and how she thinks it's cool that I volunteered to swim the fly.

This works pretty well until the last, thick glob unsticks from the bottom of the glass and slides right down my throat. I gag a little, and a pasty orange bubble forms in my mouth. My whole body shudders as I try not to heave.

CHAPTER NINE

DISGUISES

Twenty minutes later, I send Sean a text to let him know I'm at his front door.

Come in, Sean texts me back.

It couldn't have been more than thirty seconds after I'd just choked down the last of my protein shake when Sean called, all excited, like he'd just discovered a gold mine in his backyard or something. I'd told Sean I was busy, but he said I had to meet him at his house immediately. Coop was already on his way.

"There's only a small window of opportunity," Sean had said, then hung up before I could ask him what the hell he was talking about.

I open his front door and am immediately nosed in the balls by Tug, Sean's hog-shaped brown Lab.

"Nice to see you too, Tug," I say, pushing the dog out from between my legs.

When you step into Sean's house, you're hit by a squall of animal odors so strong it makes your eyes water. His family has more animals than anyone I know. They have four more dogs besides Tug, and I don't know how many cats, and a parrot who's always cursing at you. Besides all the animals that they actually own, the Hances also foster pets for rescue services, which is nice and all, but I have to say, I could never live here. Sean says you get used to the wet circus smell and the noise and everything, but I'd rather not.

"We're upstairs," Sean calls out. "In my sister's room."

I walk through the family room, and the other four dogs come out of nowhere and surround me. Yipping and panting and leaping, and wagging their tails. There's a small hairy white one, and a bigger bristly brown and black one, and there's a collie, and some sort of German shepherd mix. Don't ask me their names. I only remember Tug's name, because every time I come by, Mr. Hance is always saying, "Tug, no. Tug, no. Stop that, Tug. Tug, no. Tug down. Tug off. Tug, Tug, Tug."

I give each dog a little pat as I push through the pack, so none of them will feel left out.

Then there's the inevitable high-pitched squawk from the corner of the room, followed by, "Assbag. Assbag."

"Back at ya," I say to Sean's parrot. Her name's Ingrid, and she's an African gray. Ingrid was a rescue bird that the Hances have never been able to adopt out. She rocks back and forth on the perch in her cage like she's happy to have someone to insult.

"Eat shit," Ingrid caws.

"No thanks, Ingrid. I'm not hungry." I should know better than to get into a conversation with this bird.

"Eunuch," she says to me, but I just leave it. You learn after not so long that the parrot always gets the last word.

"They do it all the time in the movies," I hear Sean say as I enter his twin sister Cathy's room.

"They also have zombies, aliens, and dragons in the movies," Coop says. "It's called make-believe for a reason."

Cathy's room is like a haunted mansion. There are gargoyles and dark red drapes and a zillion half-melted candles all over the place. Cathy used to be all pink and yellow and girlie, and then one day she went over to the dark side. No one seems too worried about her, though, because she's an honor student and she knows three languages and can play the violin and never gets into any kind of trouble. Mrs. Hance tells anyone who asks that it's just a phase and that you can't stop people from expressing themselves. So no one really says anything. They just pretend Cathy is still the same old Cathy and not someone who celebrates Halloween 365 days a year.

"It'll work—you'll see," Sean says, his head buried in a dark wooden chest at the foot of Cathy's bed. He's pulling out all of Cathy's old, pre–Addams Family clothes. Blouses and skirts and sundresses.

"What's up?" I say.

Coop turns and smirks. "Einstein here thinks he's got the perfect plan to see Mandy Reagan naked."

"I don't like it already," I say, looking at the girl clothes piling up on the floor.

Sean gets to his feet and brushes off his pants. "You'll like it when you see Mandy Reagan with nothing on."

"Sean's still going on about how Mandy takes tae kwon do down at the Community Center," Coop says.

"So"—I shrug—"you want us to dress up like girls and take tae kwon do? I'm sure she doesn't do the class in the nude."

"No, dill weed," Sean scoffs. "We dress up like girls, a little makeup, and then hang out in the women's locker room. When Mandy's finished with her class, she'll come into the change room all sweaty and she'll shuck down to take a shower and we'll be there to witness her oh-so-heavenly body."

I shake my head. "We'll never get away with it."

"That's what I told him," Coop says.

"You're both wrong." Sean turns toward the mirror over the bureau and looks at his reflection. "Think about it. It's not like any of us have any whiskers. Put on a wig, some frilly clothes, some lip gloss, and no one's going to look twice."

"My mom works at the Community Center," I remind him. "She'll recognize me."

"Let's just see how we look before you go nixing the

idea." Sean bends over and grabs a flowery blue dress. "I'll go first if you guys are too chicken."

"Are you sure no one's coming home?" Coop says.

"Positive. My dad's at work, my mom's at the dentist, and Cathy's over at a friend's house. We've got, like, two hours."

"All right. What the hell," I say, scooping up a denim skirt and a pink button-down. "But if any one of us *can't* pass for a girl—like, *really* pass for a girl—then we don't do this."

"You guys are freaks." Coop squats down and starts rummaging through the clothes. "But if it means seeing Mandy Reagan's sweater sacks, I'd dress up as pretty much anything."

Coop picks up a green shirt, then puts it down again. He finds a tank top but discards that as well.

"Just grab whatever," Sean says.

"No. I want to look pretty. Us plump girls need to be careful what we wear." Coop finds a flowing violet velvet blouse and a white pleated skirt. "This could work."

We all strip down to our underwear and start putting on the girl clothes. This is a little weird, I have to say. The three of us playing dress-up with Sean's sister's old stuff. I've never even tried wearing girl's clothes before, but it might be fun to see what I'd look like as my own sister.

"What will our girl names be?" Sean says, adjusting

the twisted straps on his dress. "I want to be Sierra. It's mysterious yet sexy."

"We don't need girl names." Coop tugs Cathy's shirt over his head. "We just need to look like girls."

"Sean's right," I say. "We need names. If someone asks, we need to know without stumbling."

"Fine, I'll just use my cousin's name. Dominique," Coop says.

"Nah," Sean says. "You look more like a Fanny."

"Oh, yeah?" Coop pulls down on his collar to stretch it out. "And you look like a sphincter."

"Okay, girls, enough," I say, zipping up my denim skirt. "Let's just pick our own names. I'll be Topaz because it's my birthstone."

"Dude, you know your birthstone?" Coop turns around in his velvet Merlin shirt and tighty whities. "You're already a girl."

Sean looks at himself in Cathy's full-length closet mirror. He turns from right to left to right. "I'm not going to lie. I look pretty good in this dress."

Coop laughs as he pulls up his skirt. "I'm not going to lie either, Sierra. You look *too* good in that dress."

"We need makeup." Sean skips over to Cathy's mirrored bureau.

"We need music," Coop says, moving over to the iPod docked in a speaker system on the bedside table. "Girls always listen to music when they're trying on their new outfits." He scrolls through the songs and smiles when he finds one he likes. "Ah-ha. Perfect. I should have been born in the eighties." Coop hits PLAY and rolls up the volume. There's a streak of keyboard and electronic drums and a familiar guitar riff and I realize pretty quickly that it's "Girls Just Want to Have Fun." The song is bouncy and ridiculous, and I think maybe this is getting a little too bizarre.

Coop starts to spin around, twirling his skirt so it fans out, and Sean starts rocking his shoulders and bobbing his head as he puts on lipstick, and then it's like, what the hell, so I start dancing, too.

The three of us gather around the bureau and start putting on mascara and eye shadow and lip liner. Coop finds some purple nail polish and moves to the bed and starts doing his nails. All the while Cyndi Lauper squeaks out how when the working day is done she wants to be the one who walks in the sun.

"Girls are lucky," Coop says as he strokes his nails with the sparkly plum polish. "They can grow up and they don't have to stop wearing costumes."

"What do you think, Sierra?" I say, puckering up my smudgy, dark red lips and batting my rust-colored eyelids. "Is this too much?"

"Not with a name like Topaz," Sean says.

"What's that supposed to mean?"

"She means you look like your name sounds," Coop says. "Like a cheap prostitute."

"Topaz is not a prostitute's name."

"Oh, sorry," Coop says, pulling off his socks and starting in on his toenails. "A cheap stripper, then."

"You should talk, *Dominique*." I grab the blush and start brushing it on my cheeks. "I think I saw you in that movie. What was it called again? *Waving Ryan's Privates?* Yeah, that was it."

"Good one." Coop laughs and accidentally swipes the nail polish brush across his foot. "Now look what you made me do, Topaz, you bitch."

I stand up tall and jut out my chest. "I need breasts."

"Don't we all." Coop laughs.

I bop over to the dresser and locate the drawer where Cathy keeps her underwear. I start pulling out different colored bras to find one that will match my outfit. I grab two bras—a pink one and a white one—that could work. I turn and hold them up. I'm about to ask Coop and Sean for their opinion.

But I don't get the chance.

"What the hell?!" A girl's voice—Cathy's—screams over the music.

CHAPTER TEN

PAYBACK

ALL THREE OF US WHIP our heads around to see Cathy and her friend Nessa framed in the doorway. As usual they're dressed from head to toe in black. They are both as pale as Elmer's glue, and they're both wearing black lipstick and black eye shadow. The only difference is that Nessa has about a dozen piercings and her hair is dyed blue.

Nessa starts laughing. "Oh my God, Cath. Your brother and his friends are trannies."

"We are not," Sean says through smeared wine-colored lips.

I am completely numb. It's like a switch has been thrown and I'm watching everything unfold but I can't really feel it. I read somewhere that if you get shot, you don't feel it because your body goes into shock mode and it protects you from the pain. I wish I could help Sean out right now, but I can't because I'm not here. In this room. Dressed in Cathy's frilly pink blouse and denim skirt. My face made up like a cheap stripper. Listening to Cyndi Lauper.

Cathy storms over to Sean and grabs him in a headlock. "You're violating my private space, lapdog!"

Sean struggles but he's no match for his sister. Cathy and Sean are twins, but Cathy got the better end of the deal. She's smarter, taller, better-looking, more talented, and obviously stronger than Sean.

"Let go of me," Sean squeals.

"Or what?" Cathy tightens her grip. "You'll tell on me? That's a good one. You're in such deep shit, Sean."

"Ow. You're hurting me."

"You're going to get a lot worse unless you tell me what the hell you're doing." Cathy forces Sean to his knees.

Nessa turns and looks at me. She smirks and raises her eyebrows. I can tell by the expression on her face that she can't wait to tell everyone she knows all about this. Coop, Sean, and me won't be able to show our faces anywhere, ever again.

Sean's eyes are bulging. His whole face is as red as the blush on his cheeks.

Cathy twists Sean's head farther than I think it's supposed go. "Careful how you answer. If I find out you're lying, I won't stop at telling Mom and Dad—I'll take an ad out in the *Rockville Herald*."

"Okay, okay," Sean coughs out. "I'll tell you."

Cathy loosens her grip just a little.

Sean clears his throat. "We were going to sneak into the women's dressing room at the Community Center. To try and see Mandy Reagan naked, okay? Happy?"

I can't believe he gave that up so easily. It's a good thing Sean doesn't know any national secrets.

"You perv," Cathy says, letting Sean go.

Sean stumbles to his feet, rubbing his crimson neck.

"Although"—Cathy looks over at Nessa—"it would serve the Virgin Mandy right."

Nessa and Cathy share a look.

They smile.

"Are you thinking what I'm thinking?" Cathy asks.

"What goes around comes around." Nessa laughs.

"Does your mom still have those awesome wigs?"

Nessa nods. "She sure does."

"Supreme."

Cathy turns and looks at Coop, Sean, and me. "All right, you deviants. Today's your lucky day."

Cathy starts to circle each one of us. Sizing us up.

"What are you talking about?" Sean says.

"Me and Nessa are going to help you out." Cathy grins. "We'll make you up to *really* look like girls."

"No, thanks," Coop says. "We already look like girls."

This makes Nessa and Cathy nearly spit up with laughter.

"Please," Cathy says. "You wouldn't fool a blind person."

"I'm gonna go get the wigs," Nessa says. "This is

going to be stupid fun. I'll be right back." Nessa turns and rushes out of the room.

Cathy nods. "Yup. We'll make you guys up real pretty. No one'll even look twice. And Mandy Reagan will finally get what's coming to her."

I have no idea what Cathy has against Mandy, but if she's on Cathy's shit list, I don't envy her one bit. I'd rather not wind up there myself, though I'm afraid this whole situation is going to land Coop, Sean, and me right smack at the top.

CHAPTER ELEVEN

THE LOCKER ROOM

THERE," CATHY SAYS, putting the finishing touches of blush on my cheeks with a flourish like a master artist. It was hard sitting still for so long. My stomach has started churning, either from nerves or from all that protein shake or maybe a combination of both. "You guys look gorgeous."

Coop, Sean, and me shuffle over to Cathy's closet mirror. With the new dresses the girls picked out and with the wigs and proper makeup, I hardly recognize us.

"Holy crap," Coop says, his eyes wide. "Sean, you look prettier than your sister."

"Watch it, loser," Cathy says.

Nessa isn't even trying to contain herself. She's practically barking up a lung laughing. "That is some sick shit right there."

"Smile," Cathy says.

Sean, Coop, and me turn around just as Cathy snaps a picture of us with her cell phone.

"Hey!" the three of us shout, holding up our hands, turning away.

"Now, I want a full report," Cathy says. "And don't forget the photos." She grabs her digital camera off her nightstand and holds it out to Sean.

He doesn't take it. "I don't know. Maybe this isn't such a good idea."

"One click and I can send this picture of you guys looking very girlie to the entire world. If you want me to erase it, then you'll bring me back a shot of Mandy Reagan gone wild." Cathy waggles the camera at Sean. "Come on, now."

Sean reaches out and takes it. "Why do you want pictures, anyway?"

"The Virgin Mandy fooled around with your sister's boyfriend last year, dork," Nessa proclaims.

"And when we hack into Mandy's Facebook page, we're going to need something to post," Cathy adds.

"Pound it, girlfriend." Nessa offers up her fist.

Cathy bumps Nessa's fist with her own and they both laugh.

"Besides," Cathy says, "you guys are gonna want something to look at when you abuse yourselves, right?"

This sends Nessa into hysterics. She falls onto the bed, muffling her laughter in Cathy's pillow.

"All right, girls," Cathy says. "Off you go." She shoos

us from her room. "And don't come back without the evidence. Or the whole swim team will be getting copies of your oh-so-pretty debutante photo."

This idea of Sean's is turning into more of a nightmare every minute.

Coop, Sean, and me scuffle from the room and hobble down the stairs. Walking in girl shoes is not the easiest thing. I'm lucky because I snagged the pink sandals, which are less constricting. Sean's managing pretty well in a pair of red heels. But Coop has it the worst. He couldn't fit into any of Cathy's shoes, so he had to sausage his pudgy feet into a pair of Mrs. Hance's pumps. They're still too small, but at least he could get them on.

Ingrid makes a loud catcall and flutters her wings as we pass through the family room. "Fresh meat. Fresh meat."

"Shut up, Ingrid," Sean says.

"Come to Papa." Ingrid caws.

We have to walk up to the Community Center because there's no way we could ride our bikes in these dresses. And it's amazing. Nobody even gives us a second look. It's like we're just three regular girls out for a stroll. People walk past us and cars drive by, but there's nothing. I feel a little more confident with every person who ignores us.

We're about a block away from the Community Center when I get a seizing pain in my gut. I wince and grab at my midsection. Now that I think about it, it probably wasn't such a great idea to triple the amount of protein powder I put in my shake.

"Tae kwon do is over at four," Sean says, looking at his sister's wristwatch. "That gives us about twenty minutes. What should we do in the meantime?"

"Let's just go in," I say. "I have to use the bathroom. I've got cramps."

Coop laughs. "Dude, are you getting your period?"

"Very funny. I just need to use the can."

"No way," Coop says. "You'll have to hold it. We can't be hanging out in the women's locker room for twenty minutes. People will get suspicious."

"Let's walk around the block," Sean says.

And so we do. We walk up to Woodgrove Lane and then make a right onto Redwood, and with each step my intestines feel like someone is tying them into knots.

"You guys ever have a protein shake?" I ask.

Coop recoils. "Matt, buddy, I like you but not nearly that much."

Sean splutters.

"You know what I'm talking about," I say. "The powdered kind."

"Oh, you mean for gay astronauts?" Coop says.

Sean nearly falls over in hysterics.

"I'm serious," I say. "My mom had this protein powder in the closet and I drank some of it and now I think it's making me feel a little sick."

"It's probably just gas," Sean says. "Because of your nerves."

"Yeah, it's nerve gas." Coop laughs.

"Try to burp," Sean suggests. "It'll relieve the pressure."

I try to force out a burp, but nothing comes.

"Not like that," Coop says. "Like this." He swallows and swallows more and more air and then makes a huge O with his painted lips and releases a long soggy belch that sounds like a growling bear with a mouthful of porridge. The burp goes on forever, and it has Sean practically in tears. It's all the funnier because Coop looks exactly like a girl.

When Coop's finally done, he's got a proud grin on his face. "It's all in the diaphragm. My dad taught me that."

The three of us approach the doors to the Lower Rockville Community Center and as we do my stomach cramps seem to subside a bit, thank God, because there's no way I'm letting anything get in the way of me seeing Mandy Reagan naked.

Sean grabs the door handle and takes a deep breath. "Here goes nothing." He pulls the door open and ushers us in. "Ladies."

Coop stands up tall and struts inside. I can't believe he can be so confident. I'm starting to pit out my dress; I can feel it. Girls don't sweat this much. I bet my makeup will start to streak soon. All of a sudden I know we're going to get caught.

"Go," Sean orders through clenched teeth.

"I have a bad feeling about this," I say.

"Everything's going to be fine," Sean whispers. "Nobody's going to notice anything. Unless of course you draw attention to yourself. Like you're doing right now."

"I can't do it," I say.

"Just think of Mandy Reagan. Totally nude," Sean says. "And if that's not enough, think of that picture my sister has of us."

I close my eyes. There's no choice, really. I step through the door and Sean follows.

We make our way toward the front desk and I relax a bit when I see that someone other than Mom is manning the computer. It's some guy I don't know. He's got earbuds in and is reading a beat-up science-fiction paperback.

You're supposed to scan your membership card before you enter, but most of the time no one pays any attention and you can just walk by and go straight into the locker rooms. People do it all the time.

Things look pretty good for us, what with this guy so involved in his book and everything.

Coop leads the way, strolling by the desk like he's done this a million times before. Sean and I follow, trying to act just as casual. It's a breeze making it by the front desk, and we're almost at the door to the locker room when the guy calls to us.

"Oh, girls," he says.

Oh, *crap*. He knows. Of course he knows. We might

look like girls, but we sure don't walk like girls. We should have practiced that. He's going to call the police or something. He'll take us into the office and my mother will be there when they pull the wigs off us and I'll be forced to tell her everything. I knew this wasn't going to work.

Coop, Sean, and me turn around and shuffle toward the desk.

The guy squints at us. He pulls one of the earbuds from his ear. "You think you could just walk right by me and I wouldn't notice?"

The three of us stare at the ground.

"You should be ashamed of yourselves."

My eyes dart over to the front door. I think about making a run for it.

"I put a lot of work into this new schedule," he says, pulling a hot-pink piece of paper from a display on the desk. "The least you girls can do is take one." He holds the sheet out to us.

Sean cautiously reaches up and takes the page. "Sorry," he says, using a fake girl-voice that sounds more like Mickey Mouse than anything else.

"It's all right." The guy shrugs. "But make sure to tell your friends. There's a lot of great new classes this summer."

"Mm-hm," we all say, smiling.

"Okay, well, have fun." The guy tucks the earbud back into his ear, sits down, and picks up his book.

We have to swallow our laughter as we enter the women's locker room.

It looks like we're the only ones here right now, which is good. It'll give us some time to scout out the best viewing location. The women's changing room is way different from the guys'. For one thing, it's all pale yellow. The tiles, the lockers. And it smells way better, too. Not like a ripe hockey bag. The towels are all rolled up and stacked on the counters. There are potted trees in the corners. There are even private shower stalls.

We've got about five minutes until Mandy Reagan's class is over, which is just enough time for me to use the john. My gut is back in action and I want to be able to enjoy my first naked girl sighting without these annoying cramps.

"Don't rip the carpet too loud," Coop says to me. "Girl farts are different. They're more like mouse squeaks. You go letting off sonic booms and we'll be found out for sure."

"Yeah, yeah," I say. "I'll be right back."

I make my way through the maze of lockers and toward the bathroom in the back corner. The door leading to the gym and the studios is just down the hall.

I've never been in a girls' bathroom before, either, but here it's not so different from the guys'. There are no urinals, sure, but it's just as much of a mess. Wet paper towels flung all over the sink counter. Toilet paper on the floor.

I'm still marveling at all this when a toilet flushes. I'm not so nervous now that we fooled the guy at the front desk.

I take a deep breath, smile, and start toward the stalls.

And that's when one of the stall doors opens—

And Kelly West steps out.

I get that plane-suddenly-dipping feeling. Sweat on the back of my neck. Thrumming in my temples.

"Hi," Kelly says, barely glancing at me.

"Hi," I say with the same bad Mickey Mouse voice Sean just used.

Kelly stops and looks at me. "Do I know you?"

I shake my head.

"You look so familiar," Kelly says. "What's your name?"

"Topaz," I say softly, looking down. "Excuse me." I move past Kelly, toward the farthest stall.

"Wait," Kelly says.

I stop but don't turn to face her.

"Did you take ballet?" Kelly asks.

I shake my head again. My intestines seize. I'm going to die if I don't go to the bathroom right away.

"This is going to bother me all day. I know you from somewhere."

I shrug and reach for the door to the stall.

"Just turn around. Let me see your face again."

If I can just relieve some of the pressure in my gut, I

could deal with this situation better. I figure I can safely let off some quiet gas at this distance.

I relax just a bit and realize instantly that this was a mistake. There's nothing quiet about it. There's a rumbling thunderclap in my boxer briefs followed immediately by full deployment.

"Ohmygod," Kelly says, her voice horrified. "I'm sorry."

I don't have to turn around to know that she's already gone.

The cesspool stink smacks me in the nose like a baseball bat and I feel the warm stew seeping down my legs. I waddle into the stall and stand there in complete shock.

What the *hell* do I do now?

....

CHAPTER TWELVE

MANDY REAGAN

I SNAP MYSELF BACK. This is not one of those situations where you want to stand around for any length of time considering your options. You need to do damage control as fast as possible.

I lock the door, lift my dress, and step out of my underpants before all is lost. I take a seat on the toilet and release the hell hounds. It's the worst case of the sputters I've ever had.

It's lucky I'm not wearing regular old loose boxers or things might be beyond repair. My tighter boxer-briefs have kept most of the evil contained. It's nothing I can't deal with. Things will be all right. I just need a few minutes.

Someone comes into the bathroom and starts gagging. "Jesus." The voice is muffled like the woman is speaking through a cupped hand. I hear her turn and leave. Thank God.

I've been breathing through my mouth ever since I got the first whiff, but I know that the smell is toxic, because I can taste it and I have to use everything in my power not to puke.

My initial thought is to put my underwear in the garbage, but I'm afraid that will foul the entire locker room and ruin our chances at seeing Mandy.

It's probably best if I just flush everything, briefs and all. That way the evidence will be gone and the air will eventually clear.

I stand up, lift my fully loaded shorts, and plop the whole filthy package into the bowl. I flush the toilet with my sandaled foot, and everything starts to swirl around and down and I thank God I'm rid of it.

I reach down and grab some toilet paper to start cleaning myself up, but it's the really thin, cheap kind and the roll is jammed into the holder so the tissue keeps breaking off into tiny half sheets. It takes some effort to unfurl a wad that's big enough to be of any use.

As I'm wiping up, I notice that the murky brown water in the toilet is still whirlpooling. It's spinning around and around, but it's no longer going down. In fact, it's rising. And fast. Before I know what's happening, the water completely fills the bowl and starts cascading over the rim. I hurl my muddied mass of toilet paper at the swell but it just floats over the edge like a barrel over Niagara Falls.

I haven't even come close to finishing the cleanup,

but there's no time. I whip around, unlatch the lock, and tear open the door.

The dark water bleeds out of my stall and into the others. It won't be long before the entire bathroom is flooded. I bolt out of there with a who-me? quick-stride and then weave my way back through the lockers.

When I reach the guys, Sean and Coop are waiting on the benches.

"What took you?" Sean asks in a hushed tone. He glances at his girl watch. "Mandy'll be here, like, any second."

"We have to go," I say, sneaking a look over my shoulder. "Now."

"Christ, what's that stink?" Coop says, covering his mouth and nose with the crook of his elbow.

I'm about to say something, but I don't get the chance.

"Overflow!" a girl yells, sprinting by us, holding her nose.

The brown water has seeped from the bathroom and is now puddling out over the locker-room floor.

Sean scowls at me. "What did you do?"

"I'll tell you later," I say through clenched teeth. "Let's just leave."

There are screams and shrieks and splattering footsteps as the girls from the tae kwon do class bolt right past us. Mandy Reagan is the last to run by. I'd forgotten just how big her breasts are and how absolutely gorgeous she is.

"Goddamn it," Sean says, slapping the bench and standing up.

We hightail it out of the locker room just as three staff members wielding a plunger, a toilet snake, and a giant wrench storm by in the opposite direction.

Outside, we slog toward home, the fog of disappointment surrounding us. I give Coop and Sean the short version of what happened, leaving out a few of the more embarrassing details.

"I'm really sorry," I mumble, surreptitiously pulling the back of my dress away from my sticky butt.

"Don't sweat it." Coop claps me on the shoulder and laughs. "It's pretty friggin' funny, dude."

"You won't be saying that tomorrow," Sean pipes in, "when Cathy sends that photo of us to the whole swim team."

Coop shrugs. "We'll just say she Photoshopped it. No biggie."

Sean's face brightens. "Yeah," he says. "That's right. You can do anything with pictures on the computer these days."

I haven't told them yet about Kelly. How she saw me. And how when she sees the photo she's sure to recognize me as "that girl who crapped herself in the women's bathroom at the Community Center."

And then I get the mother of "Oh shit!" electric jolts up my back.

I freeze. "We have to go back."

"What are you talking about?" Coop says. "No one's getting naked in that sump you created."

"No. My underwear. I have to go back and get them."

"The ones you plugged the toilet with?" Sean snorts.

"They're going to know they're mine."

Coop breaks up. "Dude, relax. They can't ID skid marks."

I run my hand down my face. "You don't understand. My name is in them."

"I'm sorry, what?" Coop says.

"My mom sewed my name into my underwear when I went on the school's Easter break trip last year."

Coop and Sean lose it. Spit flies from their lips. They double over.

"It's not funny," I say. "When they wash your clothes, they need a way to know whose is whose."

"Did she sew the days of the week into them, too?" Coop crows.

"Do you see me laughing about this? They're going to pull those boxer briefs out of the toilet and they're going to see my name on the waistband and then they'll show them to my mom and I'm totally screwed."

Coop shakes his head, trying to catch his breath. "It's a hell of a way to go down, Mattie." He grabs my shoulder again. "I feel for you, dude."

Sean is lost in fits of laughter when all of a sudden he stops. His expression clouds over. "Goddamn it,"

Sean says. "I just realized. Matt's underpants don't just incriminate him. It's exactly the proof Cathy needs to verify her picture. Why else would Matt's underwear be in the women's locker room unless we all dressed up and snuck in?"

"You're nuts, dude," Coop says. "You think an overflowing toilet at the Community Center makes the front page?"

"No," Sean says. "But this is Lower Rockville. And it's just the kind of story people tell their friends at parties. It'll get back. You'll see. Way to go, Matt."

"This was your stupid idea, Sean."

"To see Mandy Reagan naked. Not for you to crap your pants and then try to flush them down the toilet. What the hell were you thinking?"

"Fine. I'll go back myself." I turn to go.

Coop grabs my arm. "You go back there and for sure you'll be caught. Your only prayer is that they just don't look too closely. They find the underwear and say, 'Here's the problem,' and then throw them away. I doubt they're going to bring in a detective."

I sigh. "I hope you're right."

We continue home, with me tugging at the back of my soiled dress and cursing my life the whole way.

CHAPTER THIRTEEN

CONSEQUENCES

Sean, coop, and i make it back to Sean's house to clean up and change into our own clothes. It takes way longer than I thought to get all the makeup off. Even after I shower, I have to scrub my face raw to wash away all traces of Topaz. Sean's sister isn't around, thankfully, so we don't have to explain why we don't have the pictures of Mandy or why I threw her sundress into the garbage.

I bike home, taking my time, zigzagging from curb to curb.

As I approach my house, I'm prepared for the worst. I expect Mom to be standing just inside, clenching my soggy, soiled underwear in her fist, screaming bloody murder. I put my bicycle away in the garage, leaning it carefully against the wall. Just right. Check the tire pressure. Check out an old scratch on the frame.

When I run out of things to inspect on the bike, I head out of the garage. I get to the front door of our house and open it slowly, bracing for the onslaught.

I look around.

Nothing.

Mom is nowhere to be seen.

The only sound is Grandpa Arlo mumbling to himself from somewhere inside.

I make my way down the hall and enter the family room. Grandpa's hunched over the computer, hunting and pecking at the keyboard. I can't make out what's on the screen, but I could probably guess.

"Hi, Grandpa," I say.

"Jesus Christ!" he cries, jolting in his chair. He scrambles for the mouse and quickly shuts the Web browser. "What the hell are you doing sneaking up on me like that? You want to give me a heart attack?"

"Whatcha looking at?"

"None of your goddamn business is what I'm looking at."

"It kind of is," I say.

"And how do you figure that?"

"Because you're going to get another virus on the computer and then blame it on me. *Again.*"

"That was your brother who did that," he says, his eyes sliding to the side.

"Grandpa, Pete's got a girlfriend. He doesn't need the Internet."

"Okay, Mr. Know-It-All." Grandpa reopens the browser and finds the Web page he was looking at. "There. Happy?"

I move in closer and have a look. *TheFrugalRomantic. com. The top ten most economical gestures to woo that special someone.*

"It's stupid," Grandpa mumbles. "But I'm desperate."

"Which one are you going to do?" I read down the list. "Are you going to give Mrs. Hoogenboom something handmade?" I suppress a laugh. "Like a Popsicle-stick picture frame? Or a handprint turkey?"

"I'm glad you find this so funny."

I read through a few more ideas. "All right, how about sending flowers?"

"You don't think she got enough of those when Ray died?"

"Candy?"

"Diabetic."

"A beach picnic?"

"Anyway." Grandpa sighs, slapping his hands on the desk. "Now that you've sufficiently embarrassed me, I think I'll go for a walk." He stands and pushes past me.

I follow him to the front door. "Where's Mom?"

"She's going to be late. Some crisis at work." Grandpa sits down in the chair in the foyer and uses a shoehorn to guide on his loafers. "Which reminds me. Some Tim or Tom from NutraWorld called her. If she gets home before I do, tell her that they need her entire shipment of protein powder and fiber laxative back ASAP. Stupid bastards got the labels mixed up." Grandpa snorts as he stands. "I'd hate to see the sorry chump who drinks a tall glass of fiber laxative thinking it's a protein shake. Gives a whole new meaning to squat thrusts."

"Yeah," I say weakly, forcing a laugh. "That would be pretty bad."

Grandpa opens the front door. "It's just you and me for dinner. Peter's gone over to Melissa's. But don't wait for me to eat. I may be a little while." And with that, he leaves.

I make my way into the kitchen and throw some blueberry Pop-Tarts into the toaster. I should probably take this free time to go practice my butterfly. But I'm wiped.

I think I'll just crash in front of the TV, holding my breath until Mom comes home.

CHAPTER FOURTEEN

WALNUT

THE ROCKVILLE SWIMMING ASSOCIATION is a joke, when you really think about it. We only have three swim meets all summer. The relay challenge, sectionals, and championships. Which is already three meets too many, if you ask me. But for all the swim practice they have us do, you'd think that they'd want us to compete more than every few weeks.

The relay challenge is always held at Walnut Avenue. It's the dirtiest pool in the whole town. They only paint the bottom like every ten years, and there's graffiti on every surface and broken glass all over the lawn so you have to be real careful where you lay your towel down.

And I don't know what kinds of parties they have at Walnut, but they must be pretty sick, because you always find crushed beer cans and dead squirrels and used condoms everywhere. It probably doesn't help that there's a biker bar and a pool hall and a 7-Eleven right across the street. I think they let Walnut have the relay challenge because it's the lamest of the three meets and nobody really cares too much about it.

Mom's dropping me off across the street from the Walnut Avenue pool this morning so she won't have to turn around. I'm still waiting for her to bring up the underwear incident at the Community Center, but there's been no mention of it. Yet.

Mom lights one of her organic cigarettes as I step out of the car, grabbing my rolled-up green towel, goggles, and iPod. Normally, Mom would come to the meet to cheer me on, but they've called an emergency NutraWorld summit today to discuss the recall of the protein powder and fiber laxative.

I wait for the traffic to clear, then run across the street. "Good luck!" Mom calls out, tooting her horn. I give a quick wave as she goes.

The grass outside the pool is sectioned off by teams. The Walnut Killer Whales, the Dowling Dolphins, the Bronson Barracudas, the Upper Rockville Vipers, the Lower Rockville Razorbacks, and the Sterling Seamen. Don't ask me whose bright idea it was to name Sterling Avenue's team "the Seamen," but whoever it was condemned them to an eternity of ridicule.

Coop probably has the most fun with it. He never lets up. "I'd rather not swim with all the Seamen in the pool." "Look, talking Seamen." "Ew, the grass is covered in Seamen." He's gotten a fat lip more than once over the last six years.

I have to walk through several team sections before I find the Razorbacks' blue-and-white banner strung between two trees. Most of our team is already here. Kelly and Valerie are sitting on a big blue comforter spread out on the grass. They're flipping through some magazines. Kelly's got her grape Tootsie Pop going. Both of them smile and say "Hi" as I pass.

Valerie's little brother, George, swims in the Tyke Races, so even though she's not on our team, she comes to every meet to cheer him on. George is pretty good, too. Last year he won the half-lap freestyle, and this year he'll be swimming in a full-lap relay.

I find Sean and Coop sitting cross-legged on their towels, playing Texas Hold'em. Coop cleans Sean out every time they go at it, but for some reason, Sean keeps asking Coop to play. He says that his luck is bound to change someday. What Sean doesn't seem to understand is that it has nothing to do with luck and everything to do with the fact that Coop is the world's greatest bullshitter and has no problem going all in with a seven-two offsuit.

"Hey," I say, examining the ground closely before I put my towel down.

"Full house," Coop calls, laying down two jacks.

"Are you kidding me?" Sean throws his cards at Coop. "You're such a schween!"

"The luckiest damn schween you've ever seen."

Cooper laughs and rakes in the pile of quarters and dimes. He looks up at me. "Sean's done. You want in?"

"I'll pass." I unfurl my towel and let it float to the ground.

"Can you loan me some money, then?" Sean says. "I need to try and win some of my allowance back."

"No way." I sit down and place my goggles and iPod at the corner of my towel. "I'm getting a bag of Funyuns and a Dr Pepper after our freestyle relay."

Sean and Cooper share a look and are unusually silent.

"What?" I say.

"Should we tell him?" Cooper asks.

Sean takes a deep breath and exhales forever. "You tell him."

"Tell me what? Your sister hasn't shown anyone that picture of us?"

Sean smirks. "Not yet. When I told her what happened to you, she nearly peed herself."

"You told her? Why'd you do that?"

"I had to tell her something. Otherwise she would have circulated the photo right then. Anyway, she's not letting us off the hook. She wants a shot of Mandy and she doesn't care how we get it."

"Great," I say. "Now she's got the crapping-my-pants story to go along with the tranny picture. I'm going to be this year's Hot Dog Helen for sure. I'll never live this down."

Coop turns his whole body so he's facing me, his expression dead serious. "Dude. You have something way worse to worry about right now."

"What could be worse?"

"You know how every year the three of us swim the freestyle relay with Omar?"

"Yeah . . ."

"Well," Coop says, "you're not swimming the free-style relay this year."

"What are you talking about?" I say, a little confused because that's my only event in the relay challenge.

"Ms. Luntz took you off our squad."

"Fine. Whatever." I shrug. "I'll go get my Funyuns right now, then."

Sean shakes his head. "You don't understand, dude. You're not swimming the freestyle relay, but you *are* swimming on my medley squad."

"That's stupid. Why would Ms. Luntz do that? Sid always anchors the medley."

"He still *is* anchoring it," Cooper says.

"And Gregg's still doing the backstroke and I'm still doing the breaststroke," Sean says.

"Which leaves only one stroke for you, buddy." Coop is struggling not to smile.

My chest constricts. "No way. I'm swimming the butterfly at championships. Not today. You guys are just screwing with me."

Sean and Coop both stare at me, and I can tell by the pity in their eyes that they're not lying.

"I can't swim the fly. I'm not ready. I only volunteered for championships."

"Apparently not," Sean says.

"No." I shoot to my feet. "This is a mistake. I have to talk to Ms. Luntz."

I march across the grass toward Ms. Luntz, who's over by the bleachers, laughing at something Mr. Shanker, the Barracudas' coach, has just whispered to her. She smacks at him playfully with her clipboard. Mr. Shanker has this bushy-ass mustache that he's probably had since the seventies, and you can tell that he dyes it to match his hair plugs, because it kind of looks plastic. He wears his Hawaiian-print shirts completely unbuttoned, showing off his tanned, freckled chest and round belly.

"Ms. Luntz?" I say when I've reached the bleachers.

Ms. Luntz's expression shifts like blinds flicked shut on a sunny day. "What?" She scowls at me.

"Can I talk to you a minute?"

Mr. Shanker flashes a milk-white smile. "We'll catch up later, Darlene." He turns and walks away.

"Couldn't you see," Ms. Luntz hisses through clenched teeth, "that I was having a conversation?"

"Sorry. But I, umm . . . I just heard I was swimming the butterfly? In the medley relay?"

"Yeah," she says, like I'd just asked if I should wear a bathing suit.

"But I thought I was going to swim it at championships?"

Ms. Luntz laughs. But not a that's-funny laugh. More like a you're-an-idiot laugh. "We have *three* meets, Gratton. Someone has to swim butterfly in all three of them. Or maybe we should just forfeit those events. Is that what you'd like me to do?"

"No," I say. "I just thought . . . When you asked for a volunteer . . . I just thought . . ."

Ms. Luntz sneers at me, her nostrils flaring. "You *thought*?"

I can't tell if she's asking me *what* I thought, or if I'm actually *capable* of thinking. I decide to cut my losses.

"Never mind," I say, turning and walking off.

What the hell am I supposed to do now? I can't even finish a single lap of the fly. Forget about two. I'm going to look like a moron.

"Hey, Matt."

I look up. It's Valerie. Waving me over to her and Kelly.

I hesitate, glancing over at Sean and Coop playing cards again. The medley race isn't until later in the meet. I have a bit of time. But not much.

I walk toward Kelly and Valerie. "What's up?"

"Sit down," Kelly says, slurp-popping her lollipop from between her lips. "We want to give you a quiz."

"A quiz?" I suddenly feel all sweaty.

"Yeah." Valerie laughs. "To tell us which cartoon character you are." Her French lilt makes this seem much more interesting than it should be.

"I was Bugs Bunny," Kelly says. "And Valerie was Peppermint Patty."

"Come on. Don't you want to know who you are?" Valerie pats the comforter.

"Uh, yeah. Sure. Okay."

I guess Pete was right. Volunteering for the fly made Kelly notice me.

I kneel down in between the girls.

"All right," Valerie says. "I'll read the questions and you have to answer honestly. Kelly will keep track of your answers and then do the calculations."

I look over at Kelly, who's got a pen and pad at the ready. Being this close to her, it's hard to catch my breath. My mouth goes all cottony. I have to look away, be careful not to stare. Except my eyes keep sliding over to her. I need to find something else to focus on. A loose thread in the comforter. I'll make that my beacon.

Valerie sits up and folds back the magazine. "Okay. First question. 'What would you consider a perfect date? A romantic dinner for two. Renting a video and ordering takeout. A concert. Rollerblading. Or an amusement park.'"

Huh? What does this have to do with cartoon characters? They don't even go on dates. I figured the questions would be "Do you like to eat carrots, pizza, lasagna, or insects?" Kelly was Bugs Bunny. So what would Bugs Bunny choose? Something active. Something fun.

"Well?" Valerie says.

"Umm." What if I answer wrong? What if Kelly likes hanging out at home rather than going out? What if she loves Rollerblading? "Amusement park," I say.

Kelly writes this down.

"Really?" Valerie says. "I wouldn't have guessed that." She looks at her magazine again. "Okay. 'Which of the following occupations would you choose if you only had these jobs to choose from? Plumber. Teacher. Fireman. Doctor. Gardener.'"

Man, oh, man. These don't sound like cartoon-character questions. I guess Bugs Bunny would probably want to be a gardener so that he could get free carrots. But a fireman's cooler. And a teacher shows you're a caring person. Why the hell did I agree to take this stupid quiz?

"Gardener," I say.

Kelly snorts. She starts to write.

Gardener? Christ. Way to go.

"Wait," I say. "I meant teacher."

Kelly scratches out my first answer. She writes down my new one.

"Next question," Valerie says. "'You have the afternoon completely free. What would you want to do? Go to the mall. Go to the gym. Read a book. Go to the movies. Or sleep.'"

"Mall," I blurt, thinking about what girls like to do. Then I realize. That's exactly what *girls* like to do. I'll wind up being Betty or Veronica. "Movies, I mean."

"Are you always this indecisive?" Kelly sighs, scratching out "mall" and writing down "movies."

"No," I say. "Sometimes. I don't know. Not usually."

Valerie laughs.

"I didn't know the questions were going to be so serious."

"Well, we're almost done, so you can chill," Kelly says.

Valerie folds the magazine back and finds her place. "'What's your favorite holiday? Fourth of July. Easter. Valentine's Day. Christmas. Or Halloween.'"

"Christmas," I say confidently. Who doesn't like Christmas? Jewish people, I guess. Is Kelly Jewish? I have no idea. Damn it. Why didn't I think of that? What if she's Jewish? I should have chosen a nonreligious holiday. I should have said Fourth of July.

"Last question," Valerie announces. "'What kind of person would you rather hang out with? Somebody who is funny. Somebody who is good-looking. Somebody who is intelligent. Somebody who has a lot of money. Or somebody who's adventurous.'"

Great. Save the hardest question for last. All this

quiz has done is make me realize how little I know about Kelly. Other than the fact that she's extraordinarily gorgeous. I could say I like to hang out with people who are good-looking, but that's just not true and Kelly would know it. I mean, all you have to do is take one look at Sean and Coop to see that.

"I like all sorts of people."

"You have to pick one," Kelly insists. "Otherwise the test doesn't work."

"But I like smart people and funny people and adventurous people and good-looking people. It doesn't seem fair."

Valerie swats me with the magazine. "Don't be difficult. You have to pick one. Who would you *most* like to hang out with?"

"Maybe I'm not a cartoon character," I say. "I'm probably too complex."

Valerie and Kelly both glare at me.

"Fine. Funny people. If I have to choose."

Kelly quickly scribbles this down, and her pen moves wildly across the page as she does the computations that will seal my fate.

"Give me the magazine," Kelly says, holding out her hand. Valerie passes it to her.

Kelly looks at the magazine, then at her paper, then at the magazine again. "Okay," she says. "Here we go. You are . . . SpongeBob SquarePants."

Valerie chuckles. "SpongeBob's cute. A bit nerdy, though."

I feel my cheeks burning and hope to God they aren't as red as they feel.

"'You are the classic friend,'" Kelly reads. "'SpongeBob is the friend everyone wants to have and nobody wants to lose. You like to have fun, but you should try to avoid stressful situations.'"

Perfect. I'm the friend. The guy everyone wants to talk to but no one wants to date.

"That was fun, huh?" Valerie says.

"Yeah," I lie. "Although, I think I dress a little better than SpongeBob."

"How do you think I feel?" Valerie laughs. "It's not like Peppermint Patty's got the greatest fashion sense."

"*And* she's a lesbian," Kelly adds.

"Is not," Valerie says. "Besides, my mom's friend is gay and she's, like, the coolest dresser I know."

"I don't know what you two are complaining about." Kelly throws her pen down. "At least your characters actually wear clothes. I walk around completely naked all the time."

Naked? Kelly naked? All the time? Completely naked?

Oh Jesus.

I suddenly realize my jaw is hanging open. I quickly close it. Thank God there's no such thing as ESP.

My eyes keep darting back to Kelly. I need to get out of here. If I wait another minute, they won't need ESP to know what I'm thinking.

"Okay, well." I stand quickly. Think of something else. Hairy underarms. Mr. Shanker's belly. "I better get back to Sean and Coop."

"Wait," Valerie says, glancing at Kelly, then looking up at me. "Are you going to Ronnie Hull's party next Friday?"

I swallow. I blink. I look over my shoulder. I blink again. Stop blinking, idiot. "I . . . uh . . . No . . . I didn't . . . I wasn't . . . I didn't know he was having one." Brilliant.

"Yeah. His parents are out of town." *Naked* Kelly speaks around her *naked* lollipop, tucked inside her *naked* cheek. "You should come."

"It's gonna be awesome," Valerie says. "Me and Kelly are going."

"Yeah? Okay. Sounds good." I close my mouth and bite down hard on my tongue to try and wrench control of my mind.

"You can bring Coop and Sean, too," Valerie continues. "But it's BYOB. A six-pack should get you guys in."

"Great," I say. "No prob. We'll see you there." I smile and turn and stride back to Sean and Coop.

I take a quick peek down. Somehow I've managed to avoid putting on a puppet show.

Thank God.

CHAPTER FIFTEEN

MEDLEY

WE HAVE THE MASTER PLAN," Coop says as soon as I return. He's got this I-know-something-you-don't grin on his face.

"What are you talking about?"

"Wait," Sean says, holding up his hands. "First, tell us what that was all about. You were over there an awfully long time."

"They just wanted to give me this dumb quiz that's supposed to tell you what cartoon character you are."

"Don't tell me." Coop chuckles. "Marge Simpson."

"Very funny."

"Did Valerie say anything about me?" Sean asks.

"Strangely, no." I roll my eyes. "So, what's this about a plan?"

"Let's just say you won't be swimming the butterfly today." Coop laughs, leaning in and clapping my back.

"I'm listening."

Sean sighs. "How much money do you have?"

"Twenty bucks. Why?"

Sean holds out his hand. "We need it."

"What? No."

Coop lowers his gaze at me. "Do you want to get out of the relay or not?"

"Tell me what the plan is."

"We can't do that." Sean shakes his head. "If you're in on it, then you might give it away."

"How would I give it away?"

"You need to be insulated," Coop says. "If you're not part of the plan, then you can't be blamed."

"I'm supposed to just hand you my twenty bucks without knowing what you're going to do with it?"

"Do you have a better idea?" Sean says.

"Yeah. I could keep it."

Coop cocks his head. "How much is getting out of this race worth to you?"

"What are you going to do? Bribe Ms. Luntz?"

"Look, do you want our help or not?" Sean asks.

I exhale hard. "Fine." I dig the twenty-dollar bill from the pocket of my shorts and hand it to Sean. "But if your 'mysterious' plan doesn't work, you both owe me."

"This isn't the Home Shopping Channel, dude," Coop says. "We don't offer money-back guarantees."

"All right." Sean turns to Coop. "Let's get this over with."

Sean and Coop march off across the lawn toward the shopping strip.

I grab my iPod and start watching *Sin City* to get my mind off the fact that I probably just threw away twenty dollars.

When Coop and Sean return, they empty a big plastic bag of candy and chips and fruit pies onto our towels. It looks like a vending machine exploded.

"This is your plan?" I reach over and pluck up a Whatchamacallit. "To have a party?"

Sean grabs the candy bar from my hand. "Don't!" he snaps. "This is a carefully calculated formula. How long until the medley?"

"I don't know," I say. "Twenty minutes?"

Sean looks at Coop. "We're cutting this pretty close."

"Just get to work," Coop says.

Sean kneels down in front of the pile of junk food and starts sorting it out. He mumbles to himself as he places a lemon pie into a pile with a bag of pork rinds and a pack of malted milk balls.

"What are you doing?"

Coop grabs my arm, pulls me up, and guides me off. "You should be somewhere else."

"What's going on? I don't understand."

Coop flashes me a closed-mouth smile. "That's good. Let's keep it that way. Go on." He gives me a little shove.

I glance back over my shoulder as I walk toward the bleachers. Coop does a little shooing gesture.

This is ridiculous. I should just cut my foot on a rusty beer can and be done with it.

Twenty minutes later, the boys' fifteen-and-older medley relay is called over the loudspeaker and Sean is licking his multicolored fingers as we approach the gate to the pool.

"Did you have a nice feast?" I say to him.

Sean lets out a ferocious belch.

"Maybe you can at least tell me when your little plan's supposed to kick into gear. Because the race is about to start, in case you haven't noticed."

"Relax," Sean says.

We walk by the Dolphins' relay team standing by starting block one, and that's when I see their butter-flyer, Tony Grillo, smiling and laughing and mock-punching one of his teammates in the shoulder. Tony seems to have doubled in size since last year—which makes him about four times as big as me. He almost doesn't look real. His muscles are carved too perfectly in his body, like an Incredible Hulk action figure. The scar on his upper lip gives him a permanent sneer. Girls around the swim league say it's sexy, but to me it looks like he always wants to bite you.

Tony's leopard eyes suddenly lock onto mine. He grins like he can smell my fear. Like he knows I'm the sickly wildebeest.

I stare at the concrete. The pieces of hardened gum, the putty-patched cracks. Sean and I reach starting block three, where Sid Kershower and Gregg Zuzzansky are already stretching.

"Hey," they say in unison to Sean and me.

"Hey," we say back.

I pretend to limber up, too. Shaking out my arms, rolling my head. But really, all I can think about is how I'm toast. Sean and Coop have left me hanging out to dry, and they're going to be laughing their heads off after this stupid relay. Not to mention that Kelly is about to witness the full measure of my dorkery.

"Go, Razorbacks, go!" I hear Kelly and Valerie starting up the swim-team cheer. "Go, Razorbacks, go!"

Then it's Shannon Motts who takes up the lead. She spends hours writing and teaching us her idiotic team cheers every season. Shannon gets all pissed when we mess them up or change the words. If you looked up *enthusiastic* on Google, you'd probably see a picture of Shannon Motts jumping in the air and screaming through her yellow bullhorn.

"We are the Razorbacks. We can't be beat!" Shannon calls out, her voice megaphone-amplified. About six people halfheartedly join in. "We are the Razorbacks, so take a seat! When we swim backstroke, all the other teams choke! When we swim breast, we are the best! When we swim free, it's vic-to-ry! When we swim fly, we wave good-bye! Good-bye! Good-bye!"

These cheers are supposed to energize you and make you feel full of team spirit, but right now all it's doing is making me feel like I'm about to ride a tricycle in the Indy 500.

"I need to know what the plan is," I hiss at Sean. "Now."

"The plan? The plan is to kick some ass and take names," he says a little too loudly, nodding at Sid and Gregg, who nod back.

I try to breathe, but my chest is tight and I can't get enough air.

The four of us arrange ourselves into our swim order, behind our starting block: Gregg, Sean, me, Sid.

"Backstrokers in the water," the starter calls out. She's someone's hot mom in a bikini top and track pants.

"No mercy," Gregg says, holding up a solidarity fist. He's got this totally serious scowl on his face as he steps off the ledge and into the water.

"What a tool," Sean whispers to me out of the corner of his mouth.

He's not the only one, I want to say. I could strangle Sean right here. I can't believe I call him and Coop my friends.

Gregg slips on his goggles and arranges himself into starting position.

I look back and see Kelly and Valerie pressed up against the fence.

"We are the Razorbacks, it's no mistake!" Shannon hollers. "Feel our power and eat our wake!"

"On your marks," the starter lady calls out.

I never thought this is how my life would end, but I guess we all have to go sometime.

"Get set." She raises her starter's pistol over her head. I wish she would just point it at me and put me out of my misery.

Bang! The gun fires and I jump. The backstrokers push off the wall in six simultaneous, splashing swells.

Sean's eyes are glassy, and he looks a little pale as he steps up onto the starting block.

He's probably feeling guilty. Jerk. Serves him right.

Gregg's in the lead, heading into the turn. He's an egotistical moron, but he also happens to be a strong swimmer, which just makes you hate him even more.

I shift from one leg to the other and then back again. A cold shiver rockets up my spine. The volume on the world has suddenly been cranked up. There's the roar of the crowd and the slosh of the water and the tick of the timekeeper's stopwatch all swirling around me, making me dizzy.

"Ow!" Sean suddenly screams, grabbing his middle and folding over. Everyone turns and stares. "My stomach! Oh, God! The pain!" He staggers off the starting block, his eyes rolling back in his head.

Ms. Luntz rushes through the pool gate toward Sean. She looks more furious than concerned. "What the hell's wrong with you?" she says when she reaches his side.

"Can't swim." Sean groans. "Horrible stomachache. Have to . . . forfeit. Uhhhhh."

Are you kidding me? *This* is the great plan? A stomachache?

"Omar!" Ms. Luntz calls out, not missing a beat. "Get over here! You're swimming breaststroke!"

Sean's bent over, his arm leaning on the starting block. He's not faking it, that's for sure. His face has turned a sort of yellowish blue.

Omar bolts through the fence, whipping off his hoodie and stumbling out of his sweatpants. He hops up on the starting block, fumbling with his goggles as Gregg hurtles backward with half a lap to go.

Omar leans forward, ready to take off once Gregg reaches the wall.

Ms. Luntz is trying to help Sean up, but he's not making it easy. He's all deadweight, wriggling around.

"Don't move me," Sean groans.

And that's when he makes a dive for the edge of the pool and lets fly a rainbow torrent the likes of which I've never seen before in my life. It's like an open fire hydrant plugged directly into hell.

Lifeguard whistles blow like crazy and girls start screeching and all the swimmers step away from the pool as Gregg backstrokes right through the floating psychedelic afghan.

My stomach lurches. I have to turn away or I might follow Sean's lead.

I see Cooper laughing hysterically, smacking his hand into the fence. He gives me a double thumbs-up.

I feel kind of bad now for thinking Sean and Coop wouldn't come through for me. I mean, Valerie was right there, able to see the whole disgusting thing, and Sean chucked a dummy, anyway.

I had no idea he was such a good friend.

CHAPTER SIXTEEN

PUMPING IRON

YOU CAN USE 'EM, but if you touch anything else I'll break your face." That's what my brother, Pete, said to me when I asked if I could use the weights in his room while he's on vacation with Melissa and her family for the next couple of weeks. He also said he'd break my face if I didn't put the weights back exactly where I found them. Or if I damaged them in any way. Or if I left my stink in his room. Normally I wouldn't put my face in such danger, but these are desperate times.

I got out of having to swim the fly at the relay medley, but sectionals is in two weeks and there's no chance we'd get away with pulling that same stunt again. I figure if I work out hard enough, I might be able to build up at least a bit of muscle by then.

I run an Internet search on the computer in the family room: *Building muscle workout routines.* There are 683,000 results. I need an extreme workout that will kick in superfast, so it's pretty lucky when I come across one called The Extreme Workout—Massive Muscles, Ferociously Fast. It consists of an intense series of exercises with names like Severe Squats, Deadly Deadlifts, and Kamikaze Curls. The article explains how to get maximum results out of each exercise. There are pictures and everything. If you follow what they say, you're supposed to pack on the muscle in just a few weeks. I print it out and start toward my brother's room.

"Matt, can I see you a second?" It's Grandpa Arlo, calling from the kitchen.

"I'm kind of busy, Grandpa," I call back. "Can we do it later?"

"When you get to be my age, there might not be a later."

I look down at the pages in my hand and sigh. It's not like I'm looking forward to doing these exercises, but I have to get started or I'll never get into shape.

I make my way into the kitchen and there's Grandpa Arlo, folding Christmas wrapping paper around a toaster-size box on the table. It's weird seeing dozens of Santa Claus heads smiling at you in the middle of summer. Grandpa Arlo's having a difficult time with the wrapping; there's too much paper and not enough box.

"Whatcha doing, Grandpa?"

"Just a minute." He wrestles some tape from the dispenser and secures a crumpled wad of wrapping paper at one end of the present. "There," he says. "Finished."

It's the saddest-looking gift I've ever seen. I mean, I'm no wrapping expert, but even I can manage a present that doesn't look like it's been kicked around the yard.

"What is it?"

"Never you mind," Grandpa says. "I just need you to deliver it to Mrs. Hoogenboom."

"Is it her birthday or something?"

"Don't be an idiot," Grandpa says. "Why would I use Christmas paper on a birthday present?"

"I don't know. Why did you use Christmas paper in July?"

"It's all we had. Now shut up and listen." Grandpa Arlo grabs the present and holds it out to me. "I need you to be discreet. If she sees you delivering it, she'll be suspicious. I just want you to put it on her front doorstep, then knock and run and hide."

"Can't I just leave it and she'll find it when she comes out?"

"No. You need to make sure she finds it right away." Just then, the box meows and wobbles in Grandpa's hands.

"Is there a cat in there?"

"It's a kitten. Edith said she'd always wanted a kitty, but Ray was too much of a curmudgeon. Well, now she can have one."

"Why don't you want her to know it's from you?" I say.

"Animals are risky gifts, Matt. People either love you for giving them a new friend or hate you for saddling them with a burden. I just signed it 'From Someone Who Cares.' That way, if she likes it I'll tell her it's from me, and if she doesn't, we can jointly curse the inconsiderate bastard who gave it to her. Either way it'll give us something to talk about."

"What if she's not home?"

"Where's she going? Her husband just died. Go on. Take it over there." Grandpa Arlo shoves the box at me.

I fold up my workout papers and tuck them into the back pocket of my shorts. I take the gift, but it's unsteady because the kitten keeps moving. "Shouldn't you poke holes in this or something? For air?"

Grandpa scrunches up his face and bats my idea out of the air with his hand. "No. That would give it away."

Another muted meow comes from the present.

"I don't think a few airholes will be what gives it away, Grandpa."

"Don't worry about it. Paper's porous. And there's plenty of air in the box. Just get it over there. Chop-chop."

"Okay." I turn to head out.

"When you hide, make sure you can see her answer the door. I want a full report. What she says. What her expression is. Everything."

"Sure, Grandpa."

I stop in the vestibule to put on my sneakers, and while I'm at it, I punch a couple of holes in the side of the box with my house key, just in case.

I'm out the door, trying not to appear too suspicious as I run-walk across the street holding a poorly wrapped Christmas present in the middle of summer. The kitten is really yowling now. I take a quick look, but there's nobody around. I want to unload this thing as fast as I can.

Up the Hoogenbooms' cracked concrete driveway, past their faded brown station wagon, and I'm at the house. I place Grandpa's package gently on the ground and then knock hard on the metal screen door. I should have decided on a hiding spot first off, because now I look left and right and there's no place to go.

I dash around the car and lie on my belly, in the dirt and sand, behind the front wheel. I press my cheek to the ground and look under the car. Just then, the front door opens out and smacks into the gift. The kitten lets out a loud cry, and I hear Mrs. Hoogenboom say, "What on earth?" She bends down to pick up the box. The kitten howls. "Good Lord. I hope this isn't what I think it is."

Mrs. Hoogenboom takes the present inside. I don't even want to know what she's going to say when she opens the box.

Back at the house, Grandpa grills me for details. "What did she say?" "But how did she say it?" "Did she smile?" "Did she open it?" "Did she read the card?"

I give him as much as I can, though none of it seems to satisfy him.

He starts to pace, pushing his glasses up on his nose, stroking his goatee, rolling his tongue around his mouth. "Okay, okay. I'll give it a couple of hours. Then I'll phone her up. Just to say hello. And we'll see if she mentions it."

I tell him that sounds like a plan, but he doesn't seem to be listening. I pull my workout instructions from my back pocket and head upstairs.

Pete's room is like a museum exhibit. Everything is neat and organized and clean. All his CDs and DVDs are lined up in alphabetical order. All his books are arranged in the bookshelves using the Dewey decimal system. The clothes in his closet are color-coordinated. His posters— Harry Houdini, Clint Eastwood, the Beatles—are professionally framed and hung squarely on the walls. His fancy airplane models are placed strategically around the room, strung up from the ceiling or set out on a special display table made up to look like an aircraft carrier, with little air force figures standing around and tiny brass placards describing each airplane. He spends months making these models, getting all the details exactly right, and I have to say, I don't see the big deal.

Pete's dumbbells are stacked by the weight bench in neat little pyramids. I tiptoe toward them, careful not to brush up against anything. I unfold my workout sheet and look around for somewhere to place it. I decide that the floor would be best.

I test out a few of the weights to see how much I might be able to lift. I decide on two ten-pound dumbbells and start in with the Barbaric Bench Press. Three sets of thirty reps. I barely make it through, but you're not supposed to rest in between exercises, so then it's a twenty-pound dumbbell in each hand and some Ludicrous Lunges. My legs are burning halfway into the second set.

This working-out stuff really sucks. It feels like my muscles are being torn apart. There's no need to look like Mr. Universe, so I decide to skip the last set of lunges and pick another exercise from the sheet. Impossible Push-ups are out, because I know from gym class that I can only manage three regular push-ups before I collapse. I'll give the Crazed Crunches a shot and see if they don't make me want to puke my guts out.

You're supposed to be able to do the entire routine in forty-five minutes.

It takes me three hours.

When I finally get to my last set of Insane Standing Shoulder Presses, I am spent. But I'm not giving up. I have to finish. I've got too much riding on this to short-change myself. I heave the fifteen-pound dumbbells over my head using all the force of my breath and every ounce of strength I have left. It's twenty-four . . . twenty-five . . . twenty-six . . . twenty-sev . . . sev . . . sev . . . But I can't get the dumbbells up past my ears. My legs feel rubbery. My arms are empty. With only four reps left.

I don't know why, but I get it into my head that if I can just finish these last few presses, then I will somehow be able to take second in the butterfly and I'll be able to ask Kelly out and she will be happy to be my girlfriend. I make that deal with myself.

I take a deep breath, screw up my face, and groan loudly as I force my arms up into the air. They're shaking like crazy, but somehow I get the weights up past my ears.

I smile because I know that I am going to finish now. There is no doubt.

And just as I'm thinking this, my arms lock and my legs disappear from under me, and life switches into slow motion as I fall backward, clutching the dumbbells, smashing into Pete's model-airplane display table, sending shards of wood and plastic and figures and little brass placards soaring and tumbling into the air.

I lie there on the floor in complete shock. It looks like a miniature Pearl Harbor. Pete is going to freak. He might even cry. Right before he beats me to death with what's left of his Sopwith Camel. He won't care that it was an accident. I could have taken a loose lamb-tikka-masala dump on Pete's pillow and it wouldn't have been as bad as this.

I have to think. How can I fix this? How can I make this better? I get to my feet and survey the situation. Okay. Okay. Some of the models don't look too bad. Some of the wings have just snapped off. The aircraft-carrier table is split in two, but it's a pretty clean break. I don't know. Maybe I can do some repair work.

I heave the weights back into their little pyramids and bolt downstairs.

"What the hell was that?" Grandpa calls from his bedroom.

"Nothing, Grandpa. I just dropped . . . something. It's fine."

I dash outside and over to the garage, yank the garage door open, and find the old rusty toolbox. I root around and grab some heavy-duty wood screws, a screwdriver, a little vial of SuperDuper glue, and some electrical tape.

Back up in Pete's room with my makeshift repair kit, I stand there in the middle of the wreckage and there's no friggin' way I'm going to be able to make it look like nothing happened here. I need a plan B.

And plan B is to make it look like it wasn't my fault. Something fell on the table. Like Pete's framed Harry Houdini picture. It could have happened. It's not right over the table, but who knows how these things go. The weight of the picture frame wrenched the nail out of the wall and then the rest was physics. He should have let Dad help hang the picture. But Pete was stubborn and he wanted to do it himself. I remember that. And now look what happened.

The thing is, if Pete were a normal brother and would just scream at me and let me give him some money to smooth things over, then I'd never even think about covering it up. Okay, I'd think about it, but I probably wouldn't follow through. But Pete will kill me and I'm not kidding. It will be a crime of passion. Pete loves those models more than anything. If he had to choose between Melissa and his models, there wouldn't even be a discussion. It's really just survival at this point. He'll probably thrash the poor Harry Houdini picture, but better Houdini than me.

I move to the wall and carefully lift the heavy picture frame off its hook, shuffle to the right, and then drop it into the mess. I pull the nail from the wall, throw it on the floor, and tell myself that it looks believable. It's a bit of a stretch, but I have a few weeks to try and convince myself before Pete comes home.

CHAPTER SEVENTEEN

STRATEGY

COOP HAS CALLED SEAN and me to an emergency strategy meeting. We're already three weeks into July and we are no closer to seeing a naked girl—and Mandy Reagan in particular. What with swim practice and the Kelly situation, and the fact that our last attempt backfired in such a big way, we haven't exactly rededicated ourselves to the cause. Coop says that if we don't start planning something right now, this could be the first summer we fail to achieve our goal, which, to hear him tell it, would upset the balance of the entire universe. I don't know about that, but what I do know is that if we don't somehow get that picture of Mandy, our own little universe will be more than just upset. It will be completely capsized.

"What we need is a Clamato Classic to get our creative juices flowing," Coop says as the three of us make our way into his backyard.

And sure enough, Coop's got his rickety old Ping-Pong table all set up and ready to go. The Clamato Classic is a round-robin table tennis tournament that we came up with a few years ago. The objective is not so much to come in first but to avoid coming in third. Because third place means you have to drink the most unholy of beverages: a super-sized Adventure Town souvenir cup filled to the brim with equal parts Clamato and chocolate milk. It makes me queasy just thinking about it.

"Whoo-hoo!" Sean hollers, running to the table and grabbing a paddle. "Who wants to get their butt wiped first?" He leaps around, swatting an invisible ball.

"You can *wipe* mine." Coop laughs. "But only after I *whip* yours." He picks up the other paddle along with an orange Ping-Pong ball.

I take a seat on one of Coop's wobbly foldout beach chairs.

"Volley for serve." Coop sends the ball over the net and Sean returns it. They go back and forth about a dozen times before Coop lobs a high one that just nicks the corner.

"Damn it." Sean snatches the ball off the grass and tosses it back to Coop.

"All right," Coop says, bouncing the ball on the table several times, testing it out. "Let's talk strategy. How are we going to get that naked picture of Mandy Reagan? We can't let the locker-room incident get us offtrack. That was probably too complicated. We should try to keep things simple." He grabs the ball and serves a low, fast shot.

Sean handles the serve easily. "It was a good plan. And it would have worked if it wasn't for someone's mocha mud slide."

"Yeah, yeah, yeah," I say. "Can we let that go?"

"Well, we know *you* can let it go." Coop laughs, cutting the ball underneath, trying to add spin. It doesn't fool Sean, though, even though he's laughing. He follows it perfectly and sends the ball right back.

Sean and Coop are pretty evenly matched. They can play for twenty minutes straight without anyone taking a point. It's kind of annoying.

Finally, Coop gives the ball a violent smack. It catches the top of the net, and the ball dribbles onto Sean's side, making it impossible for him to return it.

"Cheap," Sean says.

"Not as cheap as your momma." Coop points his paddle at Sean.

"My mother's not cheap, flush hole." Sean hurls the Ping-Pong ball at Coop, who catches it without flinching.

"Oh, that's right." Coop nods, apologetically. "She just let me use a coupon that one time."

"Laugh all you want now," Sean says. "We'll see how funny you find it when you get that first room-temperature taste of tomato, clams, and chocolate milk."

"I'll find it pretty damn funny because I'll be the one watching *you* suck down Satan's swill."

"Guys," I say, trying to get us back on track, "let's get focused. We have a situation to deal with here."

"Matt's right." Sean sighs. "Cathy smirks and waves her cell phone at me every time she sees me."

Coop shrugs. He balances the Ping-Pong ball on the surface of his paddle. "I'm fine with trying to see Mandy Reagan naked if we can work it out. But if we can't, and Cathy sends out the picture, I still say we can claim she Photoshopped it. I mean, it doesn't look like anyone's examined Matt's incriminating underwear too closely, so there's no proof we were in the girls' locker room."

My stomach sinks. "Yeah, about that . . ." It's not fair to hold out on them anymore. "There's something I didn't tell you guys," I say.

Coop and Sean both look at me with concern. The ball rolls off Coop's paddle and bounces on the table.

"When I went to the bathroom . . . I sort of ran into Kelly."

"Are you serious?" Sean blinks. "But she didn't recognize you, did she?"

"It doesn't matter," I explain. "If that picture of us gets out, she'll put it together. That's all the proof Cathy will need."

"Aw, man." Sean groans. "I can't believe this. If we weren't totally screwed before, we are now."

Coop taps his Ping-Pong paddle on his chin. "Okay, wait. Let's not overreact, here. So, you passed Kelly in the bathroom. Big deal. She probably won't even remember."

I sigh. "Oh. She'll remember."

Sean and Coop both bury their heads in their hands and moan.

Coop starts to laugh. He pulls his hands down his face. "Matt. Jesus, dude. I'm sure there's something worse than shitting your pants in front of the girl of your wet dreams; I just can't figure out what that would be."

We spend the next two hours playing Ping-Pong and trying to come up with any way we can think of to see Mandy Reagan naked. The ideas get progressively more ridiculous as the day goes on. There's a plan to string a tightrope between Mandy's house and her neighbor's. There's another where we hang-glide past her bathroom window when she's taking a bath. And then there's Sean's latest, where we get someone to buy us a lottery ticket and we win a million dollars and then offer it to Mandy to take all her clothes off.

"Dude," Coop says, "if we had a million bucks, we'd get to see all the woofers and tweeters we wanted."

"That's true." Sean nods, perched on the edge of the beach chair. "But that still wouldn't solve our problem with Cathy."

Coop cocks his head. "You don't think a few grand wouldn't buy your sister off?"

"All right, enough already," I say, squeezing my eyes shut. "I have to concentrate on the game."

Coop chuckles. "Ooooh. Someone's getting a little panicky."

We're down to the final match that'll decide third place. It's between me and Coop and I'm behind nineteen to eighteen and it's his serve and, yes, I'm getting a little worried. I've had to drink the clam-milk once before and it's disgusting. Plus, you end up burping it up for the next three days.

"I'm not getting panicky," I lie. "I just want to focus."

"Okay, let's focus, then." Coop bounces the Ping-Pong ball over and over again on the table. The hollow click of it is driving me crazy. "But keep your mind on the game. Two more points and I win. You don't want to go thinking about Kelly West jumping up and down on a trampoline."

This makes Sean crack up. "Yeah," he says. "And try not to imagine her doing it in a wet T-shirt. Because that would *really* distract you."

I glare at Coop. "Are you going to serve sometime this century?"

"Wet T-shirt." Coop grins. "Man, oh, man. What could be more distracting than that?" He gestures with his Ping-Pong paddle. "Unless, of course, it was a chilly day."

"Ohhh." Sean doubles over in fits, toppling out of the chair. "Do *not* think about that, Matt. Whatever you do."

"Whenever you're done," I say.

"That's just . . . wow," Coop says, his eyes glazed over. He shakes his head like he's trying to dislodge the image he's created. "Okay. Here we go."

Coop wastes no more time. He rockets the ball over the net with a ton of topspin, but it misses the end of the table and whirls around in the grass.

"Damn it!" he shouts. "I just psyched myself out."

I retrieve the ball and get set to serve.

"Boiiing. Boiiing. Boiiing." Sean makes hushed bouncing-on-a-trampoline noises.

"Okay. That's funny," Coop says. "But enough. Matt's right. This is too serious for that kind of distraction."

"*Now* who's getting panicky?" I laugh.

"Please," Coop scoffs. "I'm not the one who's going to be walking around with a chocolamato mustache."

"Of course you're not," I say. "Just put Kelly completely out of your mind and you'll be all right. As long as you don't instantly replace her with Mandy Reagan. And her beautiful marshmelons bobbing up and down in slow motion."

Coop points at me. "Screw off, okay?" He drags his hand down his face, presumably to try and erase the image of Mandy. But I can tell it's still there, because his eyes have a feverish glaze.

"My serve." I flip the ball into the air and bat a nice, hard, low shot across the table.

Coop barely manages to get it back to me.

I pretend to slam the ball hard but instead just tap it lightly onto Coop's side of the net.

He backs up, totally fooled, then tries to lunge for it. But it's too late. "Crap!"

"Nineteen all," I say, laughing.

"Man, you must really be under the spell of Mandy's angel cakes," Sean hoots.

"Zip it, Sean." Coop grits his teeth. He glares at me. "Okay. We're even now. Can we play the rest of the game fairly?" He rolls his shoulders and tilts his head from side to side.

I turn to Sean. "Are you listening to this? The cheater feels cheated."

"I know," Sean says with mock sympathy. "Look at him sweat. Imagine what would happen if we threw Miss October into the mix. And some hot oil. He'd probably have to concede defeat."

Coop grabs his head and groans. "Stop it!"

"Stop what?" I say.

"You don't want to win this way, Matt," Coop whines. "You'll feel guilty. And there will always be that nagging feeling in the back of your mind. Like you didn't deserve the win."

I look at Coop a second before completely losing it. Sean and I bust up.

"You're right," I say. "I'd feel awful."

I take a breath and send a bullet Coop's way. He smacks the ball back to me with determination.

But I'm totally confident now and I do this insane spin-o-rama move, swatting the ball high in the air.

Coop's eyes follow the arc and I can tell he thinks it's going to miss the table by a mile, so he lets it go, except it somehow grazes the side with a soft tick that makes him fall to his knees.

"Holy shit!" I holler. "Someone call Sports Center. Point, nineteen."

"Thanks a lot, Sean," Coop says, wanting to blame someone.

"What?" Sean throws his hands up in surrender. "It's not like you were ever going to return that."

"Whatever." Coop's already retrieved the ball. He hurls it at me. "You think you can get that lucky twice in a row?"

I waggle my eyebrows. "As a matter of fact, I do."

"Okay, then. Bring it."

I smile and serve, and it's like the Ping-Pong gods are killing themselves with laughter, because the ball is way overshot and still it brushes the edge of the table before coming to rest on the lawn.

"Second place is mine!" I whoop it up and throw my paddle high into the air.

Sean walks over to Coop and pats him on the back. "Sorry, dude. But better you than me."

A few minutes later, we're in Coop's kitchen. He sits at the table, his leg jiggling, wanting to get this over with as quickly as possible. But me and Sean take our time getting everything ready.

Sean places the yellowed, plastic Adventure Town cup in front of Coop. I pour the Clamato slowly, plop by foul plop. Sean follows, doing the same with the chocolate milk.

"You have to drink it all," Sean says when he's topped it up.

"Good to the last drop," I add.

Coop grabs the cup and cautiously brings it toward his lips.

The sick smell of it hits me in the face all the way over here.

"Clam, clam, clam," Sean and I chant.

Coop nearly yaks after the first taste. That's the worst part. It's like a cold, rancid chowder. When I had to drink it last year, I had to pretend that I'd been poisoned, that the clam-milk was an ancient Indian recipe and it was the only thing that could save my life.

I find myself cringing as I watch Coop chug the rust-brown sludge. At one point I actually have to turn away.

When he finally finishes, he slams the cup onto the table. "Deee-licious," he says, letting out a loud soggy belch. "That hits the spot."

It only takes about five seconds before he bolts to the bathroom with his hand cupped over his mouth.

....

CHAPTER EIGHTEEN

THE KITTEN'S OUT
OF THE BAG

WHEN I ARRIVE HOME, I hear Grandpa Arlo talking to someone whose voice I don't recognize. I enter the kitchen and see him sitting at the table, having tea with Mrs. Hoogenboom.

"Hi," I say, trying to smile.

Grandpa and Mrs. Hoogenboom both turn toward me.

Mrs. Hoogenboom has on a light purple dress with a tie at the waist and a gold dragonfly broach pinned to her chest. Grandpa Arlo is wearing his old faithful: a pale pink dress shirt, slacks, and a belt.

"There he is," Grandpa says. "We were just talking about you. Edith came by a little while ago. She was wondering if you might know anything about a kitten that was dropped off at her house this morning."

Mrs. Hoogenboom smiles at me while Grandpa shakes his head furiously behind her.

"A kitten?" I ask, stalling.

"Yes," Mrs. Hoogenboom says. "Wrapped in Christmas paper, of all things." Her voice is thin and wheezy. Like a kazoo.

"Huh," I say. "Why do you think I'd know anything about that?"

"She thought maybe you might have seen something." Grandpa takes a sip of his tea. "Or heard something from your friends."

"I can't imagine who would do such a thing," Mrs. Hoogenboom says. "I don't know if it was meant as a gift or some kind of practical joke. Either way, I just don't know what to do with the poor thing. She's such a dear. I'm calling her Daisy. Just for the time being. Oh, but I can't keep her, can I? What if she belongs to someone else?"

I'm not sure how to play this. Grandpa Arlo is making all sorts of grimacing faces behind Mrs. Hoogenboom but I can't tell what he wants me to say.

"I guess if it was wrapped up and it had a card on it, then it was probably a gift," I say.

"Oh, yes, the card. 'From Someone Who Cares.'" Mrs. Hoogenboom squints at me. "But how did you know about that?"

Grandpa Arlo grabs his forehead behind Mrs. Hoogenboom's back, like he's just had an aneurysm.

"I . . . umm . . . just figured, I guess, because most presents come with cards."

"That's true," Grandpa interjects. Mrs. Hoogenboom

turns to look at him. "And if it had a card, the cat was probably a gift. Maybe from someone who knew you always wanted one."

Mrs. Hoogenboom smiles big. "I do hope you're right. I have sort of fallen for Daisy. And it would be nice to have some companionship. I just wish I knew who gave her to me."

"I'm sure it was someone of great character." Grandpa Arlo sits up tall. "Someone who understands how much you would enjoy some comfort right now. Probably some-one who—"

"Doesn't have the slightest clue how to take care of a living creature," Mrs. Hoogenboom says. "I mean, any person who would put a kitten in a box and then wrap it up in that thick Christmas paper . . . The poor thing could have suffocated. I'd like to know who it was just so I could give them a piece of my mind."

With this, Grandpa hoists himself to his feet. "Well, if we hear anything, we'll be sure to let you know, Edith."

Mrs. Hoogenboom takes the cue and stands. She taps her lip like she's thinking. Then she nods. "I know. I'll just visit Gracie's Pets. I'll bring Daisy there and see if she was bought from them."

Grandpa's face turns ghost white. I see his Adam's apple bob hard in his throat. "Why, that's a terrific idea. I don't know why I didn't think of that," he says. "I think I'll go with you. I could do with a drive."

Grandpa puts his hand on Mrs. Hoogenboom's lower

back and guides her from the kitchen. He looks back at me, with panic in his eyes. He makes a telephone out of his hand and fingers, holds it up to his cheek, and mouths, "Call the pet store."

I wish Grandpa would get someone else mixed up in his schemes. It's not like I don't have enough of my own problems.

As soon as I hear the door close, I go over to the telephone and angrily flip through the yellow pages on the kitchen counter. I find the number for Gracie's Pets and dial. As the phone rings, I'm trying to figure out what the hell I'm supposed to tell them. Two old people will be coming in asking about a kitten, and could they please deny having sold it? They're going to think I'm a prank caller.

"Gracie's Pets," a woman's voice, cold and serious, answers. She sounds more like a Catholic school nun than a pet store owner.

"Oh, hi," I say. "I was wondering . . . My grandfather bought a kitten from you recently . . . He gave it as a present to someone and . . . The thing is . . . The lady he gave it to is bringing the kitten back to your store—"

"I'm sorry," the woman says, sounding anything but. "We don't accept returns on animals."

"Oh. No. It's not about returning it." I switch the phone to my left ear because my right one's getting sweaty. "This lady just wants to know if your store was the one who sold the kitten."

"Why? Is something wrong? Our kittens are all thoroughly checked out before we get them. We can't be held responsible for anything that happens once the animal leaves the store."

"The kitten's fine," I say. "It's not that."

"Well, then, what's the problem?"

"It's a little complicated. You see, the kitten was a surprise. And my grandpa doesn't want this lady to know that he was the one who bought it."

"I'm not sure what it is you're asking, young man."

"Okay. Look. Is there any way, when the lady comes into your store with my grandpa, that you could tell her that you *didn't* sell the kitten? That you never saw the kitten before in your life?"

A long, severe silence strangles the line like a boa constrictor.

"So you want me to *lie*?" the woman finally says.

Oh, crap. My neck and shoulders seize up. The phone is slick in my sweaty palm. I hold my breath, bracing for the onslaught.

"Why didn't you say that in the first place? You got me all worked up for nothing."

I'm not sure I heard her correctly. "So . . . you'll say you didn't sell the kitten, then?"

"Kitten? What kitten? We haven't sold a kitten in months."

I let out my breath. "Thank you."

"You're very welcome. Thanks for calling Gracie's Pets." And with that, the woman hangs up.

I put down the phone.

Now that I've solved Grandpa's problems, I can get back to tackling my own. I look over at the rooster clock on the wall. Dinner's not for another couple of hours, which gives me some time to search online for a new, less conspicuous pool to practice at in the evenings.

I can't risk practicing at Rockville Avenue Pool anymore. Not after Kelly and Valerie showed up when they should have been eating dinner like everyone else. I need to go to a pool where there isn't any chance I'll run into someone I know. A pool where I can make an ass of myself in complete anonymity.

CHAPTER NINETEEN

NARROW ESCAPE

I'M NOT REALLY ALLOWED into the Elk Hills Country Club. You're supposed to have a membership or be accompanied by someone who has one, but I'm pretty sure I can sneak in without too much of a problem. We went there once, when I was about eight. The whole family was invited by a friend of my dad's who showed us all how to do backflips off the diving board. They have a really nice Olympic-size pool and there's almost no chance of me being seen by anyone from the Rockville Swimming Association. I figure if I just dress up nice, stroll in like I belong, then no one will look twice.

I MapQuested Elk Hills and it's supposed to be, like, ten minutes by car, so I can probably get there in a half hour on my bike. Which just means more exercise.

I pull on a pair of khaki pants over my Speedo and button my only semi-clean dress shirt. It's baby blue and has a few thumb-size grease stains on the front, but I'm sure nobody's going to be looking that closely.

I clip on my tie, tug on some dark socks, and buff out the scratches on my dress shoes. Being so dressed up is going to make it a little difficult to ride my bike, but there's nothing I can do about that. I fling my towel around my neck, grab my goggles, my wallet, and my cell phone, and I'm off.

As soon as I step into the hall, I see Mom dragging the Hoover up the stairs. I get that oh-crap-I'm-caught plunge in my belly. I think about darting back into my room, when I see her heading toward Pete's bedroom. She'll freak if she sees the mess from the "accident," and maybe even call Pete. Which is why I put his big orange DO NOT DISTURB sign on the door.

Mom reaches for the doorknob, and I have to make a split-second decision.

"Wait," I call out. "What are you doing?" I hurry over to where she's standing.

Mom turns and smiles. "What does it look like I—" She squints at me. "What are you wearing?"

I look down at my outfit, my towel, my goggles.

I don't really like to lie, though I seem to be doing a lot more of it lately. I particularly don't like lying to Mom. Probably because Dad lied so much to her before they split up.

But I've already built this house of cards, and it's up to me to keep it standing.

"It's for the swim team photo."

"In your dress clothes? Don't they always take the

team photo at championships when you're all in your swimsuits?"

"They're doing it different this year."

Mom looks me up and down. "Your shirt's stained."

"It doesn't matter," I say. "It's the whole team together. The picture will be from far away. No one'll even notice."

"Of course they'll notice."

"Trust me. They want us to wear our towels around our necks and our goggles on our heads. We're supposed to be the swim team with class. It's stupid. Some photographer trying to be artistic or something." I need to shut up before I dig myself deeper than I already am. I feel the pits of my shirt getting wet. She's not buying any of this—I know it.

"You should at least have a nicer shirt."

"This is the only one I have that's clean."

"Well, I'm sure your brother has something you can wear." Mom grabs Pete's bedroom doorknob and starts to push the door open.

"No!" I lunge for the handle and yank it closed.

Mom stares at me, eyes wide. "What is *wrong* with you?"

"Nothing," I say, positioning myself between Mom and the door. "It's just . . . Pete has his do-not-disturb sign up and . . . I'm sure it's for a reason."

Mom gives me that sideways, skeptical look. "It's very nice of you to be so protective of your brother's privacy, but I'm sure he didn't mean for me *not* to clean his room for three weeks. Now please move out of the way."

"No," I say. "I can't."

"Matt. What's going on?"

Oh, God, here we go again. I take a deep breath. "Pete asked me to make sure you didn't go into his room."

"Why?"

A good question. I wish I'd thought that far ahead.

"He got you a birthday present," I blurt. Mom's birthday isn't for two months, but it's the only thing I could think of. "And it's huge. Way too big to hide anywhere. So . . . if you go in, you'll ruin the surprise."

"Okaaay," she says, regarding Pete's closed bedroom door over my shoulder with what looks like deep suspicion. "So I'm not supposed to go into his room until September?"

I realize now that I am a terrible, terrible liar. I mean, how am I supposed to get a picture of my entire swim team in dress clothes with towels around their necks and goggles on their heads? And how am I supposed to get Pete to buy Mom a giant, unhideable present? What would that even be? A statue? A totem pole?

"I guess not," I say. "Unless, of course, he decides to return it. Which he might. He was talking about it. I don't know. He wasn't sure you'd like it. Besides, how messy could his room be, right?" My eyes slide away as I picture the wreckage just beyond that door. "Anyway." I look at my wrist. There's no watch there, but I pretend there is. "I have to go. I'm going to be late. Ms. Luntz'll freak."

I make my move toward the stairs and call over my shoulder, "Don't worry. I'll give Pete's room a once-over before he comes back."

I catch a glimpse of Mom's dumbfounded look as I dart into the stairwell. I have no idea if she believes me or not, but I'm pretty sure I've stalled her for a while.

I'll deal with it later.

Right now I have more important things to do. Like sneaking into the Elk Hills Country Club and getting some practice in.

CHAPTER TWENTY

TREADING WATER

It was a big mistake to ride my bike wearing my dress shoes. I've got massive, bursting blisters on the backs of both my feet that sting like scalding bacon grease with every pedal revolution.

I pull into the circular drive of the Elk Hills Country Club and lock my bicycle up to the rack out front. The club looks like a stretched-out old-fashioned white clapboard schoolhouse. The hedges have been squared off, and the tulips in the flower beds are all evenly spaced. A flagpole stands in the middle of the round driveway, with the Stars and Stripes hanging limply above what I can only guess is the Elk Hills Country Club blue-and-white flag all curled up around itself.

Now that I'm here, I'm starting to feel nervous. I tried to remember my dad's friend's name on the ride over. But it never came to me. I'd been planning to drop his name if anyone questioned me. Now I just pray no one stops me or makes me check in.

I breathe deeply and stand up straight and tall. I don't know why I think rich people have good posture, but I just figure they do. I walk up to the front and hold the door open for a short lady in a pantsuit. She smiles at me, her teeth smudged with lipstick.

I walk into the country club and scan around for some clue as to where the pool is located. The place smells like lemon oil and ammonia. It's pretty nice—white and black tiles on the floor, dark wood beams on the ceiling—but not nearly as fancy as I remembered from when I was eight. There are some very boxy brown cross-hatched chairs surrounding a round glass coffee table. A few tall plants in the corners. Some golf-course paintings on the walls. There are quite a few people milling about. Some are dressed up, but others are more casual.

I pass by the reception desk without a hitch. The willowy woman in her navy Elk Hills Country Club uniform is too busy doing paperwork to notice me.

There's a wooden sign at the back of the lobby with arrows pointing in various directions. To the clubhouse. To the Elk Hills Café. To the ballroom. And, bingo. The swimming pool.

The hall that leads to the pool is lined with framed photographs. I have to do a sort of shuffle-walk to stop my dress shoes from chafing the backs of my raw heels. A tall man in a dark suit heads toward me, so I pretend I'm interested in the pictures. Each one has a little typed caption: GROUNDBREAKING, RIBBON CUTTING, 1995 RENOVATION.

It's pretty boring stuff, but the tall guy passes by without hassling me.

The entrance to the pool is guarded by a metal gate and a wooden table with a clipboard resting on it. I don't remember what you're supposed to do here, if you're supposed to sign in or wait for someone or what.

Several loud snaps and the sound of laughter float over the air. I peek through the fence and see a group of five boys in shorts and T-shirts, running in circles down by the deep end, trying to get away from each other. They're all around my age, and they're whipping each other with rolled-up towels. A man and a woman, both wearing straw hats, are playing Scrabble at one of the poolside tables. An older woman in a bikini and sunglasses is reclining on a lounge chair, reading a book.

There's no one here to stop me from going in. I take a step toward the gate when I hear someone walk up behind me.

"You are here for the swimming?" It's a man with some sort of Arnold Schwarzenegger accent.

I turn back and see the guy standing there. He's got spiked white-blond hair and a wiry muscular body under a tight green golf shirt. His cheeks are sunken, and darkened with a few days of stubble.

"Umm . . . Yes," I say.

He taps a black-painted fingernail on the clipboard. "You will sign in here." I notice now that all of the fingernails on his left hand are painted black. Weird.

I grab the pen that's tied to the clipboard and scrawl an illegible signature. I'm hoping that the guy won't even look.

But he does, squinting as he tries to read what I've written. "What is this?"

"My signature."

He looks at me. "What is your name?"

I have to think quick. Something wealthy sounding. "Arthur," I say.

"Arthur what?"

"Arthur . . . ummm . . . Bottomly . . . the third."

The guy nods. "I am Ulf." He holds out his hand for me to shake.

I shake his hand, wondering why I'm shaking his hand. Country club protocol?

"We must get started. Come." Ulf turns on his heel and marches through the gate.

Get started? I have no idea what he's talking about, but I follow him anyway.

We walk over to the five boys horsing around by the diving boards.

Ulf claps his hands once. "Enough!"

All five boys drop their towels and freeze.

Ulf gives us a lips-only smile. It's like the smile you get from the principal right before he announces your punishment.

Ulf starts to pace with his hands clasped behind his

back. "Welcome to Advanced Aquatic Lifesaving Skills. You are about to experience the most intense and grueling five weeks of your life. This training is not for the soft or the weak. My course is unlike any other lifesaving program in the country. In my class there are only two options: you either pass. Or you die."

I am looking around at the other kids to see if this is a joke. But their faces are gray and stony.

"They say humans cannot survive more than three days without water." Ulf bangs his fist on his chest. "They are wrong. I survived *seven* days. Treading in the middle of the Atlantic Ocean. No food. No water. Nothing."

Uh-oh. This is a mistake. I have to get out of this right now. I raise my hand.

Ulf doesn't seem to notice. He just keeps pacing.

"This is why anything I do to you here, in this puny pool, will be a piece of pie. If you want to complain, do it to your mommies, because I have lived through hell and I do not want to hear about it."

I stretch my hand higher. "Umm, excuse me."

"And so." Ulf stops right in front of me and stares into my eyes. "If there are no questions, we will start today by honoring my survival." He points to the pool. "By treading water. For one half hour."

Several of the boys start to take off their sneakers and their shorts.

"With our clothes *on*." Ulf's eyes are still locked on mine. *"Schnell!"*

All the kids immediately leap into the pool, fully clothed.

I don't move. "Uh . . . Mr. Ulf," I say.

"There is no *Mr.* Ulf. There is only Ulf."

"Okay." I feel my mouth getting pasty. "Ulf. I think there's been a mistake. I'm not supposed to be in this class."

Ulf grins, big and toothy. "You do not think I have heard this excuse before?"

"No. You don't understand. It's not an excuse."

Ulf isn't listening. He just grabs my shoulders and starts pushing me toward the pool.

"Wait. No. Wait."

But he's not waiting. He's shoving. The soles of my dress shoes have no tread and just skid along the concrete, my blisters screaming in agony.

I'm no match for Ulf, so I try to do some quick damage control, pulling my wallet and cell phone out of my pockets and flinging them toward the benches. My cell phone skitters along the pavement, and my wallet strews its contents all over.

So much for damage control.

We've reached the edge of the pool, and Ulf gives one last heave, sending me flailing into the water.

CHAPTER TWENTY-ONE

SAVED BY THE SCHNELL

You will thank me when you are stranded at sea," Ulf calls to us from the comfort of dry land. He's still pacing like a hungry tiger. "I am saving your life. In advance."

We have been treading water for twenty-seven minutes now. My clothes are so weighed down that I can barely keep my head above water. All of us are huffing and puffing. I was already in pain from my extreme weight-lifting routine, but now I am beyond sore.

Several times during this torture, I have attempted to do a dead man's float just to catch a second of rest, but every time I've tried it, I've felt a dive ring smack me in the back of the head.

"You will be diving down to retrieve every one of those rings, Mr. Bottomly," Ulf said to me after he'd hit me the third time.

There are six rings down at the bottom of the pool now.

Ulf studies his wristwatch. "In exactly two minutes you will have a sixty-second recess. In that time, I expect you to remove your clothing. Down to your swim trunks."

Ulf walks over to a pile of bricks I hadn't noticed until now. He grabs one and hurls it into the pool, barely missing one of the kids. "Heads up," he says, way too late.

Five more bricks get tossed our way, each *kerplunk*-ing loudly into the water. I don't have the energy to dodge, and I secretly wish for one of them to hit me in the temple so I can have an excuse to quit.

"Each of you will dive down twelve feet for a brick and swim it back to shore. Mr. Bottomly, you will dive for your six rings *and* your brick. Then we will swim four hundred yards of butterfly. For this I will join you. To keep the pace."

Ulf pulls his shirt off over his head to reveal a severely toned torso with a great big purple birthmark cut diagonally across his chest. If you just glanced at it quickly, you might mistake it for a supervillain insignia.

My limbs feel like deflated inner tubes. The only thing that keeps me going is the fact that I never have to come back here. Ever.

When time is called, we drag ourselves out of the pool. It takes me all sixty seconds of the "recess" to strip off my waterlogged dress shoes, socks, pants, and shirt. My wet clothes must weigh like twenty pounds.

Fifteen minutes later, I've managed to dive for all the rings and my brick, hating life all the way.

I cling to the edge of the pool like a wet newspaper.

"Now we swim!" Ulf launches himself right over my head into the water.

The other boys follow.

They finish their first lap of butterfly in no time and are headed back toward me before I can even muster the energy to push off from the side.

There's no chance in hell I'm going to be able to finish sixteen laps of fly. I'm only halfway across the pool when I have to switch to freestyle.

I've only taken four strokes when I feel someone grab my legs and yank me backward.

I stop swimming and turn to see what's going on.

"Do you think that I was born in the morning?" Ulf says, wading there behind me.

"I don't know."

"When I say swim the butterfly, I do not mean dance a waltz, I do not mean comb a sheep, and I definitely do not mean swim the crawl. Do you know what I *do* mean?"

"Swim the butterfly."

"Yes, well, at least we have determined there is nothing wrong with your hearing."

Ulf makes me swim all sixteen laps of the fly even though I have to stop every few strokes to tread water.

When I'm finally finished, forty-five minutes later,

all the other kids are long gone. I can barely move. I can barely breathe. I'm so light-headed that I have to sit down on the pavement, my head between my knees, before I can even think about getting dressed. I'm not sure how I'm going to bike home.

"We must talk." Ulf towers over me, pulling his shirt on. His matted hair drips water onto my curled-up legs.

He's going to tell me that I am not qualified to be in his advanced swim class and that's just fine with me because, like I said, I don't plan on ever coming back again anyway.

Ulf crouches down next to me. "I was picking up the pieces of your wallet while you were swimming." His face is close up to mine. I can smell his vinegary breath. "And I found this, *Matthew*." He holds up my DMV identification card, complete with my name and picture and address on it. Mom made me get the ID card for some stupid reason, like if I ever got kidnapped or something, and I've never regretted it more than right now.

"I'm sorry," I say, looking down. "I won't come back."

Ulf laughs, but not in a something's-funny way. "I am afraid you *will* be coming back. Twice a week for the next five weeks. You will finish my course. I do not care if you are a member of this club or not."

I look up in disbelief. "But—"

"*Nobody* starts my program and then does not finish it." He flicks the ID card with one darkened fingernail.

"And just to make sure, I will hold on to this. That way I will know where to send the police if you do not show up. Do you know what the consequences are for trespassing and for impersonating a country club member?"

"No," I say, looking back down, but I have a feeling he's about to tell me.

Ulf stands and smiles. "You have two choices, Mr. Gratton: my class. Or jail. What will it be?"

I hesitate, because it's a tough choice. I've never been to jail, but it's hard to imagine it's much worse than this class. Still, I can't go to prison. Mom would be pissed. "Your class, I guess," I say finally.

Ulf nods. "We will see you next Tuesday. Oh. And one more thing. Five weeks at twenty dollars a week is one hundred dollars. You will bring it next lesson."

I don't look up as Ulf walks away.

I just sit there, shaking my head. Wondering how I keep getting myself into all this crap.

CHAPTER TWENTY-TWO

BYOB

I DON'T FEEL SO GOOD," I say to Coop and Sean. I try to lift my arm up over my head, but it's not happening. I am in serious pain. My whole body feels like it's being clenched in a giant's fist.

"What do you expect?" Coop pushes a shopping cart and scans the supermarket shelves. We're "casually" strolling down the beer aisle of PriceMark, trying to figure out how we can buy a six-pack so we can get into Ronnie Hull's party tonight. "You're not supposed to do some sick Extreme Workout when you've never even looked at a weight before. Not to mention, signing yourself up for a swim-torture class."

"I didn't sign up. It just . . . happened." I look at all the different beers on the shelves and get a kind of anxious, carsick feeling.

There was talk of trying to get some kind of booze from our parents, but the only alcohol in my house is a bottle of cooking sherry and Sean's parents are trying to quit drinking, so that just left Coop, who said he would definitely lift a six-pack except that his mom keeps a strict count of all the beer in the house because his dad has diabetes and is only allowed to have two drinks a night.

"What are we doing here?" Sean says. "There's no way they're going to sell us alcohol."

"I'm thinking," Coop declares. "There has to be some way. Maybe if we buy a whole bunch of other stuff along with the beer, and we pick a cashier that looks sort of clueless. . . ."

"This is stupid," Sean says. "Why can't we bring something that tastes good? Like Red Bull or Rockstar?"

"Right, dorkus. That won't get us tagged as a bunch of tools in *too* much of a hurry." Coop shakes his head. "Besides, we don't have to drink it. We just need it to get into the party. It's like our ticket."

"Yeah, well . . ." I roll my stiff shoulders. "I don't even know if I'm gonna be able to go."

Coop stops walking and stares at me. "What are you talking about?"

"I'm talking about how I can hardly move."

"Dude. You've got to suck it up," Coop says. "You don't get invited to a party by a girl that you're trying to impress and then not show up. You're practically being handed the keys to Kelly's missile silo, and you just want to throw them away."

"First of all, you don't know that," I say. "And second, it doesn't even matter. Once Kelly sees that picture of us in drag, she'll never be able to look at me without laughing."

"All the more reason to try and plant the parsnip tonight, dawg." Coop claps me hard on the shoulder.

"Ow! Jesus!" I groan in agony and shrink away from Coop's hand.

"What?" Coop says.

"I'm in pain! Didn't you hear what I said?"

"Sorry." Coop shrugs and starts pushing his cart again. "I didn't realize you were such a wuss."

"Whatever." I try to wave Coop off, but since I can't lift my arm, I just look like a girlie T. rex.

"What if we get a six-pack of O'Doul's?" Sean says.

"What the hell is O'Doul's?" Coop asks.

"It's a nonalcoholic beer that my dad drinks. They sell it with the soft drinks."

"I don't know." Coop shakes his head. "That seems kind of . . . lame."

"No one will even be able to tell. It looks exactly like all these other beers. I'm telling you."

"You think they'll let us buy it?" I ask.

Sean shrugs. "Sure. Why not?"

Coop checks his watch and sighs. "I guess it's worth a shot. Let's go take a look."

We find the O'Doul's on the shelf in the soda aisle.

And Sean's right. It does look exactly like regular beer. Green bottles in a green cardboard six-pack carrier. You have to look super close to even see that it says "non-alcoholic" on it.

"See, I told you," Sean says, all proud, holding up the six-pack. "If you saw this at a party, you'd think it was regular beer, right?"

Coop scrunches up his face. "I guess. But what if someone's heard of it?"

"*You* hadn't heard of it," Sean insists. "Why would anyone else?"

"It's perfect," I say. "O'Doul's even sounds like a real beer. Let's get it."

We throw a bag of pretzels, some potato chips, a two-liter bottle of Mountain Dew, and a box of cookies into the cart as well. As distractions. Just in case buying non-alcoholic beer isn't as easy as Sean thinks it will be.

We go to the express line where there's no wait and load our groceries onto the conveyor belt. We put the O'Doul's at the very end so that if there are any questions we can claim that it's not ours.

The cashier is a tall dude with an accountant's hair-cut and a red vest. I try not to look him in the eyes and instead read his nametag: KENNETH — MANAGER.

Damn it.

My eyes dart over to the other cashiers, looking for someone who might cut us a break, but it's too late. Two hot girls in tank tops and miniskirts step up behind us, and Kenneth-the-manager has already grabbed the bag of pretzels and is running it past his scanner.

Kenneth is robotic in his movements, scanning an item, dropping it into a plastic bag, scanning another, then dropping it in the bag. His inattention makes me relax a little.

Until he grabs the six-pack and swipes it over the scanner.

There's a loud, prolonged beep that sounds like an alarm. My stomach does a backward somersault.

Kenneth looks at the beer, looks at us, then back at the beer.

We are screwed for sure. Stupid Sean. I don't know why we trusted him.

Kenneth grabs his red emergency phone. Presumably to call security and have us taken away.

"Wait . . . No," I blurt out, before he can dial. "Don't. That's not ours."

Kenneth looks at the two hot girls behind us, but they both shake their heads.

He narrows his eyes at me. "You aren't buying this?"

"I . . . umm . . ." I blink hard. "Why did the alarm go off? Who are you calling?"

"I need to do a price check," he says. "Do you or don't you want this?"

"Of course we want it." Coop laughs, a little too

loudly. "Don't mind Matt. He's got Tourette's. You should hear the kinds of crazy stuff he shouts out at school. It's like diarrhea of the mouth." He gestures toward the phone. "It's okay. Do your price check."

The two girls behind us turn to each other and giggle.

I feel the heat of humiliation wash over my neck and cheeks.

Kenneth looks at me like I'm a feral raccoon that might dive over the counter and attack him. He keeps an eye on me as he dials the phone.

Once Kenneth has the price of the O'Doul's, he totals our bill and Coop pays.

We exit the supermarket and I am ready to explode.

"What the hell was that all about?" I shout.

"That was me saving your ass." Coop grins, lugging the shopping bag.

"I don't have Tourette's, butt rot."

"You could have fooled me," Coop argues. "With all that blubbering you were doing. I had to say something."

"You didn't have to say *that.*"

Coop rolls his eyes and laughs. "Jesus, dude. Stop being so emo. It's worse than having Tourette's."

We walk around the corner of the PriceMark. Actually, Sean and Coop walk. I'm several steps behind them, doing a sort of Frankenstein's monster waddle. Stiff legs, stiff arms.

"Pick it up, Grandpa," Coop calls out. Several people in the parking lot turn to look at me.

I'd shake my head, but I can't. My neck has seized up.

When I finally make it around the corner, Sean and Coop are standing there laughing at me.

"I hate you both," I say.

This only makes Sean and Coop break up even more.

"I don't know why I'm friends with you."

Coop pretends to look hurt. "Can you believe this guy?" He smacks Sean's arm. "Talk about ungrateful. Did I or did I not cover for your screwup?"

"Yeah," I say. "By making me look like a jackass in front of that guy. Not to mention the two hot chicks behind us in line."

I try to storm off, but all I can do is my stiff-legged totter, which kind of dampens the desired effect.

Coop and Sean easily catch up with me, but I don't even look at them.

"Screw off."

"You're never going to see those people again," Sean says. "Why do you even care?"

"You wouldn't be saying that if it was you."

"I'm sorry, okay?" Coop says. "Jeez. You'd think you'd be happy. At least now we can get into the party."

"Not me," I say. "I'm not going."

"Oh, yes you are." Coop points a finger at me. "Don't make me have to poke you."

"Don't even think about it." I waddle faster.

Coop picks up his step. Sean is right behind him.

"Are you going to the party?" Coop's finger hovers in the air.

"No."

Coop jabs his finger into my chest.

"Ow! Crap!" The pain sends a shock wave through my whole body.

"Are you going to the party?" Coop asks.

"Can't you see how—"

Coop stabs me in the shoulder.

"Goddamn it!" I wince and cough. I'd punch Coop in the face, but the bones in my arms have turned into Twizzlers.

"Leave him alone," Sean says.

"No." Coop glares at Sean. "I'm being a good friend here." He turns back to me and sticks out his forefinger again. "Do you need more tough love?"

"Please," I say. It hurts so bad I start to laugh. "I'll go. I'll go. Just stop poking me."

Coop nods and smiles. "You'll thank me someday."

I'd like to thank him right now. By tackling him and feeding him some grass. But I have to conserve the limited energy I've got left for what is sure to be a long, excruciating traipse home.

CHAPTER TWENTY-THREE

HOT PASTRAMI

SEAN AND I ARE HAVING DINNER at Cooper's house tonight. Coop's sister, Angela, is going to drive us to Ronnie Hull's party, but she said she wasn't picking anyone up, so Coop invited us over. Mom's waived the we-eat-dinner-as-a-family rule because Pete's away.

So here we are, sitting around Coop's kitchen table with his family. My overtaxed muscles are still screaming at me, but I've muffled their cries with a handful of Advil.

I've been trying to figure out what to say to Kelly when I see her tonight, but nothing's coming to mind. Part of me thinks I'll just improvise, but most of me knows that won't work; I'll just end up all tongue-tied and stuck in my head. The more I roll it around, the more nervous I get. I need to find something to distract myself with.

I let my eyes wander around Coop's kitchen. It's way darker than mine. Everything painted olive green.

The walls, the cabinets. Even the fridge. His house smells like a mixture of sweaty socks and rubber and hard-boiled eggs.

Mr. Redmond is at one end of the table, with his elbows propped up on either side of his empty plate. There's something Ichabod Crane about him. If Ichabod Crane were a forty-five-year-old machinist with thick greasy hair and dirty calloused hands.

". . . and then I had to reach down into this vat of filthy old oil to try and find the goddamn ratchet that Al had dropped," Mr. Redmond says, chewing openmouthed on a piece of nicotine gum. "Right up to my friggin' armpit." He gives a little karate chop at his shoulder to show how far. "I shit you not."

"Walter." Mrs. Redmond shuffles her Winnie-the-Pooh body over to the table and places a platter of fish sticks down in front of us. "Language."

Mr. Redmond laughs. "These kids hear worse at school every day, I'm sure."

"He's right, Mom," Angela says, reaching her wiry arm out and forking one fish stick onto her plate. She's sort of pretty, I guess. Tanned, smooth skin. Long dark hair. But she acts like she's already an adult. A really old adult. And she bosses Coop around like he's a dog. So it doesn't make you like her very much. Or even want to imagine her naked. At least not on a regular basis. "If Lower Rockville High School were a movie, it'd be rated R for sure."

"Well, I'd like to have a G-rated dinner, thank you very much." Mrs. Redmond carries three bowls over from the oven. Creamed spinach, canned corn, and Tater Tots. "We have guests." She puts the bowls down, takes her seat, and blows a phantom string of hair from her face.

Mr. Redmond and Coop grab at the food like if they don't get theirs right away, there won't be any left. Mrs. Redmond takes her time placing her paper napkin in her lap, and Angela seems satisfied chopping up her single piece of fish into a dozen pieces.

Sean and I wait until everyone serves themselves before filling our plates.

"Anyway," Mr. Redmond says, "my point is . . ." He blinks hard, then opens his eyes wide. "I don't remember what my point was. I'm losing my mind." He pops some corn into his mouth and chews it right along with his nicotine gum.

"How's swim team going?" Mrs. Redmond asks, smiling.

"Pretty good," I say.

Coop laughs. "Matt volunteered to do the hundred-yard butterfly."

I narrow my eyes at Coop and send him a wave of hate.

Mr. Redmond turns toward me and tilts his head. The thin waddle of skin that's strung from his chin to his neck sways. "The butterfly? Are you out of your nut? Why would you do that?"

"I don't know," I say. "They needed someone."

"They're looking for people to give vasectomies to elephants," Mr. Redmond says. "You gonna volunteer for that, too?"

"No," I say.

Sean smiles. "He's doing it to try and impress a girl."

I spin my head and shoot him an I-want-to-stab-you-with-my-fork look.

"Ahhh." Mr. Redmond nods. "Now we're getting down to the nitty-gritty."

"That's pretty stupid." Angela trains her dark judgmental eyes on me.

Mrs. Redmond picks at some corn that's stuck in her teeth. "I think it's romantic."

"Mom, please, that's 'cause you're a hundred years old," Angela says. "Nobody's going to get all worked up over some guy doing the butterfly. Trust me."

"You don't know this particular girl, obviously," Coop says.

"That's not why I'm doing it, anyway." I feel my cheeks prickle. "I just wanted to challenge myself." This is great. It's not like I wasn't nervous enough about the party tonight. The last thing I need is this conversation swirling around me when I'm trying to talk to Kelly.

"Listen." Mr. Redmond gestures with a fork-speared Tater Tot. "We've all done stupid shit to impress a girl at some time or other. I could tell you stories."

"Please don't," Angela says.

"Come on, Dad." Coop sits up tall.

"Remember. We're eating, dear," Mrs. Redmond says.

Mr. Redmond puts down his utensils and rubs his hands together. "Okay." He leans forward. "This one girl. I won't name names. Your mother. She was working the counter at a delicatessen. You know, slicing meats, doling out the salads. That kind of crap."

"Not that story, Walter. Please." Mrs. Redmond's neck flushes.

"As I was saying," Mr. Redmond continues. "This unnamed girl. Your mother. She was a little ball of fire back then. A real alley cat. And the mouth on her. She pretends to be all Mother Teresa now, but let me tell you something. The words that were flying from her lips could have wilted lettuce."

Mrs. Redmond shakes her head. "That's just not true."

I look over to see if Coop is embarrassed by any of this, but he's just smiling big, watching his dad. Angela, on the other hand, looks disgusted.

"So I went in to order a hot pastrami one afternoon and I see this anonymous girl. Who looked remarkably similar to the woman sitting across the table from me right now. Only twenty years younger. And I say to myself, now here's some hot pastrami that I could *really* sink my teeth into."

Angela cringes. "Gross, Dad. I don't need to hear

this." She pushes her chair back and stands. "May I please be excused?"

"Of course, dear," Mrs. Redmond says.

Mr. Redmond waits for Angela to leave before going on. "Anyway. The deli is packed with customers, and when my turn comes, I just keep ordering thing after friggin' thing because I want to keep talking to this little spitfire. A pound of turkey breast. An entire two-foot salami. Three pounds of macaroni salad. Like that. Nothing I wanted. Nothing I could actually afford. But once I got started, I couldn't stop. And I figured that she must think I'm loaded if I can be ordering so much crap. I had her laughing and smiling and it was like we were the only two people on the planet."

Mrs. Redmond shakes her head. "It sounds all sweet and charming, but wait."

"Okay, well, then, this prick behind me pokes me in the shoulder blade with his umbrella and he's all, 'Hey, I'd like to order sometime this century.' So I said, 'Well, buddy, you better take a seat, because I'm just getting started.'"

"The poor man was in his seventies," Mrs. Redmond says.

Mr. Redmond waves this away. "I don't remember that. All I remember is this cocky bastard mumbles something under his breath and other people start laughing. So really, I don't have any other choice but to give him a little smack upside the head with my salami. I mean, he was making me look like an ass."

"You were doing a pretty good job of that yourself, Walter," Mrs. Redmond says.

"Whatever. Anyway, the guy screams and grabs his nose like I broke it or something."

"You *did* break it," Mrs. Redmond adds.

"*Fractured* it. Hey, is it my fault the guy had weak cartilage? It was a salami for Christ's sake. Of course, I realize now, hindsight being what it is, that maybe I shouldn't have whacked him with the salami." Mr. Redmond smirks. "Instead, I probably should have used the block of Parmesan."

Coop and Sean laugh.

Mrs. Redmond gives Coop's dad a disapproving stare. "That's not funny, Walter."

"The point is," Mr. Redmond fixes his eyes on me. "I lost myself because I was transfixed by a female of the opposite sex. So I know from whence you come." He grabs my aching forearm, pinning it to the table. His hand feels like burlap. "Little advice from the worldly wise. Women have no idea what's going on in a guy's mind. If they did, they'd run screaming. So keep up a good front. Never let them know the real you. My motto is, why tell the truth when a lie will do just as well?"

"Just ignore him, Matthew," Mrs. Redmond says. "Walter doesn't mean any of that. He likes to tease people."

I spread the creamed spinach around my plate with my fork. Mr. Redmond's right about the things that fly through my head sometimes. I'm sure most of the good-looking girls I meet wouldn't be too pleased to know that I'm usually picturing them in various states of undress. Of course, I don't need Coop's dad telling me not to go confessing this; I've done some dumb things in my life so far, but nothing quite *that* stupid.

I lightly knock the wooden underside of the table, hoping I haven't just jinxed myself for the party tonight.

CHAPTER TWENTY-FOUR

THE PARTY

Angela is driving us to Ronnie Hull's house in her new-to-her two-thousand-one impulse-red Toyota Corolla. Angela is in love with her car. She talks about it like it's her genius child. It gets the best gas mileage; it has the best stereo; it has the most comfortable seats. She keeps the car in showroom condition. You are not allowed to eat in it; you are not allowed to wear your shoes in it; and she would prefer you didn't breathe too much while you were sitting in it. She won't let you lower the windows, because she doesn't want the outside air contaminating the interior. She keeps the inside temperature a perfect, noncorrosive sixty-five degrees Fahrenheit.

Angela pulls the car up to the curb. "Out, brat," she says.

"Thanks." Coop hands over fifteen dollars and grabs the green plastic bag with the "beer." We throw open the doors and I slowly unfold myself from the backseat. I seem to be stiffening up with each passing hour.

When we are all out of the car, Angela drives away.

We sit on the curb, putting our sneakers back on, as the car motors down the street.

"I can't believe she actually makes you pay her," I say.

"I know," Coop says, sounding a little bitter. "That was my last fifteen bucks. But that's not all she got."

"What are you talking about?" Sean raises an eyebrow.

"I let a beef biscuit fly just before we got out." Coop nods. "She should be getting a nice lungful of sawmill right about now."

"That's classic, dude." Sean gives Coop a fist pound.

"Let's see if she keeps the windows shut now," I say with a grin.

Coop, Sean, and me head up the walkway. My waddle is more of a medicated shuffle now. I don't know if I'm going to be able to pull this off. Coop says I should find a couch to plant myself on and I'll be fine, but I'm not so sure.

All the lights in Ronnie's two-story house are blazing. The thump of the music inside rattles the windows. I was feeling pretty confident about our O'Doul's plan all day, but now that I see the two guys hanging out and smoking by the front door, I'm a lot less optimistic.

"Play it cool, Tourette's," Coop whispers, like he can feel my waves of anxiety.

As we approach, the taller of the two guys holds up his hand like a traffic cop. He's wearing an orange T-shirt with a drawing of a chimpanzee on it. Under the picture it says MY MONKEY'S BEEN BAD. IT NEEDS A SPANKING.

"What do you got?" the tall guy says.

Coop holds out the plastic bag. The other guy, the shorter one who's dressed all in black, takes the bag and opens it. I hold my breath as he looks inside. After what seems like a month, he nods and smiles. "O'Doul's. Nice."

Coop's eyes slide back and forth between me and Sean. I start breathing again.

The guy in black pulls out one of the bottles. "Can we bum one of these bad boys from you?"

"Uh, yeah. Sure," Coop says.

"Righteous." The tall guy grabs the bottle from his friend. "O'Doul's. All of the great, rich taste of beer with none of that annoying alcohol."

Both of the guys laugh.

"Are you kidding me with this sputum?" The tall guy tosses the bottle at Coop, who juggles it before getting a firm grip.

"I think you homies got the wrong venue," the guy in black says. "You're probably looking for the piñata-and-pony party up the street."

"That's right." The tall guy snickers. "O'Doul's goes perfect with ice-cream cake and cookies."

"So, what?" I say. "You're not going to let us in?"

"The real question you should be asking," the guy in

black says, "is do you actually want to go in there carrying *that*?"

I look over at Sean and Coop, who seem to be examining their shoes. "We want in," I say.

"Suit yourself." The tall guy throws his hands up. "We were just told, make sure everyone brings beer. No one said anything about a minimum alcohol content. If you losers want to go in there with this baby brew and humiliate yourselves, far be it from me to stop you."

The guy in black shoves the shopping bag back at Coop.

The tall guy opens the front door. "Please drink responsibly."

The two guys crack up as Coop, Sean, and me cautiously step inside.

The music is so loud, it vibrates my skull. The house is packed with kids holding bottles and cans of beer.

"No one's going to be able to tell," Coop mocks Sean.

"We're in, aren't we?"

Coop holds up the green bag. "Yeah, except now we're lugging a ticking bomb."

We navigate the maze of bodies, squeezing past guys and girls laughing, drinking, and trying to talk over the boom of the bass drum.

I recognize a few girls from school, a couple of guys from Ronnie's band, the guy who works at the 7-Eleven. I keep my eyes peeled for Kelly or Valerie, but I don't see either one. I don't know if I'm relieved or disappointed. A little of both, probably.

We make it to the kitchen, and thankfully, there's no one here.

"We have to hurry," Coop says. "Keep a lookout."

Coop quickly flips open the lid on one of the half-dozen coolers on the floor.

"I didn't see Kelly," I yell over the music.

"Keep your pants on." Coop buries three of the beer bottles way down into the ice. "We'll find her. After we deal with this white elephant."

Coop snags some napkins off the counter. He wraps them around three of the O'Doul's.

"Under *no* circumstances are you to reveal this label to anyone," Coop says. "If you do, I will deny any knowledge of your existence."

We each grab a napkin-cloaked O'Doul's and stroll the party. The living room swarms with kids. I nod at a few guys from swim team.

We make our way past the couch toward the glass door that leads to the backyard. Coop slides the door open, and the three of us step outside. There are tiki torches lit around the kidney-shaped pool in the center of the yard. The music is piped out here as well, but it's much softer. There must be a hundred kids standing around or sitting on lawn furniture. I scan the crowd. Still no Kelly.

I look over at Sean. Something's different about him.

"Did you grow taller since this afternoon?" I say.

Sean shakes his head.

Coop looks over at Sean and squints. "You *are* taller. What the hell?"

"Shut up, okay?" Sean whispers.

"Are you wearing high heels again?" Coop laughs. "Because if you really want to be a girl, there's nothing to be ashamed of."

"The only shame is pretending to be something you're not," I say.

"Screw off. Both of you." Sean cranes his neck, pretending to look around, like if he ignores us we'll just go away. Fat chance.

"You better tell us what's going on or I'm going to have to make an announcement," Coop says.

Sean sets his jaw and speaks through his teeth. "I'm wearing lifts, okay? And I'd appreciate it if you kept it on the q.t."

"Lifts?" I say.

"Famous people use them all the time." Sean huffs. "They add like three inches."

"So, what, that gives you like a three-and-a-half-inch hog now?" Coop says.

"To your *height,* spaz. You're such a third-grader sometimes."

Coop cups his hand over his mouth and smothers his laughter. "I'm sorry. I'm sorry. It's just so friggin' funny."

"Go ahead." Sean shrugs. "We'll see who's laughing

last when Matt hooks up with Kelly and I'm spending quality time with Valerie."

"Right." Coop nods. "The only thing is, by the time you get with Valerie, I won't be able to laugh anymore because I'll be dead. Of old age."

"There's Kelly," I say. "Over there." I casually point to a large oak tree in the corner of the yard. I can see part of Kelly's face and her right arm. She's talking to someone, but I can't make out who it is.

"Is Valerie with her?" Sean bobs his head back and forth, trying to see through the crowd.

"I can't tell," I say.

Coop takes a step to the side. "Uh-oh."

"What?" I move over to where Coop is standing. And that's when I see what Coop sees.

Tony Grillo. His black-, blue-, and white-striped polo shirt barely contains his freakishly pumped Bowflex body. He's talking to Kelly, gesturing with the beer bottle in his left hand.

"Shall we go?" I say.

Coop squints at me. "Just like that? You see the enemy and you turn and tuck tail?"

I attempt to shrug, but my aching shoulders don't obey. "What am I supposed to do?"

"I guess you weren't a Spartan in your past life," Coop says.

"She's with her boyfriend."

"And not just any boyfriend," Sean says. "I wouldn't

be surprised if under those designer clothes he was wearing spandex and a cape."

Coop shoots Sean a look. "Hey, *Lifts*. Keep your fantasies to yourself, okay?"

Sean shakes his head. "That's not—"

Coop holds up his hand, silencing Sean. "Don't make it any worse." He turns to me. "Look, Matt. Maybe they're going out. Maybe they're not. All I know is, Kelly invited you to this party for a reason."

"She was probably just being friendly."

"Matt, Matt, Matt. Why do I always have to be the one to explain these things to you?"

"Explain what?"

Coop takes a deep breath and runs his hand down his face. "Okay. I'll walk you through it. Has Kelly ever asked you to a party before?"

"No."

"Right. So, why do you think that suddenly changed?"

"I don't know."

"Have you two recently become best friends?"

"No."

"Did you save her kitty from a tree?"

"No."

"Did you chase down a mugger who stole her purse?"

I shift my weight and sigh. "What the hell does this have to do with anything?"

"I'm just trying to figure out why, if you aren't good friends, if you didn't do anything to suddenly make Kelly think she owed you something, she would invite you to this party."

"I don't know."

"Sean, help me out here." Coop turns to Sean, who is busy scoping the party for Valerie. Coop backhands Sean's shoulder.

"What?" Sean looks at Coop.

"I said help me out here."

"With what?" Sean blinks.

Coop gives Sean his best annoyed-teacher glare.

Sean is totally lost. He looks at me. He looks at Coop. "I thought I saw Valerie."

Coop throws his hands in the air. "Fine. I guess I spent all my money to get us into this party for nothing. Whatever. I'm done. Everyone for themselves. Sean, you go find Valerie and try to impress her with your three inches. Matt, you can keep on pretending Kelly doesn't have her eye on you so that you won't have to do anything about it." Coop nods. "If you need me, I'll be the one with the drunkest girl in the party, trying to convince her I'm Justin Timberlake's younger brother. Adios, amigos."

Coop walks off, leaving me and Sean standing there, looking at each other.

"What crawled up his butt?" Sean says.

"I don't know. Maybe he's pissed because he won't be able to afford his comic books this month."

"Graphic novels," Sean corrects me.

"Whatever."

"There's a difference."

"I don't give a shit, Sean. Just go away." I want to punch something. A wall. A door. Sean, if he doesn't leave soon.

Sean shrugs. He takes a sip of his O'Doul's. "You've got it bad, Matt. I know the feeling. But I'll tell you one thing. What my uncle Doug once told me. You have to get your priorities straight. Friends first, then Springsteen, then women." Sean raises his beer bottle, nods, and walks away.

CHAPTER TWENTY-FIVE

FIGHT OR FLIGHT

I DRAW IN A DEEP BREATH and let it out slowly. I try and take a tug on my "beer," but it's a struggle. I have to bring my face down and meet my hand halfway because I still can't lift my arm high enough to drink properly. I have to slurp more than actually drink and I'm sure I look like a moron, but I don't care.

I stand there for another minute and watch as Tony leans into Kelly. He whispers something in her ear. She rolls her eyes, but she doesn't move away. She just stands there and listens to everything that's coming out of his snarling scarred mouth.

Kelly's wearing tight low-rise jeans with small hearts on the front pockets and a tiny pea-green bomber hoodie that shows off her flat stomach and belly ring.

God, this is torture.

I need to leave. Coop's an idiot. And even if he *was* right, what does he expect me to do? Challenge Tony to a fight? I couldn't even beat him in a thumb wrestle. I mean, look at those hands. They're like Sasquatch paws.

I do my dippy-bird act and take another suck on my beer.

I knew this was a mistake. Coop's sister won't be back for us until midnight, which means I better find something else to do besides stand here like Charlie Bucket with his nose pressed to the candy-store window.

I turn and manage my way over to a round glass table by the side of the pool. All four plastic chairs are available. I carefully lower myself into one of them. The Advil should *not* be wearing off so quickly.

I wonder if I've done some real damage to my body. It was a Herculean chore getting out of the house tonight without my mother seeing. If she'd caught me in this state, she wouldn't have let me leave. My mother is a serious worrier. She's crazy about safety. Even more so since Dad left. She wanted me to wear a hockey helmet last year when Grandpa took me out to play golf. "What if one of those flying balls hits you in the temple?" she said. "It could kill you." It took a while for Grandpa Arlo to talk her down from that one. We left as fast as we could when she started going on about how she wanted me to wear a cup. "You only have one *you-know-what*," she called after us. "All it takes is one golf club flying out of someone's hands and . . ." We were in the car and gone before she could finish.

Yeah, if she'd seen me this way, she would have

rushed me to the emergency room, for sure. Which would be like a day with the *Maxim* Girls, compared to this.

I look down at the pool. The water is pretty filthy. The Hulls obviously don't use it much. There have to be a thousand dead worms on the bottom. Along with a big clay planter and a rusty tricycle. There's a thin film of algae, or something green, floating on the surface. I wonder if Coop could get Sean to bob for a Life Saver in that sludge.

I sigh. I don't belong here. Maybe I can call a cab. This night sucks.

"Go to hell, asshole!" It's a girl's voice.

I look up and see Kelly storming past me.

"Where do you think you're going?" Tony comes after her.

Kelly thrusts a bird high in the air and keeps walking, right through the back door and into the house.

Several people laugh. "Ouch. Stinger," someone says.

Tony doesn't follow her. "Whatever." He turns and joins a group of kids huddled around the barbecue. "What a bitch."

I hear Coop's voice in my head, like Obi-Wan: *"Dude, here's your chance. Go after her."* But I don't move. Why would she talk to me? Who am I? She hardly knows me.

"Get your ass out of that chair!" It's Coop again. Reprimanding me. I don't like that he's taken up residence in my brain. But he's right. I have a window of

opportunity here. Things like this don't happen every day. It's decision time. Take a chance or play it safe. Be a man or stay a child. Go big or go home. My palms are damp. I wipe them on my jeans, but they won't dry.

Fine, I'll go. I'll just see if she wants to talk. I grip the armrests and hoist myself out of the chair. I hobble toward the back door, hoping to God that Kelly hasn't decided to do her sulking upstairs.

CHAPTER TWENTY-SIX

WHEN OPPORTUNITY KNOCKS

I DO MY BEST march-of-the-wooden-soldiers clomp through the party. I look everywhere, my head dodging left and right. Every time I think I see Kelly, it turns out to be someone else.

I see Sean in the corner of the living room, talking to some girl with corkscrew blond hair. I guess he got tired of waiting around for Valerie. This new girl is oddly cute, I suppose. In a kind of Ashley Olsen meets Frodo sort of way. I don't recognize her from anywhere. Sean stands about two inches taller than her, which means he's one inch shorter without shoes. They're passing Sean's masked beer back and forth, and he has her laughing. Way to go, Sean.

I approach them, forcing my rigid limbs to move in as natural a way as possible. Sean gives me a chin lift by way of hello.

"Hey," I say.

"Matt, this is Tianna."

"Hi," I say.

Tianna smiles. "Hello." She takes a mouthy sip of Sean's beer.

"Have you seen Kelly around?"

"Yeah," Sean says. "I just saw her go into the kitchen."

"Thanks." I nod and I'm off again.

I hear Tianna giggle as I lumber away. I'm sure that Sean has used my pain to make this girl laugh, but I don't hold it against him.

I make my way into the kitchen and there she is. All by herself. Sipping a beer and staring out the window. My first impulse is to turn and leave. She obviously wants to be left alone. Why else would she be hiding in the kitchen? I can't tell if she's crying or not. And it's none of my business. I'll just go. That's the polite thing.

Kelly downs the rest of her beer. She turns and sees me. "Hi." She smiles.

"Hi," I say. "I was just . . ." Just what? Standing here staring at you. Thinking about what you look like naked. Wondering if I have a chance in a billion to kiss you. No. These are exactly the things Coop's dad was talking about. Keep up a good front. "I saw you outside. Are you okay?"

Kelly cocks her head and smiles again. "Aww. That's so sweet."

"I wasn't eavesdropping or anything." I clear my throat. "I was just sitting there when I saw you go by and you looked upset."

Kelly sighs. God, she's so pretty. "It's no big deal. My ex-boyfriend's just an asshole, is all. But what do you expect? He's a guy. No offense."

"Don't worry about it. I know what you mean. My two best friends are guys and they're both assholes."

This makes Kelly laugh. Wow. I feel a tingle down the back of my neck. I can't believe I made her laugh.

"You want a beer?" Kelly drops her empty into the recycle bin and moves to one of the coolers.

"Oh. No, thanks. I've got one." I wave my camou-flaged O'Doul's.

"Well, I'm getting one."

She squats down and opens the lid of a cooler. Her low-rise jeans slide just a little lower. I can see the top of her crimson thong. Jesus Christ. I swallow. I can only take in little, shallow breaths. I am suddenly aware of everything. My eyebrows. My chapped lips. The hang-nail on my left pinky. It's like all my nerves have been amplified. There's a tickle in my eardrum but I leave it alone. I don't want Kelly to turn around and see me with my finger stuck in my ear.

All of a sudden Kelly howls with laughter. "Oh, my God. Who's the loser who brought the O'Doul's?"

A rush of horror courses up my spine as I grip the beer tight in my right hand. I glance down to make sure the label is hidden. The napkin has soaked up the dampness from the bottle and is starting to shred.

Kelly stands and slinks over to me, holding up a bottle of Budweiser. "Can you open this for me?"

Oh, great. This should be interesting.

"Sure," I say, taking the full bottle in my left hand. It pulls my arm down like I've just been handed a bowling ball.

Kelly looks at me funny. "You okay?"

I let out a nervous laugh. "I sort of upped my regular workout routine. I might have done a little too much."

Kelly stays close. I breathe in her sweet cinnamon-spice smell, and it's making me dizzy.

I can feel the soggy napkin wrapped around my O'Doul's disintegrating under my sweaty palm. I have no idea if in my weakened state I'll be able to twist the top off this beer bottle using both my hands. But I know for sure I won't be able to do it with just the one. So here are my options: Use my teeth and hope Kelly thinks it's funny and not just disgusting. Put my O'Doul's down and risk her spotting the label. Or lean back slightly and tuck the O'Doul's under my arm to free my right hand so I can use it to open Kelly's beer. It's the most physically painful alternative but the least emotionally devastating, which is why I choose it.

Kelly must be able to sense my anguish because she gestures at my O'Doul's. "I can hold that for you."

"No," I say. "It's fine. Really. I've got it." I tuck my

napkin-wrapped beer under my left armpit, having to angle myself backward a little so it doesn't spill. This is even more excruciating than I'd anticipated and I feel the perspiration starting to bead on my forehead.

I reach down with my right hand and grasp the Budweiser bottle cap. I try to twist it off without scrunching up my face in agony. The cap isn't budging; it's just digging into the flesh of my fingers.

"This new workout routine," I explain. "It's a killer. Three hours straight. It really takes it out of you."

"Just don't get too pumped up, okay?" Kelly says. "Muscle-heads are all into themselves. Trust me."

I give the cap another try but to no avail. If this takes me much longer, I am going to look like the wimp of the century. I muster every last scrap of strength I have left and lean into it with all I've got, trying not to groan too loudly. By some miracle I manage to wrench the top off the bottle. But in the process I also manage to spill my O'Doul's.

"Yikes!" Kelly squeals, leaping back so she doesn't get drenched.

Panic shoots through me and I involuntarily lift my left arm, releasing the O'Doul's from my armpit. It slips from its napkin sheath and bounces off my foot and onto the floor.

The bottle spins around, releasing its carbonated froth like a rabid ferret.

"Oh, crap!" Kelly says, laughing through her cupped hand.

I have to think fast. Once that bottle stops spinning, the label will be visible and Kelly will see that *I* am the loser who drinks the O'Doul's.

"Here," I say, shoving the Budweiser at Kelly so she won't get any crazy ideas about going for my beer.

I think about diving on top of the bottle like it's a grenade, but I can't imagine that won't look suspicious. Instead, I pretend to reach down for the O'Doul's and "accidentally" kick the bottle out through the kitchen doorway, into the carpeted family room, where someone I don't care about can find it.

"Oops," I say. "Oh, well. I guess that's the end of that one."

"Wow." Kelly giggles. "That was dramatic." I'm not sure, but I think she might be a little drunk. She takes a sip of her beer.

My mind zooms in on her lips and man, oh, man. I have to lean against the door frame or I'm going over. My desire is wrestling with my exhaustion and terror, and the whole thing is making me light-headed.

"So, uh . . ." Ask questions, idiot. Change the subject. Get the conversation flowing. "So, Tony's your *ex*-boyfriend?"

"Yeah. We broke up like a month ago. But he won't let it go. It's pathetic."

"Huh," I say. Come on, Matt, something besides that. Make something up. Something interesting. Tell her you spent a month in Europe last year.

"Speak of the devil," Kelly says, and turns away.

Tony bumps past me, causing my muscles to spasm.

"Who the hell is this?" Tony jerks his thumb in my direction.

Kelly spins around and smirks. "Only the guy who's going to kick your ass in butterfly at sectionals next week."

Tony's head swivels. From me to Kelly and back to me. "This twig?"

I'm as stunned as he is. Why would she say something like that? She must be drunk. "I'm, uh . . . I . . . Actually . . . Well . . ."

"That's right." Kelly laughs. "And I'm gonna be there to watch it all happen. I can't wait. We'll see what all your hussy sluts think about that. You're going down, big boy. Whooo!" Kelly raises her beer and then takes a long, long pull.

"Is that right, Twig?" Tony says to me, his eyes on fire.

Don't blink. I blink. For Christ's sake, don't gulp! I gulp. "I don't . . . You know . . . I am swimming . . . the butterfly . . . I guess we'll just have to see."

Tony snaps his head back to Kelly. "This what you go for now? Napoleon Dynamite here?" Tony gives a quick, derisive snort-laugh.

Kelly nods. She's going for the kill, I can tell. "You bet. Mark's more of a man than you'll ever be."

Mark?

"And he's not—" Kelly uses her left thumb to cut her pinky off at the first knuckle. She waves this in Tony's face. "I've seen him in a Speedo."

Tony glares at me, his pupils narrowing to pinpoints. Like I'm the one who just suggested he's got a tiny lunch log. I don't know if he's sneering or not because of that lip scar, but he definitely looks like he wants to take a bite out of my face.

"You're such a loser, Tony." Kelly shakes her head. "I'm going home." She storms out of the kitchen.

Tony points his thick sausage finger at me. "We're not done, you and me, *Mark*." He pokes me hard in the chest, which makes me cough in pain, and then goes after Kelly.

I stand there in the kitchen. Alone. I can feel the blood pumping through my veins. I have that brick-in-the-belly, sinking feeling. It's time to leave.

I'm about to go in search of Coop, when squat little Ronnie Hull stomps into the kitchen, waving my O'Doul's bottle.

"Who's the jackscrew who's leaving their empties on the floor?" he shouts.

"Not me," I say, holding up my hands. "I don't drink O'Doul's. I think that's Tony Grillo's brand."

My eyes slide to the side as I hustle out of the kitchen before Ronnie can ask any more questions.

CHAPTER TWENTY-SEVEN

DEEPER AND DEEPER

Coop is nowhere to be found. Sean and the Hobbit girl are out on the front porch, waiting for her parents to pick her up. I start looking for a place to hide until midnight, just in case Tony Grillo returns to beat the crap out of me.

I wander out back, my seizing muscles making me walk more and more like I just got off a two-hour bull ride. I do my best to blend into the crowd, but I'm on guard, constantly looking over my shoulder, even though my stiff neck makes this nearly impossible. I may not be able to put up much of a fight when Tony comes for me, but at least I won't be blindsided.

I head past the pool and toward the play set in the far corner of the yard. It looks pretty dark back there. I'm thinking I could take up refuge in the little wooden cottage at the top of the wave slide. When I get there, though, I find Valerie sitting on a swing, shuffling her feet in the dirt, making circles and swirls.

"Having fun?" I say.

Valerie looks up and smiles. "Matt. You came."

"Yeah." I nod. "I've been here for a while."

"Have you seen Kelly?"

"Yeah," I say. "I think she left. She had a fight with Tony."

"Tony's a bastard." Only Valerie's French accent could make this sound so cute.

"I'm sort of getting that."

"He cheated on her with like five different girls. He's a pig. She deserves someone better."

"Yeah," I say. Maybe Coop was right all along. Maybe Kelly did invite me to this party for a reason. Of course, that doesn't explain why she doesn't even know my name. "You want a beer?"

"I hate beer. It tastes like piss." Valerie spins herself around and around on the swing, winding up the chains. She lets go and twirls back fast. "Push me, okay?"

"Sure." This is going to cause me much agony, I know it, but what can I do? If I'm nice to Valerie, maybe she'll tell Kelly.

I move behind her and place my hands on her back. Her skin feels warm through her shirt. "Ready?"

"Go for it."

I give her a little push, and my muscles are cursing me for doing it. She pumps her legs lightly. We get into a nice kind of slow rhythm. Valerie swinging out into the night air, kicking her feet up, swaying back down into my hands for another push. This would all be picture perfect if my arms didn't feel like two blazing Duraflame logs.

"You doing anything fun this summer?" Valerie asks. "Any exciting plans?"

The only thing that jumps to mind is our goal to see a naked girl.

"Not really," I say. "How about you?"

"We have a cabin on Lake William," Valerie says. "We go there sometimes in the summer."

"Sounds nice."

"It's okay."

"I've never been to Lake William." I give Valerie another gentle push. "Do they have boats and stuff there?" I'm trying to figure out a way to bring this conversation around to Kelly. To try and find out what she really thinks about me. But it's got to come naturally. I don't want to sound too pushy.

"Yeah," Valerie says. "My brothers love all that stuff. Waterskiing, windsurfing, tubing."

"Not you?"

"Swallowing mouthfuls of nasty lake water is not my idea of fun. I'm more of a book-on-the-beach girl."

"I can see that." Another push. "So, you ever bring friends up there?" I'm hoping she says she brings Kelly, so that we can start talking about her.

Valerie shoots me a mischievous look over her shoulder as she swings back toward me. "Oh, real subtle, Matt."

Oh, my God. Can she read my mind? "Sorry. I'm, uh . . . just . . . I was only wondering if—"

"I don't think my parents would be too happy if I brought a *boy* with me to our cabin." Valerie laughs. "Though I'd love to see their faces if I asked."

"No, I wasn't . . . That's not . . ."

"Besides," Valerie says, "I can't imagine Kelly would be too happy with me."

What does she mean by that? Is it because Kelly likes me? Or is it because she usually invites Kelly? I can't tell if she's serious or not. She must be making fun of me. What's going on here?

"That's pretty forward of you, inviting yourself to my cabin like that." Valerie chuckles. "And I thought you were shy."

"But I wasn't inviting . . ." The words are fish-hooked in my throat. I feel my whole face get hot. "Never mind. Let's just . . ."

Valerie is laughing hard now. "It's okay, Matt. I'm just teasing you."

"Oh." I exhale.

"I bet you're blushing," Valerie says. "I bet your cheeks are beet red."

"Yeah, well . . ." I keep pushing Valerie on the swing. I don't know what to say anymore. We're both quiet.

"I'm sorry." Valerie drags her feet on the ground and stops the swing. My arms rejoice. She turns to look at me. "I didn't mean to embarrass you. Well, I *did* mean it.

A little. But I'm sorry." Valerie smiles at me. She's trying not to laugh, I can tell.

"It's okay." She's looking at me so sweetly. I figure I might as well take advantage of her feeling sorry and go for broke. "But . . . I was curious—"

"There you are!" It's Coop striding toward us. "I've been looking all over for you, dude. You're harder to find than a first-edition Watchmen." Coop gives a half smile to Valerie. "Hey, Val."

"Cooper."

Coop grabs my shoulders and steers me away from the swing. "Excuse us. I just need to borrow Matt here for a little while."

"Sure," Valerie says.

I look back over my shoulder, desperate to finish talking with Valerie. But I don't have the physical or emotional strength right now to resist Coop.

"What are you doing?" I say. "I was talking to her."

Coop shakes his head like whatever I'm saying means nothing. "It's *Mission Impossible* time, dawg."

Coop's got his arm around my shoulder. We're headed back toward the house.

"What the hell does that mean?"

"It means," Coop says, "we're about to accomplish our summer's goal *and* get that picture for Sean's sister. As long as you don't shit your pants again."

CHAPTER TWENTY-EIGHT

BEST-LAID PLANS

It's MANDY REAGAN, dude. She's here. And I overheard her asking her friend for a condom," Coop whispers to me as we head upstairs. The steps are a challenge for me, but if I lean from side to side, I manage them okay.

"So what?" I say.

"She said she's meeting a guy up in Ronnie's parents' bedroom at eleven thirty." Coop raises his eyebrows. "So, we hide in the closet and get a live sex show, dude. Just like they have in Amsterdam."

"You've never been to Amsterdam."

"I've seen movies about it."

"Who's the guy?" I say.

Coop laughs. "Who cares? He could be Ronald McDonald and it wouldn't matter, because that's not where I'll be looking."

I'm torn, actually. The idea of seeing a hot girl having sex is more than a little enticing. But I really wanted to hear what Valerie was going to say about Kelly.

Sean's waiting for us in the upstairs hallway. "All clear," he says.

We make our way into the room at the end of the hall. It looks very much like a parents' bedroom. The bed perfectly made with a brown comforter, pillows on both sides stacked three deep. Nothing on the floors. Perfume and cologne bottles neatly placed on the dresser, right beside a glass jewelry box. It even *smells* like a parents' room. A sort of swirling mix of leather, soap, and lavender.

"Over here," Coop says, pointing to the walk-in closet. "If we keep the door cracked just a bit, we'll be able to see out but they won't be able to see in."

"I don't know." My mind is still out in the yard with Valerie. "What if we get caught?"

"We're not going to get caught," Coop says. "Trust me."

"And even if we do," Sean says, "what are they gonna do? Chase us into the party buck naked?"

Coop looks at his watch. "Five minutes to showtime." He walks over to the bedside table and clicks on the lamp.

"What the hell are you doing?" I say.

"He's setting the mood," Sean says. "We want it romantic."

Coop laughs. "Yeah, that's what we want. Romance. Followed quickly by some filthy, raunchy monkey love."

"They're going to know someone was in here," I say.

Coop looks skyward. "People leave lights on in their rooms all the time. They won't even think twice about it. Besides, this way we'll get a better look and get a clearer picture." He waves his cell phone camera in the air.

Coop moves to the closet and holds open the door. "Gentleman, please." He gestures inside. Sean hurries in. I go next and Coop follows, pulling the door shut behind him, leaving a one-inch slit for us to peer through. "Okay, we need to arrange ourselves for optimum viewage. Sean, you kneel on the floor. Matt, you stand behind Sean."

Sean and I get into position.

"Good," Coop says. "And I'll just peek in from the side here. Like this." Coop stands next to Sean and leans over, his head floating around my chest.

We have a pretty good view of the bed. The light Coop turned on does make it easier to see. Now that we're here, I feel myself getting fired up.

"This is gonna be awesome," Sean says.

"We should've made some popcorn." Coop laughs at his own joke.

"We should be quiet now," I say. "Just in case they're early."

"Okay, Mom," Coop says.

"Hey, Coop, can we switch? My legs are cramping up."

"Suck it up, dude." Coop swats the top of Sean's head.

"I'm serious," Sean says.

We hear voices down the hall.

"Shut up," Coop orders. "They're coming."

I hear a guy's voice getting closer. "Ronnie won't care." It sounds slightly familiar.

"Are you sure?" A girl who I assume must be Mandy.

"Whatever. He's passed out in the backyard."

Mandy enters first. She's wearing a tight pink belly shirt and a short denim skirt. Oh, my God. This is going to be good.

The guy enters. And he's definitely not Ronald McDonald.

Tony Grillo shuts the bedroom door and locks it. Mandy does a sexy twirl that brings her up close against Tony. She pulls a condom from the back pocket of her skirt and holds it up like she's doing some kind of commercial. "Lexi loaned me one."

"Really?" Tony laughs. "Are you gonna have to give it back to her when we're done?"

Mandy laughs and smacks Tony's chest. "Gross."

I am excited and terrified all at once.

Sean emits a small soft groan. I don't know if it's pain from his leg cramp or if it's an I-can't-believe-what-I'm-about-to-see moan. Either way, he better shut up or I'm going to kill him.

Tony pulls Mandy's T-shirt up and over her head. She's wearing a lacy pink push-up bra, and I think I might faint. It's really going to happen. My first live naked girl.

Mandy returns the favor and lifts Tony's polo shirt over his head. His chest is carved from stone. His stomach is ripped. Mandy runs her hands down Tony's body like she's worshiping it. "Wow," she says.

Sean whimpers again. It's definitely pain this time.

Mandy unbuttons Tony's pants and lets them drop to the floor. His legs are like sequoias.

Tony unzips Mandy's jean skirt at the side. He squats down and tugs the skirt off her hips, pulling it to the floor. She helps him out by doing a little hip shimmy, which makes me have to shut my eyes before I totally lose control.

I hear the faint, electronic click of Coop's cell phone camera taking a picture.

Mandy freezes. "Did you hear something?"

"No," Tony says, burying his face in her neck.

Sean grunts loudly. I feel him shift on the floor.

"There. What was that?" Mandy asks.

Sean loses his balance and the back of his head smashes hard into my groin.

"Ooof." All my breath is forced from my lungs. I lean forward, cracking my head against the door—

—which flies open.

"What the fuck?" Tony stares at us huddling in the closet.

Mandy shrieks and clutches herself.

"Here it is," Coop says, picking a phantom something off the closet floor. "Found it, guys. Sorry to interrupt. You can go back to whatever it was you were doing."

Coop is the first to bolt. He runs to the bedroom door, unlocks it, and flees before Tony can get his pants back on.

Sean is right on Coop's heels.

I'm momentarily paralyzed. Tony meets my eyes.

"You!" He straightens and points. His pants fall back around his ankles.

I don't wait to confirm his accusation. My legs are still in horrible pain, but it's amazing how a shot of pure fear can get you moving.

★ CHAPTER TWENTY-NINE ★

DROWNED

SPLIT UP!" COOP YELLS as he bounds down the staircase, with Sean right behind him. "He can't get all three of us."

I scramble down the steps after them. I think I'm running fast, but Coop and Sean are leaving me in their dust.

My left heel slips off the edge of one of the steps, and I'm bobsledding down the stairs on my ass. I feel the burn of the carpet through my jeans. The staccato pounding on my tailbone. Despite the pain, it works out pretty well because I make it down to the first floor much faster than I would have otherwise.

Some kids in the family room are laughing and pointing at me, but I don't have time to be embarrassed. Tony is charging me, pulling his shirt over his head, taking four steps at a time.

"You're going to die, Twig!" Tony roars.

I don't doubt this, but I sprint anyway. It's pure instinct.

I use the party guests as obstacles. I dodge in and out of everyone. Around this girl. Past that guy. In between this group. Sidestepping that couple. Some people reel back, raising their beers out of harm's way. Others barely even give me a look.

"Excuse me," I say. "Excuse me. Just need to . . . Thank you."

I can tell by the "Heys!" and "What the hells?!" that Tony Grillo is whipping like a tornado through the crowd. I imagine bodies flying through the air as he tosses them aside like dirty socks.

I wanted to head for the front of the house, but somehow I've ended up at the back. The sliding glass door is stuck. I pull on the handle, but it doesn't budge. I rattle it like crazy but still nothing.

"Come on."

"Door's locked, my nezzy." It's some guy wearing a wool hat and track suit. He smiles at me, his eyes puffy and half closed. He flicks the latch and the door glides open.

"Thanks," I say.

"Ain't nathan, dawg." He winks and shoots me with a finger gun.

I bolt outside, swiveling my head back and forth, searching for a place to hide. I start toward the play set, but I'm instantly jerked back.

"Forget it, Twig." I feel the weight of Tony's hands on

my shoulders at the same time I hear his voice. He spins me around. We're the same height, but it feels like I'm looking up at a basketball player. "You like to peep, peeper?"

I shake my head hard. "I wasn't . . . I didn't see anything."

"You think Kelly goes for pervs? Is that it? You think she'd like to know how you hide in closets?"

"It was a mistake."

"Damn right it was a mistake. Your last one." Tony squeezes my shoulders up into my ears and lifts me off the ground. "How about we see how good you swim the fly, huh? I'd like to see what I'm up against." He grins out of the snarly scarred side of his mouth.

I want to plead my case, but Tony's already thundering me toward the skanky pool like a SmackDown wrestler. The party crowd divides, stepping back like I'm contaminated. My one comforting thought is that Kelly is not here to witness my humiliation.

"Tony! Stop being such an asshole. Put him down." It's Valerie storming toward us. Great. So much for Kelly not finding out about this.

"Stay out of it, scrag," Tony barks.

If everyone in the party wasn't watching, they are now.

I shut my eyes and brace for the cold and the slime.

"Tony! Cut the shit!" I hear Valerie scream this as I go soaring through the air.

It seems like I'm falling forever. I still haven't opened

my eyes, and I expect the splash to come way before it does. The smell hits before the water. It's sort of fishy. Kind of like a five-day-dead salmon left out in the sun. I wonder why I didn't smell it before.

When I finally land headfirst in the pool, it's almost a relief. Because now I'm wet and covered in gunge and the suspense is over. Plus it's warmer than I had imagined, so there's that.

For a split second I think that I ought to just let myself drown because, really, it would be easier than having to deal with the load of crap I've gotten myself into. But then, in the same instant, I think of all the things I'd miss if I wasn't around. Like the next sixty Stanley Cup finals, and maybe actually *having* sex someday instead of imagining it, and all the laughs and good times with Coop and Sean, and Grandpa Arlo, and Mom, and even, believe it or not, my brother.

And it's too bad that I've come to this realization now because that's when I feel a smack to my temple. If I had to guess, I'd say it was the planter, but it could just as easily have been the tricycle. And really, it doesn't matter, because either way, I'm over and out.

★ CHAPTER THIRTY ★
FIRST KISS

THERE ARE SEVERAL THINGS I didn't know about being unconscious. First, it's not like sleep. You don't dream. Really, there's nothing. I want to say there's blackness, but that doesn't quite capture the feeling. It's more like you disappear for a certain period. Could be a minute. Could be a day. But there's no sense of passing time. Which is weird.

And second, when you finally wake up, you're very disoriented. So much so that you may even think Tony Grillo is trying to make out with you.

Everything's blurry, but I swear I see an out-of-focus Tony coming toward me with his mouth open. There is no way I want my first kiss—or any kiss, for that matter—to be with Tony Grillo. I try to back away, but I feel like I'm pressed against a wall. Tony puts his lips over mine.

But he's not kissing me. He's pinching my nose and blowing air into my mouth. Down my throat.

I feel my stomach convulse and I cough, and then I turn my head and puke all over Tony's fancy polo shirt.

I'm instantly aware that I'm in Ronnie Hull's backyard. Lying on his lawn. Surrounded by a group of kids. Tony Grillo is kneeling beside me. His hair is wet, and his shirt is spray-painted with half-digested fish sticks and Tater Tots.

"Fuck me," Tony says, clambering to his feet. His arms are wide like he's hugging an invisible beach ball.

"Sorry," I croak. I sit up and wipe my mouth with the back of my wrist. My head *wah-wahs*. My skull feels like someone took a bat to it.

Tony glares at me. "You weren't supposed to drown, loser. You sure aren't much of a swimmer."

Everyone laughs. But it's more of a relieved laughter than anything else.

Tony points hard at me. "You owe me, shit head." With that, he turns and stalks off.

"Are you all right, Matt?" It's Valerie. I didn't realize she was there beside me. She brushes my wet hair out of my face.

I nod. I have to force myself to swallow. "Fine," I say. My throat is raw, like I swallowed a handful of razors. "Just sort of soaking wet."

"You're lucky Tony's a lifeguard," Valerie says.

"Yeah," I manage to rasp out. "He's a real hero."

"Do you need to go to the hospital?"

"I'm okay." I touch my temple and wince. Not so much from the pain but from the shock of the golf ball that seems to be sticking out of my head.

"You need ice," Valerie says. "Let's get you to the table."

Valerie leans over and helps me to my feet. It's a struggle, as my burning legs aren't cooperating. I feel the water trickle down my back.

Valerie leads me over to the table by the pool and gently lowers me into a chair.

"I'll be right back," she says, dashing off.

The crowd of people has dispersed. I guess it was interesting at first to see if I might die, but now that I'm just some kid with a lump on his head, it's not so fascinating anymore.

I'm trying to focus. Everything feels so foggy. I'd kind of like to go home, but I should wait until Valerie comes back with the ice. I'm sure she wouldn't be doing any of this if she knew what really happened. Stupid Coop and his stupid ideas. I'm sure this will all get back to Kelly, and if dressing up like a girl doesn't completely turn her off to me, then the Peeping Tom act should seal my coffin.

I'm rubbing my closed eyelids, trying to get all these scenarios out of my mind, when Valerie returns with a plastic grocery bag half-filled with ice.

"Here." Valerie places the bag gently on my head. "It'll bring down the swelling."

I smile. "Thanks, Nurse Valerie."

"It's *Dr.* Valerie," she says, sitting down next to me. "Dr. Devereaux, actually. At least it will be someday."

"You want to be a doctor?"

"That's the plan."

"Wow," I say. "That's cool. I have no idea what I want to be."

"Oh, really? I thought you wanted to be a gardener." She laughs. I can't believe she remembers that stupid quiz.

"Hey. You only gave me *five* choices. Besides, I changed my answer to teacher. Even though I don't really want to do that, either."

"What *are* you interested in?"

I try to think but nothing comes to mind.

"I don't know," I say. "When I was, like, ten, I saw *Rocky* on TV, and for about a week I thought I wanted to be a boxer."

This makes Valerie giggle.

"I know. I'm not exactly heavyweight material." I lift the ice to show my injury as proof. "At the time, it seemed like a good idea. I drank raw eggs and chased my cat around the house to try and get my reflexes in shape."

"Raw eggs can give you salmonella," Valerie says.

"Yeah, well, Rocky did it, so I figured that's what boxers do."

"You're pretty gullible."

"Tell me something I don't know."

"Okay. I bet you didn't know that *gullible* isn't in the dictionary?"

"Seriously?"

Valerie smiles. "You see? Gullible."

"Yeah. Thanks for that." I laugh weakly. "I wasn't feeling like enough of an idiot already."

"Any time," Valerie says. Her cell phone rings. She digs it out of her little green purse and looks at who's calling. "My dad's here. Are you sure you don't want to go to the hospital? We could take you."

"I'm okay, really. But thanks."

"How about a lift home, then?"

"I'm good. I've got a ride with Coop and Sean." As *if.* I can't believe they bailed on me like that. Bastards.

"All right, then." Valerie stands, looking very serious. "But I'm going to call you tomorrow, anyway. Just to make sure you're okay. What's your number?"

I give her my cell number, and she plugs it into her phone.

"Keep that ice on for twenty minutes."

"I will."

Valerie waves, then turns and walks away.

I wait a minute before hauling myself up from the table. I keep the ice pressed to my head as I hobble my way around the side of Ronnie Hull's house. I could call my mother, I guess, but it's only a few miles, and I could use the walk home to clear the cobwebs from my brain.

CHAPTER THIRTY-ONE

THE MORNING AFTER

MY EYES ARE OPEN, but I stay in bed, lying on my side, staring at the putty blue wall of my bedroom. I have an apocalyptic headache that's radiating from the lump on my skull.

Last night I dreamed that I was over at Coop's house eating dinner but my teeth were loose and they kept falling out. I was really embarrassed by it, and I kept hiding the teeth in my napkin. It was pretty disturbing.

I run my tongue over my teeth now just to make sure they're still all there and solidly embedded.

Coop and Sean both left messages on my voice mail while I was walking home last night, wanting to know if I made it out okay. So, even though I'm still a little ticked off at them, at least they didn't completely forget about me.

My cell phone vibrates on my dresser. Last time I checked the clock it was ten thirty. Anybody who knows me knows that I sleep till noon on weekends.

And then I remember Valerie.

I throw my covers off and leap from my bed. My still-sore body grouses, and my brain slams against the inside of my skull. I have to steady myself as I grab the phone and flip it open. Valerie's name is on the screen.

"Hello?" I say, hanging on to the dresser for support.

But there's no answer. It's gone over to voice mail. Which is just as well. I'd rather not start answering questions about why Tony was so pissed at me. Once Tony and Mandy spill the beans about me hiding in the closet, I'll be as welcome as a hernia check from Jack Frost.

My bed calls to me. The tangle of the covers, the soft down pillow. But I'm already up. Might as well face the day.

I pick a few shirts off my bedroom floor and give them the sniff test. The only one that seems relatively clean is my bright yellow BIG BONE LICK STATE PARK, KENTUCKY T-shirt that Cooper got me for my birthday last year. He thought it was the funniest thing ever.

I slog out into the hall, toward the bathroom. As I look over at Pete's closed bedroom door, my insides tighten up. It's like a bear trap ready to snap on my leg. He won't be back for another two weeks, but I don't think I could make the accident look convincing even if I had two years.

After a half-gallon pee and a splash of water on my face, I notice I have a zit the size of Mount Vesuvius on my chin. My first instinct is to pop it, but Mom's words echo in my head. "Leave it alone or you'll get an infection. It could disfigure you." It takes some willpower because there's something very satisfying about the bursting snap of a whitehead. Instead, I use the cranberry acne mud mask that Mom bought me last week from a kiosk in the mall. It's supposed to draw out the oil and pus naturally. Or at least that's what it says on the label. I slather the thick red goop all over my face. It smells like a fruit cocktail and feels cold on my skin. When I'm finished, I look like some kind of crazed, masked wrestler. I growl at my reflection and do a Mr. Universe pose.

I head down to the family room to check my e-mail while I wait for the mud to dry.

Grandpa Arlo, in his frayed tan terry-cloth robe, is at the computer, talking to the screen.

"Nope. Haven't seen him this morning," Grandpa says. "I think he's still sleeping." He laughs. "This is amazing. I didn't even know you could do this kind of thing. It's like *Star Trek*."

"Who you talking to, Grandpa?" I step up behind him, and there's Kelly and Valerie on Skype. I drop to the floor like I'm dodging machine-gun fire.

"Speak of the devil." Grandpa glances down at me crouched under the desk. I wave him off like mad. "Jesus," he says, recoiling when he sees me. "What the—?"

"Hey, Matt," Valerie calls out. "Come back. Sit down at the computer."

How the hell did they get my Skype address? And why did Grandpa answer it? My eyes dart every which way, searching for an escape route.

"I, um . . . I can't," I call.

Grandpa looks back up at the screen. "He's not decent."

Kelly laughs. "Ohmygod. Do you walk around your house naked?"

"No," I say. "I'm just . . . I just woke up."

"We don't care." It's Valerie. "We need to talk to you. I couldn't get you on your cell, so I searched for you on Skype."

"I'll call you later." I feel the drying mud mask start to crack on my face.

"Oh, come on," Kelly says. "We won't be here later. So you have a little bed-head. Big deal. Poor Val was worried about you."

"I'm fine," I say, starting to commando crawl across the floor. It's a slow, tedious, muscle-straining process. Not to mention, the rug is burning the hell out of my knees and elbows. "I'm good. Thanks for asking."

"Matt's grandpa. Can you help us out?" Valerie is leaning on her accent and using a very cute pretty-please voice that I'm not sure Grandpa Arlo will be able to resist. "Could you tell him to come to the computer?"

"He's kind of embarrassed, girls. He doesn't want you to see him in his Little Mermaid PJs."

The three of them laugh.

"Thanks a lot, Grandpa," I growl through clenched teeth.

"I'm kidding, I'm kidding," Grandpa tells them. "You were right before. He's actually naked. Walks around the house that way all the time. Says it's how God made him. But that doesn't make it any easier sitting at the breakfast table with him."

Valerie and Kelly crack up again. Grandpa's having a great time.

"Hey, Matt," Valerie says. "Kelly and I are going to the mall this afternoon. Meet us at Guess at two o'clock, okay?"

"Sure, fine." Anything to get them to hang up.

"But wear some clothes," Kelly says, chuckling.

I've nearly crawled my way to the stairs, when I hear the electronic bleep of the call ending.

"You can get up now," Grandpa says. "They're gone. Come over here. I need your help."

I labor to my feet and approach the computer cautiously, just in case. But Valerie and Kelly have been replaced by a huge picture of a fluffy white kitten.

Grandpa Arlo points to the screen. "I'm trying to make a found-kitten poster for Edith."

"You expect me to help you after you embarrassed me like that?"

"You embarrassed yourself, Kabuki boy. I was just

trying to diffuse the situation with a little levity. What the hell is that on your face?"

"It's a mud mask." I touch the thick hard plaster on my cheeks. "It's supposed to help your complexion. I wasn't expecting to see anyone."

"Oh, that's your excuse? What else are you doing when you aren't expecting to see anyone? Painting your nails, maybe? Shaving your legs?"

"Mom got it for me."

He frowns. "There used to be such a clear line between boys and girls. I don't know what the hell's happening to the world."

I gesture at the monitor. "Why are you making a found-kitten poster? The kitten's not even lost."

Grandpa lets out a long heavy sigh. "When Edith and I went to the goddamn pet store, the lady there said she'd never seen the kitten before in her life."

"Isn't that why you had me call?"

"Yes, but now Edith's absolutely convinced that the kitten's stolen." Grandpa shakes his head. "I tell you. I don't know how I get myself into these messes."

"Why don't you just tell her it was you?"

"You heard her going on about what kind of awful person would wrap an animal up in a box. I can't have her thinking I'd do something like that."

"But you did."

"Anyway," he says. "I told her we'd take a picture of

the kitten and put up posters around town, and if nobody claimed the kitten in a couple of weeks, then she could keep it without feeling guilty." Grandpa turns back to the computer and starts working the mouse. "Now I've gotten the damn kitten picture into the computer, but this program won't let me type over it."

"Here. I'll do it," I say. "What do you want written on it?"

Grandpa Arlo stands and lets me take over the chair. "It's written there on the sticky note." He points to a yellow square beside the keyboard. "'Lost kitten found.' Along with Edith's name, phone number, and address."

"All right." I click on the text box and drag it to the bottom. "What color do you want the words?"

"Oh, I don't care." He waves dismissively. "It's just bullshit, anyway. But make it look nice. I want Edith to see that I made an effort. I'm going to get some coffee. Do you want something? A loofah? Or some cucumbers to put over your eyes?"

"Very funny."

He totters off to the kitchen as I finish up the poster. I use a big purple comic font so that it looks like Grandpa really went to town. I add a few cat paw prints in the corners for good measure. I think Mrs. Hoogenboom will be impressed.

When Grandpa returns, he glances at the computer screen. "That looks pretty damn good." He nods and takes a sip of his coffee. "I like how I put the little cat prints in there."

"How many posters do you want?"

"Let's run off an even dozen. We don't want to waste too much paper."

I send the poster to the printer. As it whirs to life, all I can think about is why Kelly and Valerie invited me to the mall. The wishful-thinking part of me hopes it's because Kelly wants to hang out, but the get-real part keeps asking the same question over and over.

Did Tony say something about last night?

CHAPTER THIRTY-TWO

ALL FOR ONE AND ONE FOR MALL

I WASH THE MUD MASK OFF and examine my face in the mirror. The treatment doesn't seem to have helped much, because the angry pimple is still protruding from my chin.

I take a shower and dry off and attempt to do something with my hair. It needs to be cut, but I've been putting it off because I can't find anyone who can make it look cool. The last hairdresser got really creative and ended up making me look like that woman from *The Sound of Music.* Right now there's this one piece that keeps curling up, away from my ear, and I can't get it to stay down. Why does everybody else always look like they've stepped out of a fashion magazine, and all I can manage is to look like I stepped out of a comic-book convention?

Whatever. I give up. I throw on my most expensive jeans and a black polo. I use a little of Mom's cover-up on my chin, which I'm sure Grandpa would love.

I take the bus to the mall and make it there a few minutes before I have to meet the girls. I decide to buy a fruit smoothie to use as a prop. I never know what to do with my hands when I'm around girls, so it'll be good to have something to hold.

I come around the corner, and there's Kelly and Valerie sitting on a bench, surrounded by several Guess shopping bags. There's a lump of dread in my stomach, but I play it cool as I approach, sipping my drink.

"Hey," I say.

"Hey there." Valerie smiles. "How's your head feeling?"

"Better. Thanks." I touch the bump by my hairline. "That ice you gave me really helped."

Kelly smirks. "Val told me what Tony did. Asshole. I didn't think he'd go all ballistic on you like that. I was just trying to get him back a little."

My belly relaxes because this means they haven't heard what *really* happened at the party.

"It's no big deal. He snuck up on me, otherwise I would have put him down with some of my Jackie Chan moves." I glance over my shoulder at the store window. "So. What'd you guys buy?"

Kelly peeks into each of the Guess bags. "Just a couple of tops and some shorts and a pair of jeans and some shoes. Oh, and a cute jacket. It was a light shopping day." She laughs.

"What about you?" I ask Valerie.

"I didn't get anything."

"Val doesn't shop. She's saving her pennies for college," Kelly says. "It's so boring."

Valerie's neck goes pink. "I shop. Sometimes."

"It's okay, Val. You don't have to apologize. We're just different. I'm the girlie one and you're the sensible one. Just know that when you're a rich doctor someday and I'm poor and homeless, you'll have to bail me out."

"Don't be so sure."

"Oh, please. You're a giver, Val. That's what you do." Kelly stands and grabs her bags. "Come on. Let's go to DeLuca's. I need a white-chocolate mocha, like, yesterday."

We make our way through the mall toward the coffee shop. I sip my smoothie and try to come up with something to say. I don't know why I get so tongue-tied when I'm around Kelly. She's just a girl. Like anyone else. Except exponentially hotter. I'm about to ask them if they've seen any cool movies this summer, when Kelly leans over to Valerie and me.

"Don't look now," Kelly whispers. "Hot Dog Helen's here. Ugh, like she could ever wear anything from Betsey Johnson."

I try to look without seeming like I am. Out of the corner of my eye I can see Helen Harriwick, a round-faced girl with stringy brown hair and braces, staring in the window of Betsey Johnson.

"I feel bad for her," Valerie says.

Kelly groans. "You feel bad for everyone."

"No, I don't. It's just got to be hard to always have people whispering about you."

"I heard it wasn't true," I say. "I heard that Craig Altman started that rumor when she wouldn't let him cheat off her on a math test."

"Whatever." Kelly sighs. "She's still a freak. And she should, like, get away from Betsey Johnson before people start to think that her kind shop there."

And it's as if Helen can hear Kelly from all the way across the mall, because at that very moment she turns away from the store and walks off.

I suddenly realize that this is how it's going to be for Coop, Sean, and me if people find out about the Peeping Tom episode. Not to mention our stint as cross-dressers. What are they going to call *us*? The Three Perverteers? I'm going to have to beg my family to move, for sure.

When we get to DeLuca's, I dump my smoothie and order a white-chocolate mocha, like Kelly. I want her to think that we like the same sorts of things, though I'm not sure that she even notices. She just gets her coffee and finds us an empty table.

"Aren't you getting anything?" I ask Valerie as I wait for my drink.

She shakes her head. "Too much caffeine makes me shaky. Maybe you'll give me a taste of yours. As repayment for my doctor services last night."

"Sure. Seems like I'm getting off cheap, though."

Valerie smiles. "Consider it a down payment."

When my drink's up, we join Kelly at the table. She's on her cell and she's rolling her eyes.

"Whatever you have to say, Tony, I don't want to hear it," Kelly insists.

Tony? Oh shit. This is not good. My belly resumes its earlier twisted-up yoga position.

"My voice mail's working just fine. I *heard* the eight thousand messages you left this morning. *And* I got the gazillion texts. Maybe you should get a clue." And with that, Kelly snaps her phone shut and tosses it on the table. "God!"

"You should change your number," Valerie says.

"Please. I'm not gonna change my entire life because Tony's a lunatic."

"Why's he calling so much?" I ask, taking a "casual" sip of my mocha and searing the hell out my mouth.

"*Pffff.* Like I even care. Honestly, you have to feel sorry for him. The moron can't even take a hint." Kelly pulls the lid off her mocha. "Let's change the subject. What do you want to talk about, Mark?"

"Matt," I say.

"Who's Matt?" Kelly asks. "Do I know him?"

"*He's* Matt," Valerie chides. "You called him Mark."

Kelly laughs. "Oh. That's funny. I thought we were going to rip on some guy named Matt." Kelly blows the steam off the surface of her coffee. "You look more like a Mark."

"You think?" I ask, because I don't want to embarrass her any more than she probably is.

"Anyway, don't listen to me." Kelly finally takes a sip of her drink. "I can't even remember my *own* name sometimes."

Kelly's cell phone vibrates on the table. She grabs it and looks at the screen. "Oh, Jesus Christ."

"Just turn it off," Valerie says.

"You have to admire the retard's persistence." She sighs. "I better see what the hell's so important or he'll never stop." Kelly flips open her phone. "You have three minutes and then I'm hanging up and we're never speaking again." She stands and gives us a "be right back" gesture.

My armpits are suddenly wet. I feel like throwing up. My eyes follow Kelly as she walks out of the coffee shop and into the mall. I watch as she sits on a bench. I try to read her lips, but I can't make out what she's saying.

"Ahem." Valerie clears her throat. "Am I going to have to wait all day?"

"Huh?" I turn back to Valerie, confused.

"Your mocha. Remember? You were going to let me try it."

"Oh. Right. Yeah. Sure." I push the cup over to Valerie. "Be careful. It's nuclear."

Valerie takes the coffee gingerly in her hands and lifts it to her mouth. She sips it cautiously. Her face scrunches up. "Youch. How do they expect you to drink that?"

"I told you." I look back out to Kelly, who's now lying down on the bench. Has it been three minutes yet? "What do you think he wants?"

"To prove how big a jerk he is?" She shrugs. "Who cares?" She tries to take another drink of the mocha and appears to be more successful this time. "Not bad. I think the first sip destroys most of the nerves in your mouth so that by the second sip you can actually taste it a little."

"Really?"

"Here. Try it."

I take the cup from Valerie and give it another try, but it's like lava on my tongue. "Still hot," I say, my mouth half open.

Valerie chuckles. "Well, it worked for me." She grabs a packet of raw sugar from the little basket on the table and starts fiddling with it. "So, tell me something about you I don't know."

"That could take all day." I glance out to the mall and see that Kelly has disappeared from the bench. Goddamn it. My right leg starts to jump.

"Just one thing. And then I'll tell you something about me."

"Okay. Let's see. All right. I'm a pretty terrible guitar player."

Valerie laughs. "Most people would just say they're learning to play the guitar."

"Yeah, well, I've been learning for over a year and

I'm bad. Just in case you ever hear me play. You've been forewarned."

"What kinds of things do you play?"

"Lots of songs you probably know, though I manage to make them all completely unrecognizable."

This makes Valerie giggle again.

"Now you," I say. I press down on my leg to stop it from jiggling. There's no use worrying, I tell myself. Whatever's going to happen is going to happen.

"All right. I'm going to tell you something, but you can't make fun of me."

"Uh-oh. This sounds like it could be good."

"No, it's just . . . kind of dorky."

"You're talking to SpongeBob SquarePants here, remember? Your dorkiness can only pale in comparison."

She smiles. "I'm the president of the chess club at school."

I blink hard and try not to laugh. "Whoa. Chess club. That *is* pretty geeky of you."

Valerie slaps my arm. "Shut up. You said you wouldn't make fun."

"No. Seriously. That's cool. Well. Actually. No, it isn't. But . . . I never would have guessed. You must be supremely smart. I don't even know how to play chess."

"I could show you sometime." Valerie opens the packet of sugar and pours a bit into her mouth.

"I'd be terrible at it. I can barely manage checkers."

"You might surprise yourself."

"I doubt it." I attempt another sip of my coffee. It's almost reached a drinkable temperature. "How did you get involved in that? I mean, you don't look like a . . . chess person."

"My dad taught me. I just took to it. It's like I can see all the possibilities and how they'll play out. I don't know. I like it for some reason."

"Well . . . I bet you have all the chess kids fogging up their glasses."

Valerie smiles. She pours more of the raw sugar into her mouth. She must have caught me watching her because she suddenly stops. "Oh. Sorry. Do you want some?"

I laugh. "No, thanks."

"It tastes good. It's like rock candy."

I shake my head. "That's okay."

"I know. It's a bad habit. My mom's always on me about it. But I can't help it. I've got a killer sweet tooth."

Just then Kelly returns and plops down in her seat. "My life's worse than a soap opera, I swear."

"Do we even want to know?" Valerie asks.

I brace myself for the accusations.

"He's, like, all schizoid. One minute he's grilling me about last night. Asking me a million questions—What have I heard? Who told me what?—And the next minute he's all wanting to get back together. And I'm like, yeah, right. Let's do that. *Not.*"

I can only assume by all this that Tony didn't say anything about the peeping incident. And now that I really think about it, why would he? It implicates him as much as it does me. Of course, that's not going to stop Mandy from blabbing.

I'm trying to think of a way to ask Kelly how well she knows Mandy Reagan, when Coop and Sean suddenly appear at our table.

"Hello, ladies." Coop beams, wielding the better part of a two-foot churro.

Sean stands next to him, with his hands tucked into the pockets of his jean jacket.

"We need to talk to you, Matt," Coop says.

"I'm a little busy right now." I motion toward Kelly with my eyes.

"It's okay." Kelly stands, grabbing her Guess bags. "Val and I have some more shopping to do. You guys can have our seats."

Valerie gets up and waves. "See you later, Matt."

I watch as the girls leave.

When I turn back, Coop and Sean are already sitting at the table.

"Thanks a lot," I say.

Coop smirks. "Oh, please. Like you were going to get anywhere with Kelly while Valerie's hanging around."

"I wasn't trying to *get* anywhere. We were just talking."

Coop turns to Sean, who's busy working the buttons on his cell. "What the hell are you doing?"

"One sec. I'm texting Tianna."

"The girl from last night?" I ask.

"Yeah." Sean smiles, his thumb working like crazy. "I think she kind of likes me."

"Give me that." Coop snatches the phone from Sean's hand and snaps it shut.

"Hey!" he protests.

"Do you want to blow it with her or what?" Coop says, taking a bite of his churro.

"What are you talking about?"

"I'm talking about being overeager, dude. You look desperate if you text her back every single time she texts you."

Sean grabs his phone back. "How would you know?"

"It's basic psychology, dude. Girls want what's hard to get. But you do whatever you want. Just don't say I didn't warn you."

Sean looks down at his phone like he's not sure what he should do.

I shake my head. "Don't listen to him, Sean. If you like getting messages from her, she'll like getting messages from you."

"Ugh. I'm surrounded by amateurs." Coop groans.

"Can we *please* move on to the reason we're here before I'm infected by your painful ignorance?"

"And that would be?" I ask, still annoyed about them scaring off Kelly.

"We need your opinion." Coop takes out *his* cell phone and punches up the picture he took from last night.

It's a pretty clear shot of Mandy in her underwear, partially blocked by Tony in his boxers.

"We're not sure if Cathy will accept it," Sean confesses.

"You'd know better than us, Sean," I say. "How nitpicky is she?"

"You've seen her," Sean retorts. "She's a pain in the ass. But if she knows that it's the best she's going to get, she might be willing to bargain."

I shrug. "It's worth a try, I guess."

Coop studies the picture. "I'm just worried she might think we're trying to scam her and then do something rash." He bites off another piece of churro. "Let's think it over while we go see *Alien vs. Predator vs. Anaconda*."

CHAPTER THIRTY-THREE

BEACH BUMMER

Coop, sean, and me make our way through the mall toward the movie theater. Sean keeps sneak-texting Tianna, while Coop busies himself trying to embarrass me by waggling his churro around like it's his schlong.

I'm trying to ignore Coop by looking into the store windows, when I spot Kelly in Beach Bums, standing in front of a three-way mirror, wearing a black string bikini. The sight of her wearing practically nothing nearly makes my head explode. She turns this way and that, looking at herself. I knew she had a great body; I just didn't know how great. Bikinis are way hotter than the one-pieces the girls wear on swim team.

"Holy crap," I say.

Coop and Sean must have heard me, because now they're staring into the swim shop, sniggering like two depraved leprechauns.

"Oh. My. God. Does anyone else suddenly have an overwhelming need to buy a swimsuit?" Coop says.

Sean nods, his mouth agape. "Me. Yes."

Coop starts toward the store entrance.

"Wait." I grab Coop's arm. "Isn't it going to seem obvious?"

"Not if you don't make it obvious." Coop yanks his arm away from me. "We just need some new bathing suits. Big deal. Besides, Kelly might want my views on some of the various swimming apparel she's trying on. I happen to have a degree in bikiniology. It would be awfully selfish of me not to at least offer my expert opinion."

"Yeah," Sean says. "And my second cousin is a professional bathing suit model. For Lane Bryant. Still . . ."

"All right," I say. "But we have to play it supercool. When they see us, make sure you act surprised."

The three of us walk into Beach Bums with its fake palm trees and surfboards on the walls. We head over to the men's section. It's a pretty small store, so we still have a direct sight line to the changing area.

I take a pair of board shorts off a shelf, but I can't tear my eyes away from Kelly.

"I don't know," Kelly says. "Is it sexy or just slutty?" She turns around and tries to look at herself over her shoulder.

Valerie leans against the wall, looking sort of bored. She shrugs. "I guess it depends on your definition."

I glance over at Sean and Coop, who stand by a rack of sandals with their jaws hanging open. I half expect long strings of drool to start streaming from both of their mouths.

Kelly continues to look at herself in the mirror.

I have to be careful I don't pass out. It's crazy how the sight of a beautiful girl in a bikini can make you feel so weak-kneed. My whole body is flooded with a warm buzz, like huddling around a fire after a day in the snow.

"Okay. Maybe it is a little too revealing." Kelly slides her fingers inside the back of the bikini bottom, adjusting it over her butt.

Oh, man. I can't breathe.

"I completely disagree," Coop says, marching over to the mirror like he's trying to stop something unconscionable from happening.

Jesus Christ, what's he doing?

"It's perfect." Coop gestures with his churro. "That's the greatest bathing suit I have ever seen in my entire life."

Kelly and Valerie turn to see Coop, then Sean and me.

Valerie waves and smiles. "Hey. What are you guys doing here?"

Me and Sean walk over to join Coop and the girls.

"Wow," I say. "You guys are here, too. That's . . . What a coincidence. We were just . . ." I hold up the swimsuit in my hand and swallow. "Looking to buy some board shorts."

"You guys really like this one?" Kelly asks.

"For sure," Sean drones. "The greatest bathing suit ever."

"I don't know." Kelly studies her reflection. I can't believe it. She doesn't seem shy at all. "What about you, Mark?" She winces. "I mean, Matt. Sorry."

"Me? Huh." I put my hands in my front pockets. I take my hands out again. I cross them in front of me. Behind me. Damn it. I wish I still had a drink to hold. "It looks, uh . . . good. I think. I mean. Yeah. I like it. But . . . I don't really know that much about bathing suits."

"Okay. Let's see what you guys think of these other ones." Kelly spins around again. "But keep this one in mind."

"Oh. I will," Coop says.

"Be right back." Kelly disappears into her changing room.

"Cool," Sean and Coop say in tandem. The two of them sink into the orange velvet couch by the three-way mirror like they're getting ready to watch a movie or something.

Coop gnaws on his churro as a middle-aged saleswoman with red rhinestone cat glasses approaches them.

"Excuse me," she says. "There's no food or drinks allowed in the store. You'll have to eat that outside."

Coop stares at his churro and then stuffs the rest of it into his mouth, folding it as it goes. He smiles with bulging cheeks and holds out his empty hands. "Aaa gah."

The saleswoman sniffs disapprovingly and marches off.

Valerie glances at the changing rooms, then looks at us. "You guys should escape while you can. She's got like thirty bikinis in there. This could go on for hours. I'm sure you have better things to do."

"Better than this?" Sean points to the dressing rooms. "*Is* there such a thing?"

Coop swallows and clears his throat. "What Sean's trying to say, in his caveman way, is that there's nothing we could think of that would be better than helping a friend to look her best."

Valerie laughs. "Okay. Suit yourselves."

"Oh, we will," Coop says. "We'll suit ourselves right here until this couch takes on a permanent impression of our butts."

Jeez, so much for playing it cool.

CHAPTER THIRTY-FOUR

PEEK-A-BOO

I'M STARING AT THE CHANGING ROOMS, waiting for Kelly to emerge wearing her next bikini, when I notice that if you wanted to, you could easily peek over the stall divider and spy on the person next to you.

I look over at Coop and Sean and I can see by following their gaze that they're thinking the exact same thing.

"What do you think about this one?"

I turn back and see Valerie holding up a powder-blue bikini with a kind of halter top and miniskirt bottom.

"What?" I say, keeping one eye on the guys. "Oh. I don't know. It's nice, but it doesn't seem like Kelly."

"Not for her, silly." Valerie spins the hanger around, considering the suit. "For me."

"Oh." I get a jolt of panic. I'm suddenly feeling protective of Valerie. Like I don't want Coop and Sean ogling her. Maybe because she was so nice to me last night. "You don't really want to try on bathing suits, too, do you?"

"Maybe," she says. "It's something to do, right? We're going to be here for a while." She takes another suit off the rack. A wine-colored tankini with streaks of white. "I'll give these a try. I'll be right out."

Valerie heads back to the changing rooms before I can think of anything to say that would stop her.

As soon she's out of earshot, Coop and Sean leap from the couch and hurry over to me.

"Dude, this is our chance," Coop says.

Sean is practically vibrating. "You could totally see over that stall divider if you stood on a chair, and don't tell me you didn't notice that because I know you did."

"Yeah, it crossed my mind," I say with a mixture of excitement and apprehension.

"All we have to do is take turns pretending to try on bathing suits in one of the stalls next to the girls." Coop's got his sinister half smirk going. "It's perfect. It's almost as if God wants us to succeed in our summer goal."

"Right," I say. "I'm sure God's got nothing better to do than to help us see a naked girl."

"*Two* naked girls," Sean corrects.

"Besides," I say, "shouldn't we be focusing on trying to see Mandy Reagan? Just in case Cathy doesn't accept that picture."

"Mandy Reagan isn't naked right now just beyond those doors," Coop says. "Come on. Opportunity is ringing the damn doorbell and we're wasting valuable time here. I'll take Kelly first. And Sean, you can check out Valerie."

Sean crosses his legs like he's got to take a piss. "Holy crap. I can't believe this is going to happen. If I get to see Valerie nude, you can kill me because my life will be complete."

"Hold on a second," I say. "What if we get caught? I mean, it's pretty easy to see someone peeping over the stall wall from out here."

"That's where you come in, dawg." Coop smacks my back. "You run interference while we're in there and then we'll do the same for you."

"I don't think we should do this." I can't believe I just said that. I've been imagining Kelly naked ever since I laid eyes on her. And seeing Valerie would be an amazing bonus. But I don't know. I feel weird about this. Like it's not right or something. Jesus, what the hell's happening to me?

"That's hilarious, dude." Coop laughs. "You almost had me. Come on, Sean. Let's go get something to try on. Before it's too late."

Sean and Coop head over to the men's section, and I'm standing here feeling like one of those cartoon characters with a devil on one shoulder and an angel on the other. "Naked, naked, naked." That's all the devil is saying. Like he's got a one-track mind. Or just a very limited vocabulary. "Naked, naked, naked."

And then there's the angel whispering, "What about

Valerie? All she wanted to know was if you were feeling okay. And now you're going to help your friends spy on her? What kind of person does that?"

Just then, Kelly steps from her stall, wearing a shimmering rainbow bikini that changes color as she moves.

"This one's pretty cool, huh?" Kelly says. "It's like a party." She shimmies back and forth in front of the three-way mirror, entertaining us both with the disco-ball effect.

"It's hypnotizing," I say, totally hypnotized.

"Where's Val?"

"You inspired her. She's trying on a couple of bathing suits."

Kelly stops dancing and looks at me through the reflection. "Really?"

"Yeah. She found a couple bikinis she liked."

"That's so unlike her." Kelly laughs and then goes back to admiring herself. I don't blame her; if I looked like that, I'd spend my entire life in front of the mirror. *"Naked,"* the devil whispers in my ear.

"I'm going to get this one," Kelly says. "You almost can't stop looking at it."

"I know *I* can't," I say before I can restrain myself.

Kelly laughs.

I feel my cheeks, my neck, prickling.

"Okay, that's one. I need two more." She turns and heads back to her changing room.

Coop and Sean approach, each of them waving a couple of swim trunks.

"Wish us luck," Coop says.

"Wait." I reach out and grab both guys by the arm. "Don't. This isn't cool."

Coop looks down at my hand like it's covered in slime. "I'm sorry, what?"

"This isn't cool," I repeat.

"What are you talking about? This is the coolest thing ever. Now, let me go." Sean pulls his arm from my grip. "Valerie's only got two suits in there. I don't want to miss anything."

Coop gives me an are-you-nuts? look. "What's gotten into you, dawg?"

"Nothing," I say. But clearly something has.

"Good." Coop nods. "Then keep an eye out for any trouble."

"We need a signal," I say, stalling. "What should I do if someone's coming?"

"I don't know." Coop huffs. "Just say something like, 'How are you doing in there?' Then we'll know to stay down. Okay?"

"Sure." I take a deep breath. "That's good."

Coop and Sean head back to the dressing rooms. They aren't in there five seconds when I see Coop's head start to poke up from his stall.

He's just about to peek over the wall into Kelly's stall

when I am hit with a wave of guilt like you wouldn't believe.

"How you doing in there?" I call out.

Coop's head drops down immediately. "Fine," Coop says. "Just trying on these suits."

A moment later and Sean's head starts to rise ever so slowly as he attempts to peer over at Valerie.

And I don't know why I do it, but I grab my cell phone and speed-dial him. Sean's ringtone starts to blare "The Real Slim Shady" and his head disappears as he falls off his chair, making a huge racket behind the door as he scrabbles to answer the phone.

"Hello?" Sean says. "Hello?"

But I've already hung up because Coop is making another play for Kelly.

"How's it going in there?" I shout out, causing Coop to duck down again.

"Could be better," Coop grumbles. "Maybe you could go get me a larger size in this one."

A pair of red swim trunks fly out of Coop's stall and hit me in the face.

Valerie calls my name softly from her changing room.

"Sorry," I say to Coop, throwing the swimsuit back over the door. "I'm needed elsewhere."

I make my way over to where Valerie is poking her head out from the stall.

"I don't know about this one," she says, her head tipped down, her hair falling in her face. "What do you think?" She creaks open the door and stands there. Her feet crossed over one another and her hands pressed into her thighs.

Wow. Valerie's got the powder-blue bikini on and she looks awesome. She's curvier than Kelly but in a smokin' hot way. I don't remember actually ever seeing Valerie in a bathing suit. When she comes to the swim meets, she's usually wearing shorts and a T-shirt.

"You look pretty," I say.

"Yeah?" Valerie looks up, biting one side of her lip, like she doesn't quite believe me.

"It matches your eyes." Which it does but, honestly, that wasn't the first thing I noticed.

"Should I get it?"

There's something so shy and sweet about the way she says this that I have to smile. "Definitely," I say. "But only if you want everyone at the beach to be jealous of you."

I'm not sure why I said that, but I'm glad I did because it seems to make Valerie happy.

She laughs and her ears and neck go red as she waves me off. "Don't be silly." She shuts the door quickly and latches it.

The warm feeling I get at putting that smile on her face makes me all the more determined to stop Sean and Coop from doing what they are doing. It's like I've been given the responsibility to protect the honor of these girls. I know it sounds sappy, but the nagging, pain-in-the-ass angel on my shoulder wants me to do the right thing.

Which turns out to be nothing more than stepping aside as the saleslady heads back to the changing rooms.

It's perfect timing, because both Coop's and Sean's heads just start to pop up over the stall walls once again.

The look on the woman's face is priceless. A giraffe could walk in the store right now and this woman's eyes couldn't be any bigger or rounder.

"I beg your pardon!" she calls out. "Just what is it you boys think you're doing?"

Sean and Coop freeze for a split second, their mouths stuck in a comic-book surprised O shape.

Then, their heads drop down in unison.

"Both of you boys." The woman pounds on their stall doors. "Come out of there immediately."

"What's going on?" Kelly calls from her changing room.

But nobody answers her.

Coop and Sean yank open their dressing-room doors and bolt past the saleswoman, who tries in vain to grab them.

"Come back here!" she shouts. But they don't, of course. She glares at me, and I try to look as innocent as possible. "I'm calling security." She huffs as she storms over to the front counter.

My cell phone beeps a second later. I get it from my pocket and flip it open. There's a text from Coop. *Payback's a bitch!* It makes me smile because I can just picture how pissed Coop and Sean are.

When Kelly and Valerie come out, they want to know what happened with Coop and Sean, but I just say that they were horsing around and got kicked out. I've accomplished what needed to be done; there's no reason to narc them out.

CHAPTER THIRTY-FIVE

WHO'S AFRAID OF THE BIG BAD ULF?

WHAT IS THIS?" Ulf is holding up the Ziploc freezer bag I gave him, pinched between his thumb and forefinger at the corner like it's full of baby vomit instead of crumpled bills and change.

"It's the money," I say. "For the class. A hundred dollars."

I got to the country club a half hour early because I wore my sneakers this time instead of dress shoes and the ride's a whole lot faster without blisters. So it's just Ulf and me standing by the side of the pool. He twirls the bag around, studying it. I only had seventy dollars in bills, so I had to scrounge the rest up in quarters, dimes, and nickels.

"Do you think I am a bubble-gum machine?" Ulf says.

"No." I shake my head.

"Most people, they get their parents to write a check."

"Oh."

"I do not like counting out change." He shakes the bag, jingling the coins. "This cup of tea is not mine."

"I can count it for you," I say.

"Ah, yes. That is a very good idea." Ulf unseals the Ziploc and pulls the paper money out.

I hold out my hand, expecting him to pass me the bag. But instead, he just smiles.

"You will count out the coins for me." Ulf's expression shifts like one of those hologram cards you dig out of a cereal box. Stone-faced, he flings his arm out, sending the change hurtling through the air, splishing into the water. "As you pick every one of them up off the bottom of the pool." He looks at his watch. "You have twenty-three minutes. If you are not completed by the time class begins, you will do it all over again. I suggest you get started." Ulf moves to a lounge chair and gets comfortable. He snaps open a newspaper and that's that.

Goddamn it. There must have been like two hundred coins in that bag.

I start to tug my pants off when I hear Ulf call out from behind his paper, "In your clothes."

I stare at the pool, at the glint of the coins scattered on the blue bottom, their shapes morphing with the soft ripples on the surface.

Think of Kelly. That's what this is all about. Make it a game. Each handful of change you bring to the surface is one step closer to being her boyfriend.

I suck in a deep breath and dive in. My clothes soak up the water like a sponge. I clear my ears as I kick down, air bubbles streaming from my mouth.

Picking coins up off the bottom of a pool is harder than you'd think. It's not like you can just scoop up a handful. You have to pluck them one at a time; otherwise they kind of flutter off, this way and that, like you're on the moon. Nickels are easiest because they're thick and you can get a good grip. Quarters are not too bad because they're bigger around. It's the dimes that are a pain in the ass. Why the hell are they so small? Shouldn't they be bigger than nickels? Who was the idiot who designed these things?

Stupid dimes.

When I can't hold my breath anymore, I swim to the surface, clutching my handful of loot. I dump the wet change onto the concrete and imagine Kelly leaning in to kiss me. What will that be like? Her warm breath. The taste of her lips.

It's pretty good motivation.

Another suck of air and I plunge down again. My saturated clothes make the whole process so much harder. Which I guess is the point, but it's starting to piss me off. I toy with the idea of taking my pants off and leaving them at the bottom of the pool until I'm finished. Ulf would freak if he found out. I can't even imagine what he'd do. Which is why my pants stay on.

By the time I'm finished, it has taken me the full twenty-three minutes and I'm completely drained.

Hanging on to the ledge of the pool, I separate the coins and stack them up into piles of dollars. There's thirty bucks here, just like I knew there was.

Ulf approaches and stands over me, studying his watch. "Twenty-three minutes, fourteen seconds. Very close. But not close enough. You will do it again Thursday. Please arrive thirty minutes early next class. I will have already poured the change into the pool by the time you get here. Next time, you will have only twenty-two minutes."

Are you kidding me? God! I need to reconsider this whole going-to-jail thing. How bad could a trespassing sentence be?

The rest of the swim lesson is even harsher, if that's possible. We have to swim laps with our legs tied together, laps with our arms tied behind our backs, laps dragging one of the other kids behind us. All topped off with another sixteen laps of butterfly.

And I thought Ms. Luntz was sadistic.

Once again I'm the last one out of the pool by a long shot because I still can't finish more than a couple of laps of fly without having to stop and tread water.

I've come to the realization that, while I might just barely be able to complete four laps by championships, there's no way I'm going to be able to compete in sectionals this weekend. Not a chance. I'll need to figure a way out of it. Something more convincing this time.

I'm completely bagged, and I struggle to get my body out of the pool. Ulf reaches out and gives me his hand. He pulls me up from the water and tosses me my towel.

"You are a terrible swimmer," he says.

"Yeah. Thanks."

"But you keep going. Even though you are terrible."

"It's not like you're giving me a choice."

"There is always a choice."

I huddle inside the cocoon of my towel, trying to get warm.

"Why do you come here?" Ulf follows me to the bench where my clothes lie in a soggy heap. I reach for my khakis and start to tug them on.

"You're making me. Remember?" The pants are cold and clingy and feel gross on my skin.

"No. Before this. The first time. I am curious."

"It's a long story."

Ulf sits on the bench. "There are many pools to swim in. Ones where you do not have to lie to gain entry. Did you come here just to take my class?"

"No," I say, maybe a little too quickly. "I mean, I didn't even know there was a class here. I just needed somewhere to practice. Someplace where nobody knew me."

"Why where nobody knew you?"

I grab my drenched shirt and wring out some of the

water. It falls on the concrete like heavy rain. "I told you. It's a long story."

"You are not very old. How long could the story be?"

"Long enough that I don't want to talk about it." What's up with this guy? Why does he even care?

Ulf scratches at his cheek with his black-painted nails. "My great-grandmother once said to me that the things we do not want to speak about are the very things we need to speak about most. What do you think about that?"

"I don't know."

"What if I offered you a deal? You tell me why you came here, and I will no longer require you to come to my class." And, as if Ulf was planning this all along, he pulls my ID card out of his back pocket and waves it in the air.

"Seriously? What's the catch?" Because there's always a catch with Ulf.

"Yes. There is one catch."

He's probably going to put my ID in a safe and then throw it into the pool so I'll have to pick the lock while holding my breath.

"The catch is, I think you will return to my class anyway. On your own."

I let a quick, forceful are-you-kidding-me? laugh burst past my lips without meaning to. I clear my throat to try and cover.

Ulf raises his eyebrows. "Do we have a deal?"

"Yeah. Sure." Now all I have to do is make up some bogus story and I'm out of here, scot-free.

I reach for my ID, but Ulf pulls it back and smiles. "I know what you are thinking. But the deal is for the truth. I can tell when there is wool in my eyes. I knew from the minute you arrived something was not as it seemed. And I am a man who enjoys to have a row of ducks. Do you understand what I am saying?"

"Sort of."

"Because if you lie to me. Well. All I can say is, if you thought things were hard now, you do not have any idea of what hard can be."

Ulf holds the card out to me again.

Something drops into me as I slide the card from his hand. Like a conscience, maybe. Or that damn shoulder-angel again. I don't know. But I feel like I have no choice except to tell him the truth.

Or, at least, most of it.

"Fine." I take a deep breath and sit down next to Ulf. "Obviously, I suck pretty bad. I mean, you've seen how awful I am."

"But not as awful as the first week."

"Yeah, well, not anywhere near where I need to be. That's why I came here. To practice in private. So people I know wouldn't see how bad I was."

"I still do not understand. You are dancing a jig."

"I was trying to impress a girl, okay? So I volunteered to swim the hundred-yard butterfly for my swim team."

"Was she?"

"Was she what?"

"Was she very impressed?"

"I guess. I don't know. She said she thought it was cool."

Ulf makes an *mmmm* sound, like he's mulling this over. "Okay," he says. "You are free to go." He stands.

"That's it?"

"Why? Is there more?"

"No."

"Then you have said it. You have owned it. Now we shall see."

"See what?"

"If you are as Ulf-like as I think you might be." Ulf walks off, leaving me there, sitting on the bench, staring down at my ID card, wondering what the hell he meant by that.

CHAPTER THIRTY-SIX

THAT'S WHAT SHE SAID

OH, BY THE WAY," Coop announces as he weaves his DeathBot ship through a barrage of space debris on his laptop screen. "In case you didn't know. It's national 'That's What She Said' Day."

I give him the thumbs-up. "I like it."

"That's what she said." Coop laughs.

We're camping out in Sean's backyard tonight. It's another one of our traditions. One night, every summer, we buy a ton of junk food and energy drinks and set up Sean's six-person tent in the far corner of his yard.

We've got an extension cord running from the garage so that we can rough it in style, with computers and a TV and DVD player. There's a citronella candle burning in the middle of the tent to ward off mosquitoes and to mask the thick stink of mildew. Everyone's brought sleeping bags and pillows, but we aren't planning on logging too many Zs.

Sean enters the tent carrying his Xbox. "I don't think there are enough sockets for all these."

I waggle my eyebrows at Coop. "That's what she said."

Coop busts up.

Sean stands there, looking confused. "I don't get it."

"That's what she said," Coop says, sending him and me into hysterics.

Sean sighs and puts the Xbox down. "I can see this is going to be a long night."

"That's what she said," me and Coop howl in chorus.

"Are you guys done yet?"

Coop is practically in tears. "That's what she said."

"Okay. I'll just keep my mouth shut," Sean grumbles.

"That's what she said." I can barely talk I'm laughing so hard.

"Enough. No more. My cheeks hurt," Coop says, rubbing his face.

I point at him. "That's what she said."

And with that, the three of us fall over in fits.

"Oh, man, now look what you made me do." Coop motions to his computer. "That was my last DeathBot ship."

"That's what she said," Sean blurts out, laughing at his nonsensical joke.

Coop and I stare at him, and then simultaneously, we hit Sean in the face with our pillows.

"What?" Sean shrugs. "It's funnier when it doesn't make any sense at all."

"No, it isn't," Coop says.

"Well, I think it is." Sean grabs a bag of Doritos from our mountain of snacks.

The screen door to Sean's house creaks open and slams closed. Someone's approaching.

"Hey, morons. Put your wieners away; I'm coming out there." It's Cathy, Sean's sister. She pulls back the tent flap, crouches down, and looks inside. "Mom said you girls wanted to see me. This better be good." She grabs a bag of salt-and-vinegar potato chips from our junk food stash but doesn't open it.

I'd say something about her stealing our snacks, but I don't want to piss her off.

"We have a picture for you," Sean says. He turns to Coop. "Go on. Show it to her."

Coop digs his cell phone out of his overnight bag and flips it open. He hits a few buttons, then hands the phone over for Cathy to see.

"Well, well, well. The Virgin Mandy having a panty party. Who's the muscle-head with her? I can't see his face."

"It's Tony Grillo," I say.

"The deal was for naked." She hands the phone back to Coop. "Why didn't you wait a little longer? It looks like they were about to get busy. What happened? Did you guys wet yourselves?" Cathy reaches over and grabs a Kit Kat bar and an Almond Joy.

"No. But there was . . . an interruption," Sean says, his eyes darting to the side.

"Matt?" Cathy laughs. "Were we incontinent again?"

"No," I say, looking away, shaking my head.

Sean leaps in. "Come on. She's practically naked."

Cathy ponders this as she rummages through our pile of chips and candy. She grabs a package of Ring Dings. "I know. I'll just crop the picture of you guys so it's just from the waist up. That seems fair. Half a cross-dressing picture for a half-naked Mandy."

"Oh, come on," Sean says. "If you posted that on Facebook, it'd be good payback. I mean, it's pretty embarrassing."

Cathy glares at her brother. "Are you kidding me? There are dirtier pictures in a Sears catalog."

"Okay." Sean sighs. "How about the picture of Mandy *and* I'll be your slave for a week? Would that work?"

Cathy taps her finger on her lips. "Two weeks."

Sean groans. "Aw, come on."

"Three weeks."

Sean's shoulders slump. "Fine. Okay. God." He glances between Coop and me. "But we want to see you erase the picture of us."

"Where has the trust gone in this world?" She takes her cell phone from her pocket and finds the photo. She smiles wistfully. "It's a shame, really. You girls look so pretty."

"Okay, okay. Just do it." Sean makes a get-on-with-it gesture.

Cathy turns the phone so we can see. She presses DELETE, and the picture of us vanishes. "Happy?"

The three of us sigh with relief.

Cathy laughs. "I'll let you guys get back to playing show-and-tell." She plucks another bag of chips from our rapidly dwindling store. "Thanks for the free snacks, losers. Bah-bye." Cathy stands with her loot, then leaves.

"What if she made copies?" I say.

Sean shakes his head. "No chance."

"*I* would have," Coop says. "Just in case my phone died or something. She probably downloaded it onto her computer."

"Yeah, I'd be worried about that," Sean says, "if Cathy was even remotely organized. But I know my sister. It would have been too much of a hassle. Just like putting her plate in the dishwasher." He collapses onto his sleeping bag. "You guys can stress, but I, for one, feel like I can breathe again."

"Yeah, well, enjoy it. Because I'm still holding my breath until I figure a way to get out of swimming the butterfly this Saturday."

"Too bad you screwed us at the mall." Sean lies back with his hands behind his head. "Otherwise we'd help you out."

"You're just mad because I outsmarted you guys."

"No, actually," Coop says, "we're mad because we had a chance to achieve our summer goal and you blew it."

"You would've been caught, anyway. I probably saved you from going to jail."

Sean's staring up at the top of the tent with a dopey grin on his face. "It would have been totally worth it."

"Besides, I owed you guys for bailing on me at the party. Tony the Gorilla nearly killed me."

Coop groans. "Oh, God. How long are you going to milk that one?"

"I'm just saying—"

"Okay. Fine." Coop sits up. "But this doesn't mean that we're square. I came up with this wicked idea last night, and the only reason I'm offering it to you is that I'd hate to see my genius go to waste."

"What's the idea?"

Coop nods. "It's big—"

"That's what she said," Sean interrupts, laughing.

Coop cuts him off with a death stare. He turns back to me. "It's going to take an Oscar-caliber performance. Do you think you're up to that, Mattie?"

"What do I have to do?"

"You have to know exactly how to act. It's the only way you'll pull it off."

"Act what? What is it?"

"It's the one thing you can fake that'll even fool a

doctor. The one thing there's no definitive test for." Coop grins big and pauses for dramatic emphasis. "Appendicitis."

"Are you kidding me? What the hell's wrong with a simple migraine?"

"Look, if Ms. Luntz hears you have a headache, she'll know you bailed. And then *everyone* will know you bailed. But if she hears you had appendicitis? Who's going to fake that? Nobody. It's foolproof."

"Coop's right," Sean says. "I'd never even think to fake that."

"You have to end up in the hospital. And you have to have a doctor confirm it. That way, no one will even question it."

"I don't know. That sounds extreme."

"It *is* extreme. That's the point," Coop says. "My cousin had appendicitis last year, and he was out of commission for, like, a week. It's perfect. You're exactly like him. You have all the risk factors. You're under twenty. You're male. And you eat a low-fiber diet."

"How do you know what I eat?"

"It doesn't matter. That's just what you say when the doctor asks. You eat mostly meat and cheese. You have a severe pain in your lower right side. Here." Coop reaches over and points to my right side just above my pelvis. "You wince in pain as soon as you feel any kind of pressure. It's hard to walk. And you feel nauseous."

"What if they take an X-ray or something?"

"That's the beauty of it. They can't see it with an X-ray. All they did was make my cousin piss in a cup. They'll just keep an eye on you for a few days and give you antibiotics, and when you're feeling better, they let you go."

"Is that what happened with your cousin?"

"No. He had to have an operation. But that's because his appendix burst. Just don't go over the top with your acting and you'll be fine."

"It can't be that easy," I say.

"It isn't. You have to convince them first. But after that, it's just hot nurses giving you sponge baths and all the Jell-O you can eat."

CHAPTER THIRTY-SEVEN

WARRIOR

I TOLD YOU THAT YOU would return," Ulf says, when I enter the pool on Thursday.

"Yeah, well. I'm kind of stuck." I don't want to disappoint him, but the only reason I'm here is to see if there is any way I can possibly complete four laps of butterfly before Saturday's meet. Otherwise, I might actually have to resort to Coop's ridiculous plan.

"You have taken the step of a baby," Ulf says, looking uncharacteristically content. "This is the first step in becoming a warrior."

"I don't feel much like a warrior." I put my towel down, then take out my wallet and cell phone and tuck these inside the towel. I want to get the coin-collecting part of the "lesson" over with as soon as possible, but Ulf is blocking my way to the pool.

"When a horse falls on you, you can stay there and say, 'I am squished by a horse.' Or you can find another horse. Today, you have made the choice to find another horse. There are many people who would not do the same."

"Yeah, I guess," I say, looking down at Ulf's left hand. I keep wanting to ask him what the deal is with those black nails. Is he Goth or GI Joe or some weird amalgam? I figure since he's in such a talkative mood, I might as well try and get an answer. "Why do you paint the nails on your hand?"

Ulf glances down at his nails. "They are as a reminder. Something I do not want to forget."

"Like what, though? To pick up milk on your way home or something?"

"No. They are to remind me of a person." He closes his hand. "It is time for you to collect my coins. Go. Nineteen minutes." Ulf turns and walks toward the office.

Okaaay. Doesn't like talking about the nails. Check.

I trudge over to the water's edge and stare down at all those damn coins.

I take a deep breath.

And jump in.

CHAPTER THIRTY-EIGHT

SET THE STAGE

I COULDN'T SWIM FOUR CONTINUOUS LAPS of butterfly on Thursday. I barely managed two before I started sucking pool water.

I've been racking my brain for a better plan than Coop's appendicitis hoax, but for the life of me I can't come up with one. It scares me that an idea of Coop's seems like the only logical option.

It's the morning of sectionals and I'm lying in bed, pressing my fingers into the soft area where my appendix is supposedly located. I practice grimacing in pain when a little pressure is applied. I've never lied on quite this scale before, but I've never had to deal with anything this big, either. A few days in the hospital is a small price to pay to save face and keep my chances with Kelly alive. It might even gain me a little sympathy. Maybe she'll bring over some chicken soup and do a get-well striptease.

There's a knock on my door. "Time to get up, honey." It's Mom. "We have to leave in an hour and you want to have time to eat something."

I can't believe I'm actually going to do this.

"Mom," I say, "I don't . . . feel so good."

The bedroom door pushes open and Mom pokes her head in. "What is it?"

"I don't know." I try not to sound sick. Coop says the I'm-dying voice is a dead giveaway. "It's hard to sit up. There's like this cramp in my stomach or something."

Mom enters the room and moves over to my bedside. "Where? Show me."

I pull back the covers and place my hand on the right side of my abdomen. "Here."

Mom reaches over and lightly presses on the spot. "There?"

"Ssss." I wince at her touch, just like I practiced with Coop. "Yes."

Mom's face goes pale. She cups her hand over her mouth. "Okay. Let's not panic." She's not doing a very good job of hiding hers. I really hate having to lie to her like this. "Did you lift anything heavy yesterday?"

"No. I don't know. I don't think so. I'm sure it'll go away. I better get ready." I swing my legs around gingerly and get to my feet with just a flicker of the "agony" it's causing me.

Coop says you have to make sure that you downplay the pain. It's got to be a perfect balance between what you say and how you act. Never ask to get out of the thing you're trying to get out of. Always soldier on, like you're being brave. It's important that someone else suggest that you stay home. And even then you can't give in. They have to insist you stay home. Otherwise there will always be suspicion.

I shuffle over to where my swim stuff is.

"Do you want to go to the doctor, honey?"

"No," I scoff. "It's not a big deal. I'm actually feeling a little better now that I'm up."

This is another Cooper suggestion. You don't want anyone thinking you're lying about being sick, so make them think you're not being completely honest about feeling well.

"You don't look so good."

"Thanks a lot, Mom. You're a real confidence booster."

Mom gives a hesitant laugh, just like Coop said she would. "That's not what I meant."

She looks so worried. God, I feel guilty.

Just not guilty enough to stop.

"Let's see how you're feeling after breakfast."

"I'll be fine," I say.

At breakfast Grandpa reads the newspaper, shaking his head. "I don't know why I subject myself to this goddamn paper every morning. It's like a catalog of everything bad that's happened in the last twenty-four hours."

I'm pushing the bacon and scrambled eggs around on

my plate with my fork in an effort to appear not to have an appetite, even though I'm starving.

"You haven't touched your food," Mom says, watching me over a bite of her toast.

"Yeah. I'm just not that hungry."

Mom glares. "You're not going to a swim meet on an empty stomach, young man. You need your energy. Now eat."

I spear some egg with my fork and lift it slowly. I examine it before I place it in my mouth. It tastes good. Mom mixed Parmesan cheese and ham in, which makes it all the more difficult not to eat. I pretend that it's hard to get the food down, but really I'm savoring the one bite I'll let myself have.

I flinch a little and grab at my side.

This does not go unnoticed by Mom. She drops her fork on her plate. "You're not being truthful with me."

I look up at her. "What are you talking about?"

"You said you were feeling better, but clearly you're in pain. You won't eat. Something's wrong. I think we should take you to the hospital."

"What's going on?" Grandpa says, folding his paper and setting it aside.

"Matt woke up with a bad pain in his side and now he says he's not hungry."

"Where's the pain?"

"It's right here." I place my hand exactly where I did before.

"Sounds like appendicitis. That's nothing to screw around with. I saw a couple-a guys go down with that in Korea. If your appendix bursts, it's *sayonara*."

"That's it." Mom stands. "We're taking you to the emergency room. Let's go. Get your shoes on."

"Mom, please. It's just a stomachache."

"Fine," Mom says. "We'll let the doctor be the judge of that. I'll call Ms. Luntz and tell her you won't be able to make the meet today."

"They need me to swim."

"I don't care. They'll get someone else. Some things are more important."

"Mom—"

"You don't have a choice here, Matt. I'm not going to have my son die because he's too stubborn to see a doctor."

I can't believe this is really working. It's exactly how Coop laid it out. The stage has been set.

Things couldn't be going any smoother.

....

CHAPTER THIRTY-NINE

THE STAGE COLLAPSES

WE'VE BEEN SITTING in the waiting room of the ER for almost two hours now. Our family doctor only works weekdays, so the hospital was the only choice. Mom and Grandpa Arlo are both here with me, and I'm feeling more and more guilty with every passing minute.

There are people here with real emergencies. There's a guy who got bleach splashed in his eyes and a woman whose arm has inflated to the size of a watermelon and a kid with his hand wrapped in a bloody towel. I'm glad they're making us wait because, honestly, I don't want to be the reason any of these people don't get seen as soon as possible.

I realize now that I didn't think this all the way through.

I keep glancing at the fenced-in clock on the wall, wondering how the swim meet is going, trying to guess what event they're up to. I kind of miss being there. *Not* swimming the fly, but all the other stuff. Hanging out with everyone, eating chips, seeing Valerie and Kelly, playing cards, and rooting for my friends to win their races. I even kind of miss the stupid team cheers.

There's a small TV mounted in the corner of the room. It keeps fluttering from color to black-and-white. One of the Rush Hour movies is playing, but the sound is off, so you really can't tell what's going on. Still, I keep catching myself staring at the screen.

It's surprisingly quiet here, save for the hum of the fluorescent lights, the flip of magazine pages, and the occasional whisper. The swirl of ammonia and rubbing alcohol is burning my sinuses.

"Matthew Gratton." A wizened nurse with a scowl and a manila folder calls out my name. If there are going to be any sponge baths, I can only hope she won't be the one administering them.

Mom, Grandpa, and me all stand and make our way toward her.

"This way," the nurse says as she turns on her heel and walks down the hallway.

The three of us follow. We take a left at the corner and pass a long row of makeshift curtained-off rooms. There is a lady sobbing and sniffling behind one of the curtains and an old man moaning weakly behind another.

The nurse leads us to a free cubicle with an examination bed, a chair, and a small cabinet. She makes me sit on the bed and takes my temperature and my blood pressure and then writes something down in the folder, which she places in a plastic file-holder at the end of the bed.

"The doctor will be in to see you shortly," the nurse says before leaving.

"Goddamn it, I hate hospitals," Grandpa announces. "The smell and the cold lighting and the attitude they serve you. It's enough to make you never want to get ill."

Mom gives Grandpa a look. "Everyone here's over-worked, Dad."

"Please. That's no excuse. It's not like people get sick on purpose. Speaking of which, did you see the lady with the elephant arm in the waiting room?" Grandpa says. "Christ. What the hell do you think caused that?"

"Dad, please."

"Must have been some kind of allergic reaction or something, don't you think? She was a pretty good-looking gal, too, but if that swollen-arm thing were per-manent? I don't know that I could overlook something like that."

"I'm sure your opinion's the first thing on her mind." Mom turns toward me. "How are you feeling, honey?"

"I'm feeling kind of nauseous." Which is com-pletely true. I don't know if it's the anxiety or all the sick people or what, but my head is light and I feel like I might pass out.

Grandpa huffs. "We should have said you were

having heart pains. They always take the heart-pain cases first."

"Right," Mom says. "And what happens when the doctor comes in and Matt says it's his stomach?"

"We blame it on Nurse Sourpuss."

Mom shakes her head. "Sometimes I don't understand how we could be related."

"Of course we are, Colleen. You just got the Goody Two-Shoes gene. Don't worry, Matt. It usually skips a generation."

This makes me laugh, and I use the opportunity to grimace in pain.

Mom glares at Grandpa Arlo. "Now see what you did?"

A small but stately woman with a great shock of gray-blond hair enters our cubicle. She's wearing a long white coat and a stethoscope. "Hello. I'm Dr. Kesler."

Mom introduces herself, Grandpa, and me.

Dr. Kesler grabs the folder at the foot of the bed and lifts a pair of black-rimmed glasses that hang from a thin chain around her neck. She positions them on the end of her nose and proceeds to read.

She closes the folder and looks at me. "So. What seems to be the problem?"

"Sounds like appendicitis, Doc," Grandpa Arlo says.

"Dad. Let the doctor do her job."

"You're having pain in your abdomen?" Dr. Kesler asks.

"Yes," I say. "Right around here." I show her.

"Why don't you take off your shirt?"

If I could snap my fingers and be back home right now, I would. But that's not going to happen, and I'm too scared to tell the truth. So I slowly pull my T-shirt up and over my head, making sure not to play the pain too big.

The doctor moves in closer, and I get a whiff of her Popsicle-stick smell. She listens to my heart with her stethoscope. Has me breathe in and out. She looks down my throat, in my ears, in my eyes.

"Sit up tall." Her hands are cold as she presses on the left side of my belly. "How's that feel?"

"Fine," I say.

She moves her hand right below my belly button and puts pressure. "That?"

"Sore," I say, because I figure she's getting closer, so it must hurt a bit.

When she presses down on the right side of my abdomen, I give her my best it-hurts-like-hell-but-I'm-not-going-to-show-it face, accompanied by a minor gasp.

"That?" she says.

"Pretty bad."

"Okay. Lie down on the bed for me."

I do as I'm told. She has me sit up and lie back down again. She makes me bend my legs and lift them to my chest. Coop didn't go over any of this, so I have to improvise when to wince and when to play it cool.

The doctor scribbles something down on my chart. "How long have you been feeling like this?"

"Since this morning," Mom leaps in. "Sorry. I'll let you answer, honey."

"Actually," I say, "I woke up in the night and felt it, too." I just remembered Coop telling me to say this, because if you suddenly feel sick in the morning, it's more obvious you're trying to get out of something. But if you felt it in the night, it's easier to believe.

"Okay, well," Dr. Kesler says. "We'll take some blood. Get a urine sample. See what shows up."

"What do you think it could be?" Mom asks, rubbing her arm nervously.

Dr. Kesler places my file back on the counter. "I thought maybe gastroenteritis, but the pain's localized so I'd say it's most likely his appendix."

Mom swallows loudly. "What do we do about that?"

"To be honest, I don't like to fool around with something like this," Dr. Kesler says gravely. "I'm inclined to just go in and remove it."

"What?" I say. "An operation? I thought you only operated when it bursts."

Dr. Kesler gives a little patronizing laugh. "No, no. We'd much rather get it before it progresses to that point. If it had burst already, you wouldn't be able to talk right now. We have a saying when it comes to the appendix: when in doubt, take it out."

CHAPTER FORTY

GET OFF THE STAGE

SHOULDN'T WE WAIT?" I say. "To see if it gets better?"

Dr. Kesler studies me. "We could wait. But I wouldn't recommend it. If we go in now, it's a very simple operation. If we hold off and it ruptures, we're talking about a much more serious situation."

"You don't want that, Matt," Grandpa says. "Trust me. My buddy Arthur Gertzen had that happen, and he said it was like someone was stabbing at his intestines with a red-hot knitting needle."

Oh, crap. What have I done? My whole body starts to sweat.

"Are you sure it's his appendix?" Mom says.

"Am I one hundred percent sure? No, because there's no way to tell until we get in there. We can only diagnose appendicitis by symptoms. Does he have most of the symptoms? Yes, he does."

"All right. I'm going to call work," Mom says. "Tell them I won't be able to make it in today." She starts digging in her purse for her cell phone. She pulls out her cigarettes, her compact, her wallet.

"When was the last time he ate?"

"Just a mouthful of eggs at breakfast." Mom has found her phone. "He wasn't very hungry. Maybe three hours ago?"

"Good. By the time we get prepped, he should be fine for the anaesthesia."

My face is buried in my hands.

"Don't worry." Dr. Kesler pats my leg. "It'll all be over before you know it."

Mom and the doctor both leave. One of them pulls the curtain closed, but I don't look up to see who.

Grandpa Arlo sits in the chair. "Well, at least you'll have a cool scar to impress the ladies with."

"Yeah," I say into my sweaty palms. "Lucky me."

"Speaking of ladies. Guess who knew the whole time that I was the one who sent the kitten?"

I lift my head and look over at him.

"I knew that'd get your mind off things." Grandpa's smiling big. "I came clean yesterday when Edith wanted to expand the search. Put up a few hundred more posters. She laughed at me when I finally told her. Said she'd known all along. She was just waiting for me to say something. I thought it was just your grandmother, but it turns out all women are psychic. You think they have no idea what you're thinking, but they know. They know everything."

"Everything?" I say, wondering if Dr. Kesler could see right through my charade the way Mrs. Hoogenboom saw through Grandpa's.

"I know." Grandpa Arlo nods. "It's scary. And if they don't know right away, they'll find out soon enough. Trust me on this, Matt: there's nothing you can get away with as far as women are concerned."

"Nothing?" I say.

"It's taken me seventy-six years to learn the few things I know about women." Grandpa counts these off on his fingers, starting with his thumb. "Tell them the truth. Tell them about your feelings. And tell them in excruciating detail. If you can remember even one of these things, you'll get more jazz than I could have ever imagined at your age."

My eyes shoot over to the closed curtain. I don't want to wait around for Dr. Kesler to call my bluff. I look over at Grandpa Arlo in the chair. He's the only one who'd understand. "Grandpa, I need your help."

Grandpa sits up. "What is it?"

"I lied," I whisper. "I don't have appendicitis. I was just trying to get out of the swim meet today."

"Holy crap." Grandpa's eyes look like they're going to shoot across the room. He leaps to his feet. "What the hell were you thinking?"

"It had to be something big or my coach wouldn't believe it."

"Well, we have to tell them."

"Maybe they know already," I say. "Like you said about women."

"They don't know, Matt. Believe me. Give them some time and they'd probably figure it out, but we don't *have* time. We need to say something. Now."

"No. Please. Can't we just—I don't know—pretend I'm feeling a little better or something. Otherwise it'll get back to Ms. Luntz and if it gets back to her—"

"They want to operate on you, Matt. Do you understand that? It can't be worth getting sliced open for."

I look down at the floor. I don't know what to say. You'd think it'd be more clear-cut, but there are good arguments for both sides.

"What's all this about?"

"It's a girl. I was trying to make her think I was a jock, so I volunteered to swim the butterfly for our team. I thought I'd be able to practice enough so that I could actually swim it, but I'm not ready yet."

Grandpa laughs and smacks my shoulder. "Uh-huh. I told you it skipped a generation."

"Can you help me?"

Grandpa does his tongue-rolling thing as he mulls this over. "All right. All right. Let me think." He moves over to the small cabinet in the corner. He finds a box of latex gloves and pulls one out. "Here we go. This could work."

"What are you going to do?"

"No time to explain. You just play along." Grandpa starts blowing up the rubber glove like a balloon. It gets bigger and bigger until it's the size of a beach ball. He pinches off the end with one hand and tugs his dress shirt up with the other. "Let's hope this does the trick."

"Grandpa?"

"On three, I need you to groan, but not too loudly, okay?"

"Groan?"

Grandpa doesn't wait to clarify. "One. Two. Three."

I have no alternative, so I let out a soft low moan.

Grandpa Arlo licks his right hand and wets the loose skin on his belly. He presses the closed-off end of the inflated glove to his stomach and then starts to let the air out.

It makes a very realistic farting sound. "Groan a little louder," he whispers.

"Ohhhhhh," I wail.

And with that, Grandpa releases even more air, creating an even louder, floppier fart noise.

He nods to me. "Now for the grand finale."

"Oh, my God!" I scream. "Uhhhhhhh!"

Grandpa Arlo lets the last rush of air fly from the glove through the soggy folds of skin on his stomach, and it's the loudest, wettest fart I've ever heard in my life. It echoes through the emergency ward.

"Whoa-lly Jesus!" Grandpa calls out. "Clear the area. That was some explosive flatulence. Whew!" Grandpa

Arlo rips open the curtains and flaps them in the air like a crazy man. "Nobody light a match."

The nurse, the doctor, and Mom all rush back in.

"What the hell's going on?" Mom demands.

"I think we might have to make a new diagnosis," Grandpa says to the doctor as he continues to flutter the curtains. "That boy had more gas than the *Hindenburg*."

"Matt? Are you okay, honey?" Mom asks.

I glance up at Grandpa, who gives me the slightest smile.

"I can't believe it," I say. "I feel so much better." I stand up and press my hand into my right side. "There's no pain at all. It's like a miracle."

CHAPTER FORTY-ONE

UP ON THE ROOF

Dude, you should have totally let them take your appendix out," Coop says. "That would have been awesome."

"Yeah." Sean laughs. "*Then* it would have been the greatest story ever."

The three of us are hanging out on the roof of my house. We had planned to go to the movies tonight, but Mom says I have to take it easy just in case today's stomach issue hasn't been totally resolved. The doctor wasn't completely convinced that my "gaseous release" solved the problem. If anything, she thinks it might be indicative of a more serious intestinal virus. We promised Dr. Kesler we would keep an eye on it, but really, Mom's just happy I'm feeling better and eating my usual portions again.

"I wasn't about to get sliced open just to have a good story to tell."

"I would have," Coop says. "And I'd have asked the doctor if I could bring it home in a jar so I could take it to school to gross out Mrs. Zuzzolo."

Mrs. Zuzzolo is one of our cafeteria ladies and probably the most squeamish person you'll ever meet. A real, gray, gelatinous appendix in a jar would definitely make her yak.

"That's nasty, dude," Sean says.

The night air is sticky, and the sweet smell of our neighbors' jasmine and honeysuckle bushes drifts up to us. We're passing around a two-liter Mountain Dew bottle that Coop brought over.

"The whole team totally sucked today," Coop says, taking a swig from the bottle. "So don't feel too bad about bailing, dawg. Even if you would have won the fly, it wouldn't have helped. We came in, like, sixth place. I thought Ms. Luntz was going to have a kangaroo."

"Yeah," Sean says. "Halfway through the meet, she Frisbeed her clipboard across the lawn and nearly took off Nicky Bowmester's zucchini."

Coop laughs. "You should have seen him dodge that thing. It'd be nice if he was that fast in the pool."

Coop hands the soda bottle over to Sean, who's staring at the upstairs window on the Goldsteins' house. "It's too bad your neighbors are prehistoric, Matt; you can see right into their bedroom from here." Sean lifts the bottle to his mouth and drinks.

"Just 'cause they're old doesn't mean they still don't get busy," Coop says. "I bet if we got some binoculars, we could watch them bang their walkers together."

"Do *not* go there," Sean groans.

"You're the one who brought it up," I say, egging Coop on.

Coop taps his temple. "Think about it, dude. The Goldsteins are the same people who were having wild orgies back in the sixties."

"Ewww." Sean plugs his ears. "I don't want to think about it. Talk about something else. Immediately."

"All right," Coop says. "Let's talk about how we're more than halfway through the summer and we're still screwed as far as our goal is concerned. And then we can discuss how it's pretty much all your fault, Matt."

"Excuse me?" I protest.

"Coop's right," Sean says. "I mean, between pooping your pants and sabotaging us at the bikini store, not to mention you're always busy practicing your stupid butterfly—"

"Facts are facts, dude," Coop adds. "But fear not. You are looking at the savior of the summer." Coop pulls a folded-up piece of paper from his back pocket and waves it in the air. "What I've got right here is our ticket to heaven. And when I say heaven, I mean a place where countless girls run around without any clothes on."

"What is it?" I try to grab the paper but Coop pulls it away.

"Ah-ha. Wouldn't you like to know?"

"Not if you're going to be a big dick about it," Sean says.

"I'll ignore that because I know you're under the influence of Mountain Dew." Coop unfolds the page and lays it out on the shingles of the roof. By the moonlight I can make out a topographic map of some woods near the ocean. "What would you say if I told you that this is a map to a nude beach?"

"Seriously?" Sean says.

Coop nods. "This map was e-mailed to me by a very reliable member of Naturists for Life dot com."

Sean and I both give Coop a questioning look.

"Don't ask. Anyway, the nude beach happens to be located at Jasper Cove. Which is in Greenhead."

"Well, that does us no good. Greenhead's, like, fifty miles away," Sean says.

"Let me finish," Coop insists. "As it turns out, my sister happens to be going to Greenhead tomorrow with a friend so they can shop at the outlet stores. And I've paid her in advance to give us a ride." Coop holds up both hands. "It's okay. There's no need to bow down."

Sean grabs the map and studies it. "Holy crap, Coop. You're the man."

Coop fakes a yawn and pats his mouth. "In other news, the sun is hot and math is boring."

I take the map from Sean and have a closer look. "This could be anywhere," I say. "How do we know this guy wasn't just screwing with you? Maybe he's one of those weirdos who likes to lure young boys to his cabin in the woods."

Coop snatches the page back. "Trust me. It's legit. But if you don't want to go, I'm sure Sean and I can handle seeing all that nude-age on our own."

"I want to go," I say. And I do. Because who wouldn't want to go to a nude beach? "I just don't want to be sent into the forests and wind up meeting Leatherface. That's all."

"Mattie, Matt, Mattington." Coop sighs and slings his arm around me. "What are we going to do with you? Haven't you ever heard the saying 'No risk, no reward'? This is an adventure, buddy. Sometimes you just have to strap in and go for the ride."

I don't mind going for a ride; it's just that any ride with Coop generally turns into a runaway train.

CHAPTER FORTY-TWO

ON THE BEACH

HER LAST NAME IS *NOT* BAGGINS, okay?" Sean says, punching Coop in the shoulder. "It's Beggs. Tianna Beggs."

"Does she?" I ask.

Sean turns and looks out the backseat window of Angela's hermitically sealed Toyota. "You know what? Talk to me when you actually *have* a girlfriend."

"Oh, so she's your *girlfriend* now?" Coop says.

"That's right." Sean grins. "We've been talking and texting almost every day since the party, and last night I finally asked her out and she said yes. So eat it."

"But . . . What about poor Valerie? Isn't she going to be destroyed by this?" Coop laughs.

"One day, when you actually grow up, Coop, you'll realize that when you have something real, someone like Tianna, you understand the difference between what's *really* real and what's just pie-in-the-sky fantasy."

Coop turns to me and laughs. "We've lost him, Mattie. He's trapped in the tractor beam of the golden doughnut. We may have to do an intervention."

"You're a little pig, Cooper," Angela says, looking in the rearview mirror. "Keep that filthy trap of yours shut or I'm throwing you out."

We're all crammed together in the backseat. It's taking way longer than it should to get to the beach because Angela drives ten miles under the speed limit to save gas and cut down on the wind damage to her car's paint job. Britney, Angela's friend, has been doing her makeup in the sun visor mirror for the entire hour we've been driving.

We pass a fire station on the right and see a sign for Jasper Cove. Angela hangs a left and continues on for a bit before pulling into the beach parking lot.

We're out of the car, our towels around our necks, our sneakers back on our feet, almost before Angela has a chance to shift into park.

"I'll meet you back here at two," Angela calls out her window. "On the dot. Or I'm leaving without you."

"Two, okay, fine," Coop says, giving a thumbs-up as we walk off.

When Angela's car disappears, Coop stops. He pulls the map from the back pocket of his shorts and unfolds it. "Hold on a second." He looks down and then points to what appears to be an entrance into the woods. "That's it. The path to glory."

We make our way over to the trail, checking to make sure no one spots us going in. As the three of us head into the woods, I get a jolt of excitement about what we might get to see.

"There's the pond," Coop says, pointing to a swampy bog up ahead. "We're on the right track."

Sean rubs his hands together. "This is going to be so sweet."

"You do realize that we're going to stand out like Shaquille O'Neal at a midgets convention?" I say.

"Nah, we'll just shuck down and blend right in." Sean hops over a small ditch. Coop and I follow.

"Yeah, you're right," I say. "No one'll notice the three naked, drooling high school kids."

"Relax." Coop holds up his towel. "Super Cooper's got it covered. We won't even have to set foot on the beach." He unrolls his towel and removes a pair of binoculars. "We'll just hide out at the edge of the woods and take in the show under the cover of trees."

"Cool," Sean says. "This is going to be the greatest day of our lives."

We continue along the dirt trail. It's an obstacle course of roots, plants, and downed trees. You can smell the ocean salt from here. A woodpecker does a drumroll on a tree somewhere nearby.

We're about halfway to the beach when all of a sudden there's a middle-aged couple in sweats coming from the other direction.

"Just act cazh," Coop whispers.

When the couple reaches us, the guy with the sagging cheeks points at Coop's hand. "This is no place for binoculars, young man."

"It is if you're bird-watching," Coop says, waving the binoculars in the air. "We have to identify ten different species of birds for our summer school project before we can go home."

The woman, whose hair is in a long dry ponytail, stretches her lips to the point where they drain of color. "Jasper Cove is an adults-only beach."

"Why?" Sean asks innocently.

"It just is because it is," the man says. "There are plenty of other places to bird-watch."

Coop looks around. "I don't know. We were told we'd be able to spot a masked booby around here. I don't want to miss that opportunity."

The middle-aged couple shake their heads and continue walking. We hear them mumble to each other as they go.

Coop cringes when they are out of earshot. "Glad we didn't see *them* naked. She reminded me of my second-grade teacher, Mrs. Katin."

"Yeah, and the guy looked like my uncle Doug," Sean says, laughing.

"You think we're gonna see any better at the beach?" I reach down and pick up a large stick and whack away some ferns.

"They can't all be uggs," Sean says.

Another five minutes down the trail and we can see light through the trees. We can hear the gentle lapping of the ocean.

"Keep 'em holstered, boys." Coop starts to jog. "This may be more than your little minds can handle."

We make it to the edge of the woods and crouch behind a large tree. In the distance, the beach is speckled with what looks like naked people. I can't make out if they're men or women or what. We might as well be standing at the top of the Empire State Building looking down at a group of tourists. This is not what I had in mind.

"Good thing I brought the specs," Coop says. He lifts the binoculars to his eyes and scans the beach.

"What do you see?" Sean smacks Coop's arm.

"Not a whole lot when you do that," Coop says.

"Sorry."

I squint hard, trying to force the vision of the nude people closer.

"It's just a whole lot of big hairy dudes," Coop says. "It's like a Discovery Channel show on woolly mammoths."

Sean scoots a little closer to Coop. "There have to be some babes. Give me the binoculars. Let me see."

Coop ignores Sean and continues to pan the horizon. "Wait. Wait. Got one," he says. "Come to Cooper, baby." He rolls the focus wheel, smiling. "Oh yeah, there she—"

Coop's smile evaporates. "Oh no." His voice is laced with alarm. "Oh, God, no."

"What? What?" Sean taps Coop's arm again.

Coop pulls the binoculars away from his eyes and blinks hard. "You don't want to know."

Sean tilts his head and gives Coop a look.

"I'm serious," Coop says, looking stunned.

"Try me."

Coop closes his eyes. "It's Ms. Luntz. Jesus, I think I'm gonna puke."

"You're so full of shit," Sean says.

"I'm not kidding."

I rip the binoculars from Coop's hands and take a look for myself. "Where? Where is she? I don't see—" But as soon as I say this, I *do* see. Ms. Luntz stands on a towel and slowly slathers suntan oil all over her marshmallow-white naked body. She bends over to reach for her feet and I throw the binoculars away like they just scorched my eyes. "Oh, Christ. It *is* her. It's Ms. Luntz." I start laughing because it's disgusting and ridiculous and horrific all at once.

"Let me see." Sean snatches up the binoculars.

"Don't do it, Sean." Coop tries to grab the binoculars back, but Sean shrugs him off.

"Seriously, Sean. You don't want to see." I shut my eyes tight. "I'm telling you. The image will burn into your brain."

But Sean is having none of it. He presses the binoculars to his eyes and points them in the direction we were looking. He uses the wheel to focus the lens and then—

Sean drops the binoculars and retches. "You bastards. Why didn't you tell me it was so horrible?"

"We did tell you, idiot," Coop says.

Sean scratches at his closed eyes. "Oh, God. It won't go away. I want to poke out my mind's eye."

"I bet it never fades," Coop says. "I bet when you finally get Tianna in the sack you won't be able to think of anything else but Ms. Luntz."

"Shut your piehole right now," Sean demands. "I'm out of here. Before we see anymore Ms. Luntzes." He stands, then scurries away.

Coop and me are up and on Sean's heels. There's no way we're letting him off the hook that easy.

"You should have listened to us, Sean," I say. "How are you ever going to forget Ms. Luntz's superdroopers? They'll be swaying in your mind for all eternity."

"And all that pasty whiteness." Coop scrunches up his whole face. "Damn!"

Sean plugs his ears and stomps ahead of us. "Shut up shut up shut up shut up!"

Coop and me catch up.

Coop taps Sean on the shoulder. Sean turns and glares.

"Slow down. We'll stop, okay?" Coop says.

Sean unplugs his ears and sighs. "You promise?"

"I swear." Coop holds up his right hand. "I'll never mention Ms. Luntz's complete and total bare-nakedness again. Or all that loose in her caboose. You can count on me. The words 'Ms. Luntz's well-oiled, slicked-up, lewd nude bod' will never leave my lips."

Coop and me laugh hysterically while Sean steams.

"You're such a shit," Sean says.

"I'm sorry. Really. I'll stop." Coop tries to catch his breath. "Seriously. I'm done."

We walk along in silence for a moment.

"Ms. Luntz's vagina," Coop coughs through his fist.

I totally lose it, doubling over.

Sean stuffs his fingers back in his ears and storms ahead.

As we make our way out of the woods, Coop claps me on the shoulder. "Well, dawg. Mission accomplished."

"Does that actually count?" I say.

"For sure." Coop laughs. "She's a woman. She was live. And she was naked. Done, done, and done."

"Yeah, I guess."

"And now, thanks to Ms. Luntz, we are one step closer to actually having sex."

"No!" I cringe and shudder. "You did *not* just say that."

Coop chuckles. "It's the truth."

"How could you even put those two things together?"

"Because it's the natural progression of things, remember?"

I look at Coop like he's lost his mind.

Coop cracks up. "Okay, so maybe we're only a quarter-step closer."

I shake my head. "You are totally and completely whacked."

"I'll take that as a compliment." He stands up tall as we walk along, side by side.

CHAPTER FORTY-THREE

HOUSE CALL

I'M LYING ON THE WOODEN lounge chair in my backyard with my eyes closed. The late-afternoon sun feels good on my face. Grandpa's just mowed the lawn, and the smell of warm fresh-cut grass fills the air. There are some kids playing Wiffle ball next door. I listen to their pretend play-by-play, the *whoosh* of the pitch, the *thwack* of the plastic bat connecting with the ball.

I have to say, it's nice to just lie here. Everything's been so nuts lately. And this morning's beach adventure really wore me out. I feel a sleep wave pulling me under, and I might just let it.

I'm just drifting off when I hear the phone inside the house ring. I'll let someone else get it. I shift and try to get comfortable again. But the ringing phone reminds me that I haven't called Valerie back. She left a bunch of messages on my voice mail last night and this morning, wanting to know if I was okay. I've been putting off calling her because I'm not up to playing the whole appendix story over again.

Still, I don't want her to worry.

I sit up, run my bare feet over the bristly blades of grass, and pull my cell phone from the front pocket of my shorts. Flipping it open, I scroll down and find Valerie's number. I highlight it and press the CALL button.

"Who you calling?" It's a girl's voice behind me, along with a muffled ring tone.

I whirl around and blink into the sun. It's Valerie. I can make her out even though she's backlit and silhouetted.

"I'm calling you," I say.

"Oh, okay." Valerie opens her purse and takes out her ringing phone. She looks at the screen and her eyes light up. "It *is* you. What a coincidence." She clicks a button and holds it up to her ear. "Hello?"

"Hi. It's me, Matt."

"Hey, Matt. How you doing?" Valerie walks over and sits down next to me on the lounge chair. "I've been pretty worried about you. I was thinking maybe I should stop by."

"Sorry I didn't call you earlier," I say into the phone. "I'm doing much better."

"Oh, good. I'm glad. But maybe I should come over anyway. To see for myself."

"Oh. Yeah. Sure. Come on by. I'm here."

"Okay. I'll be there in a second." Valerie hangs up her phone and holds out her hands, palms up, like she's just performed a magic trick. "Ta-da."

"Wow, impressive." I shut my phone and slip it back in my pocket.

"I know, I know." Valerie takes a seated bow.

"How did you find out where I lived?"

"A woman has her ways." Valerie places her fingers on her temples and closes her eyes like she's using her psychic abilities.

"Now you're scaring me."

"It's called White Pages dot com." Valerie opens her eyes and smiles. "Lucky for me you happen to be the only Grattons in Lower Rockville."

"You might want to drop the whole doctor thing and think about becoming a private detective."

"Or I could be both. Valerie Devereaux, PI, MD."

"That sounds like a television show."

"Yeah. A really bad one." Valerie laughs. "I'm glad you're feeling better. Everyone was saying you had to go to the hospital."

"Yeah," I say. "I did. The doctor thought it might be appendicitis."

"Oh, no. Did they operate?"

"They were talking about it. But it turned out it wasn't anything serious."

"You've had some bad luck lately, mister."

"Tell me about it."

Valerie leans in close. "At least your head looks better." She pushes my hair back and touches my forehead with her fingers. It sends a tingle down my spine. "It's coming along nicely. That's because I made you put ice on it immediately. Otherwise you might still have a lump."

She's wearing perfume. It smells like tangerine and the ocean. I wouldn't mind staying here for a while, breathing her in. I have to stop myself from moving closer and pressing my nose into her neck. I lean back before the temptation gets too great.

"You're going to be an awesome doctor," I say. "Because you're so nice. And you make house calls. I mean, who does that anymore?"

The corners of Valerie's eyes crinkle with her smile. "That's very sweet." Valerie rummages around in her purse. "Speaking of sweet." She takes out a pack of candy and holds it out to me. "Want a Jolly Rancher?"

"Sure." I pry one of the foil-wrapped squares loose. "Thanks."

Valerie holds up a blue candy. "Blue raspberry. What did you get?"

I look at the green square in my hand. "Green apple, I guess."

"Do you like blue raspberry better?"

"Why? Do you like green apple better?"

"No," Valerie says. "You're not supposed to do that. I'm trying to figure out which one you want."

"Oh. No. Green apple's good." I don't really like green apple, so I'm assuming she doesn't, either.

"Phew." Valerie pops her blue raspberry candy in her mouth. "I would have traded with you, but I don't really like green apple."

I put the Jolly Rancher in my mouth. It's pretty tart. Really tart, actually. Much more than I remembered. My mouth feels like it wants to curl up inside itself.

"You don't like it, either." Valerie cracks up. "I can tell."

"Really? I thought I had a pretty good poker face."

"You look like someone squirted you in the eyes with a lemon. You should have said something. Spit it out and take a different one."

"Nah. This is good. Really. Once you get past the shock of how sour it tastes, it's not so bad."

We sit in silence for a moment. Tasting our candies.

"So, did you hear about Tony and Mandy Reagan?" Valerie says.

"Hear what?" My heart skips a beat because I know what's coming.

"Someone posted a picture of them on Facebook. It's pretty compromising. Everyone's saying it's from Ronnie Hull's party."

"Huh," I say. "Has Kelly seen it?"

"Oh, yeah. She went ballistic. I don't know why she even cares anymore. Tony was all apologetic and saying that it wasn't him in the picture, but it's pretty obvious if you ask me."

"Do you think they'll ever get back together?" I hope this is subtle enough, but maybe not, because Valerie's kind of looking at me funny.

She shrugs. "Who knows? It's like a bad habit with her. But honestly? I'm a little sick of it. Kelly's always going on and on about him. It's like the only thing we ever talk about."

"Yeah," I say because I can't think of anything else.

"So, what *really* happened between you and Tony at that party? I never got the whole story."

There it is. The question I don't want to answer. And suddenly, instead of a devil and an angel, it's like I've got Coop's dad whispering in one ear and Grandpa Arlo whispering in the other. Coop's dad wants me to lie like crazy. *"She won't understand,"* he says. *"It's beyond her female comprehension. She'll be disgusted and run right to Kelly and blab the whole thing."*

At the same time, Grandpa Arlo reminds me that women are all-knowing and to think otherwise is fool-hardy. *"She probably knows already,"* he says.

Which I hadn't thought about. What if she does know? What if it's like what happened with Mrs. Hoogenboom and the kitten? Maybe Valerie's just testing me.

I'm weighing my options, back and forth, when Valerie clears her throat. "Matt? Are you all right?"

"Yeah. I'm fine," I say, feeling the candy getting thick and sticky on my drying tongue.

"Your eyes, like, glazed over. Are you sure you're feeling better?"

"It's not that." I take a deep breath. "Here's the thing. I'll tell you what happened at the party, but you have to promise me you won't tell anyone else, okay? Because it's pretty embarrassing."

"More embarrassing than chess club?"

"Uh, yeah. Just a little."

Valerie nods. "Okay, I promise." And I can tell by the way she says it, the way her sapphire eyes look at me, that she means it.

"It's kind of ridiculous, really. Okay, so. The thing is. That picture of Tony and Mandy. It *is* from Ronnie's party. I know, because Coop took it."

"What?" Valerie has a surprised smile on her face.

"It's a long story, but . . . me and Coop and Sean sort of have this tradition, right? Every summer we've set ourselves a goal. Ever since we were, like, eight. Stupid things. Like trying to collect a hundred frogs, or building a clubhouse out of old boxes, or playing a thousand Ping-Pong games."

"That sounds like fun," Valerie says.

"Yeah, well. This summer it got kinda out of hand. We decided that—well, Coop actually decided—that our goal would be to try and see . . . a naked girl. In person."

Valerie tries not to crack up, but she's not doing a very good job of it.

"I know. It's dumb. Anyway, so Coop overheard Mandy at the party say she was going to get busy with some guy in Ronnie's parents' room. I had no idea the guy was going to be Tony. Believe me. Anyway, that's why Coop came to get me when I was talking to you. We were going to hide in the closet and watch."

Valerie's eyes are wide. "Oh, my God, seriously?" And she can't help herself anymore. She completely breaks up.

And because she's laughing, I start to laugh, too. "I know. It's warped. But it gets even worse. So we're all crouched down, hiding in this closet, the door just slightly open, when Mandy comes in with Tony. The two of them start making out and undressing each other, and then Sean suddenly gets this massive leg cramp."

"Oh, no." Valerie cups her hand over her mouth.

"That's right. He starts to groan and then he falls over and whacks into me and I smash my head into the door and it flies open and there we are. So obviously, we're not hiding anymore. Anyway, that's kind of why Tony was so pissed at me."

By this time, Valerie's in fits. She's got tears streaming down her face. "That's hilarious," she says.

"Not one of my prouder moments."

"Are you kidding me? Tony totally deserves it. He's

such a slut." Valerie's still laughing. She sniffs. "You have to let me tell Kelly. She'll love it."

"No," I say. "You promised."

"Oh, please. Just Kelly. She'd so appreciate it."

Valerie must be able to tell by my face how uncomfortable I am because she jumps in before I can say anything. "Never mind. It's totally between you and me. I won't say a word."

Relief washes over me. "Thanks."

"It was brave of you to tell me," she says.

I shrug. "I didn't want to lie."

Valerie looks down at the grass. "Matt?" She glances up at me. "Can I tell you something?"

There's a quiver in her voice. And something in the way she's looking at me. I feel a catch in my breath. An edge-of-the-cliff adrenaline shot. Like, maybe she's going to say that Kelly really does like me. "Sure," I say.

Valerie rocks gently forward. She bites the corner of her lip. "I . . . I wanted to tell you," she says, "that—"

"*You* are a dead man!"

Valerie and I both spin around to see Peter standing on the back porch pointing hard at me. Oh, God. I completely forgot he was coming home today.

Pete storms over to where we're sitting. He grabs my arm and yanks me to my feet.

"Excuse us," he says to Valerie. "I have to kill my brother."

I shake my head behind Peter's back to try and assure Valerie that he doesn't really mean this.

Even though he probably does.

Pete drags me off toward the house. I'm not sure if there's a connection or not, but Valerie does seem to be around to witness all of my drubbings.

I look back over my shoulder.

"I'll call you later," I say to Valerie, whose eyes are wide with concern.

"Yeah?" Peter says. "And how are you going to dial a phone with ten broken fingers?"

CHAPTER FORTY-FOUR

PANIC ROOM

PETER TOSSES ME INTO HIS ROOM and then slams the door behind us so there can be no witnesses.

"Oh, my God!" I say, feigning shock. "What happened?"

"That's what you're going to tell me." Pete's voice is shaky. He's beyond pissed.

"Jeez. It looks like your Houdini picture fell onto your aircraft-carrier table. Oh, man. That blows."

He shoves me toward the wreckage. "Don't bullshit me! There's no way that picture fell three feet sideways. Unless we had an earthquake I wasn't aware of."

"You didn't hear about that?"

He ignores this. "So, either Mom went medieval with her vacuum or you fucked up."

"Well, now that you mention it. I did hear a racket going on when Mom came in here to clean. She can be pretty clumsy with that Hoover." Normally, I'd never throw Mom under the bus. But I know for a fact that Pete would never punch her in the face.

"What. Did. You. Do?"

Not that I think being honest will get me any mercy, but it's all I've got now. I cling to the fact that when I was honest with Ulf and with Valerie, I felt a whole lot better about myself.

I take a deep breath and let it out slowly. "All right. It was me. But it was an accident, I swear."

Pete's eyes start to fill up. Tears of rage.

I keep talking, because once I stop talking the beatings will begin.

"I was using your weights, right? Like you said I could, remember? And I was careful not to touch anything. Supercareful. Except, I sort of worked out a little too much and I got tired and on my last set of shoulder presses my arms kind of locked."

Peter shuffles over to the pile of broken airplanes. He squats down and picks up one of the pieces. He turns it over, examining it. I'd feel really bad for him if I didn't know that he was probably contemplating all the ways he could rip out my heart.

"That's when I sort of fell over. And the weights kind of smashed into your model airplane table. I got scared, so I tried to cover it up. Which was wrong. I know. I'm really, really sorry. It was totally an accident and I'll make it up to you. However you want. I'll give you all my money. I'll buy you a rickshaw and pull you around. Anything. Just please don't beat me up too badly because I've got to swim championships in a couple of weeks and I need to have use of my arms and legs."

I brace myself.

Pete is still looking at the splintered fuselage of the fighter plane. "Do you have any idea how long it took me to make all of these?" He's speaking softly. It's scarier than if he was screaming. "How many hours I spent?"

"A lot. A ton. I know. If I could destroy something of mine and it would bring back all your planes, I would do it in a second. You have to know I would never do this on purpose."

Pete crushes the plastic hull in his fist and drops it to the floor.

Oh, crap. Here it comes.

I'm ready to run if he lunges.

But Peter just slogs over to his bed and sits down, the mattress squeaking under his weight.

And then he starts to sob. His whole body shaking. He buries his face in his hands.

I knew he'd be upset, but I didn't think he'd be so broken up he wouldn't even be able to beat the crap out of me. I don't think I've ever seen him cry like this.

Part of me feels like I should go over and give him a hug. But my survival instinct reminds me that you don't hug a bear with a sore head, even if he's sad.

"I'm really sorry, Pete," I repeat myself in lieu of an embrace.

"Go away," he croaks. "Just leave me alone."

And that's when it hits me. This is not about his airplanes. Something else is going on.

"Pete?" I say, taking a tentative step closer. "Why are you crying?"

He wipes his cheeks with both hands and sniffles. "They're stupid, anyway. Dad's the one who started me on them. We used to do them together. I just never stopped. I'm glad they're broken. You did me a favor."

I move to the bed and sit next to Peter.

I put my hand on his back and he lets me.

"It's funny." Pete clears his throat. "Melissa and I had this huge fight last night because I was doing a model the whole time we were away. She wanted to know why it was so important that I'd spend more time on a toy than with her." Pete laughs. "I said I didn't know."

We sit there. Quiet.

I get a flash of an image. Peter and Dad sitting at the kitchen table, carefully placing decals on a Spitfire. And I don't know why, but I feel my eyes welling up, too.

I'm thankful when Pete finally speaks. "Was that the girl you were telling me about?"

"Who? Valerie?" I turn my head and surreptitiously blot the corners of my eyes. "No. She's a friend of hers."

"Huh. Too bad. She's cute."

"Yeah. She is."

"Well. You better go call her and tell her you're alive. She looked pretty terrified back there."

"She wasn't the only one." I stand and make my way to the door.

"Don't talk too long, though," Pete says. "You've got a mess to clean up here."

As I leave Pete's room, it occurs to me how weird it is that you can imagine every possible outcome of a situation and never come up with how things will actually turn out.

CHAPTER FORTY-FIVE

MORE ULF THAN YOU CAN SHAKE A STICK AT

VALERIE'S OFF TO LAKE WILLIAM with her family for the week. I had called her to let her know I wasn't dead, which she kind of figured out when she heard my voice. I tried to get her to tell me what she wanted to tell me earlier, but she said it was something she needed to talk about in person. I said I understood, but really, it's going to drive me insane. She wouldn't even give me a hint. She just laughed and said I'd have to be patient.

I can't imagine it could be anything else besides Kelly. Of course, I haven't been able to imagine anything else besides Kelly since the beginning of the summer, so who knows.

Valerie and I agreed to get together next week when she comes back. Barring someone else dragging me off, we'll discuss whatever it is then.

I decide that I need to redouble my efforts, so that I don't disappoint Kelly when championships roll around.

I ride my bike to the country club. Ulf has agreed to meet with me every day around dinnertime for the next two weeks, until the meet. He said he lifeguards at the pool, anyway, so it's no big deal. Plus the pool's pretty empty in the early evening, so we should have the place mostly to ourselves.

I'm not sure why he's taken such an interest in me. When I asked him about it, he just said that strength of character is more important than strength of body. He also said that it didn't seem like anyone else was teaching me this, so he felt he'd better get started.

Honestly, I don't have a clue what Ulf is talking about 90 percent of the time. But if he wants to help me swim the fly better to impress Kelly enough so that she will date me, then I'm not going to stop him.

When I arrive at the pool, I'm ready to dive in and collect the change from the bottom like always. But for some reason Ulf hasn't thrown the coins in.

He is sitting high in the lifeguard stand, drinking tea from a HAVE A NICE DAY mug.

"Where's the change?" I say.

"Today there is no swimming. Today there is only hanging."

"What?"

"You are swimming too hard against yourself to finish the one-hundred-yards butterfly. I have realized this."

"What are you talking about?"

"You have an obstacle course in your brain." Ulf

takes a sip of his tea. "I should have understood this sooner. You must hang from the high-diving board. By your hands."

"For how long?"

"Until you wake up and smell the music."

"I don't get it."

"You will. Now go. Hang."

So I do. Though I have no idea why.

I climb the ladder to the ten-foot-high diving board and situate myself so that I'm hanging down over the water. The board bends a bit from my weight. I have to reposition myself a few times as my hands get raw and my shoulders get tired.

After around five minutes, I can't hold on any longer and I have to let go. I fall with a splash into the pool and swim over to the lifeguard stand.

"There," I say. "I did it. I smelled the music."

"You did not. Otherwise you would still be hanging. Try again."

We go through this same routine for the next hour and a half; me hanging and dropping and Ulf continually refilling his mug with hot water from a thermos.

Each time I try to hang on a bit longer, but it's never long enough for Ulf.

"You have to let go inside to hold on outside," he says.

What the hell is that supposed to mean?

Finally, I give up and get my towel and collect my

clothes. I walk over to the lifeguard stand and look up at Ulf. "I could hold on forever and you still wouldn't be happy."

He just sips his tea. "I am happy whether you hold on or you do not hold on."

"Then what's the point?" I say.

"If you think that it is to make me happy, then you have not hung on long enough."

"I don't get it."

"There is nothing to get. You just hang on. And when you want to stop hanging on, do not stop hanging on. This is not a puzzle."

I clench my jaw. There have been times over the past few weeks when I actually found myself almost liking Ulf.

This is not one of those times.

But still, I am back the next day.

And the day after that.

And every day I hang from the diving board. And while I hang from the diving board, I wonder, Why the hell am I hanging from this stupid diving board when I should be swimming?

I've started actually looking forward to Lifesaving Skills class, if you can believe it, because at least I get to do something other than hang.

"We are going full pig, today!" Ulf shouts at the start of Thursday's lesson.

He is having me and the five other guys tread water in our clothes again, this time for an entire hour.

I'm a little embarrassed to admit it, but I don't actually know any of these guys' names. I've been so focused on my own pain and exhaustion, I haven't taken the time to talk to them very much. Not that I've actually *had* the time. I'm usually an exercise or two behind them, and they're long gone when I finally drag myself out of the pool.

Still, I've always wanted to ask them about Ulf. Like maybe it would help me understand what he's talking about a little more. And since I need something to take my mind off the fact that I am almost completely spent, I figure this might be a good time to bring the subject up.

"Hey," I say to the guy treading water next to me. His head is shaved, and his face is sort of pinched up, like he's always wincing.

"Hey," he grunts.

"This is fun, huh?"

"Yeah." He rolls his eyes. "A barrel of friggin' monkeys."

"So . . . what's *his* deal?" I motion with my head to Ulf, who's pulling kickboards out of the supply closet.

"What do you mean?"

My chin starts to sink below the water, so I kick a little harder. "I mean he's, like, sadistic, right? Was he in the military or something?"

The guy shakes his head. "He was some kind of championship swimmer in Germany."

"Really?" I catch my breath. "Why's he teaching here, then?"

He shrugs. "How the hell should I know? Supposedly he moved here after his son drowned or something. Maybe it's the only job he could get."

"Drowned? How?"

"Some boat accident. Probably the same one he keeps flogging us with every time he wants to make a point." The guy smirks. "What's with all the questions, dude? You got a hard-on for him or something?"

"No," I say, puffing. "I'm just curious, is all. Forget it."

He glances over at the wall clock. "Yeah, well, save your breath. We still have twenty minutes of this torture." He spins and treads away from me.

I look over at Ulf lining the kickboards up against the fence. I kind of feel bad now for all the nasty things I've thought about him. And just as I'm thinking this, he turns and catches me staring.

"You are sinking!" Ulf shouts. "Keep your head above the water!"

I quickly avert my eyes. And a second later, I feel a dive ring smack me in the ear.

CHAPTER FORTY-SIX

VENICE

THERE'S ABOUT A HALF HOUR before I have to meet Val at the bus stop, and my palms don't want to stay dry no matter how many times I wipe them on a towel. I try rubbing them with antiperspirant, but that just makes them sticky, so I have to wash it off. I have gotten myself so worked up about what Valerie wants to say to me that I've had a weeklong stomachache.

I've been keeping a close eye on Kelly at swim practice, to see if she might give something away, but so far nothing. She probably wants Valerie to feel me out first. That's how these things go. Or at least it's how they go on TV.

I stand at my dresser, looking into the mirror, wondering if my hair looks weird or if I should change my shirt or brush my teeth again.

Mom knocks on my open door and stares at me. "I can't believe it," she says, her eyes filling. "My baby's growing up."

"Don't, Mom. Please." She's been making a big deal about this ever since I told her that I was going to the movies with a girl.

"Sorry." She sniffles. "Look what I found." Mom holds up a small blue sheet of paper. "It's a free movie pass for two. I got a bunch of these with my Visa points."

"Thanks, Mom, but no. I'm not going to use a coupon to get our tickets. It's cheesy. And it'd make me look cheap."

"Why?" Mom asks. "Just tell her you had it lying around and that you wanted to use it before it expires. You get free popcorn and a drink, too. She'll be happy."

I'd argue this more, but Mom looks so pleased that I take the free-movie pass even though there's no way I'm going to use it. "Okay," I say. "Thank you." I fold the coupon and tuck it in my back pocket.

Mom looks at her watch. "You better go. You want to get there before she does so she's not worried you're going to stand her up."

"This isn't a date." I groan. "We're just friends."

"I know. I know," she says. "Still. It's important. For when you do have a date."

I get to the bus stop ten minutes early, but Valerie's already there, sitting on the bench, reading a book. She's all dressed up in a black skirt and a silky blue blouse, and I can smell her familiar perfume.

"Hey," I say. "You're here already."

She closes her book and smiles big. "Yeah. I always give myself too much time." She waves her book. "That's why I always carry something to read."

I'm not really sure what to talk about. I'm so much in my head, wondering how this is going to go.

"What's the book?" I finally say, my voice cracking a bit.

"This?" Valerie laughs. "It's kind of embarrassing. It's a travel guide to Venice."

"Oh. Are you going there?"

"No. That's the embarrassing part." She looks down, her red hair curtaining her face. "I just like to imagine. So sometimes I read travel guides and pretend I'm going to the different places. I know, it's bizarre. My family makes fun of me all the time."

"No," I say. "It's not. That's half the fun of going on a trip, anyway. Imagining what it'll be like."

"That's what I think, too," she says. "And, anyway, I'm going to go someday. It's beautiful. Here, sit down. I'll show you."

I take a seat next to her on the bench, and she shows me some of the pictures in the Venice travel book. Churches and paintings and canals.

"It's hard to believe there's a real city like that," I say.

"Yeah. It's supposed to be one of the most romantic places in the world."

I glance up from the book and see that Valerie is looking at me.

"Hi," she says, smiling.

"Hi," I say, feeling my heart pound. Like just before a roller coaster takes off.

"So. What I was trying to tell you last week . . ."

"Yeah?" Here it comes: the Kelly's-interested-in-you speech.

Valerie takes a deep breath. I don't know why she's finding this so difficult.

"I like you, Matt."

"I like you, too," I say.

"No." She shakes her head. "I *like you* like you."

Oh.

Oh.

If my brain could make a noise, it would be the sound of a thousand screeching brakes.

Right. My God. How could I not have seen that coming?

Now that I think about it. The swing. The ice. Asking for my number. Asking my opinion about the bikini. Coming over to see how I was feeling.

And me, like an idiot, trying all the time to get her to talk about Kelly. I mean, Kelly can't even remember my name. And then, it's like my mind starts running a bloopers reel of all the things that bug me about Kelly: The way she rips on people like Helen Harriwick. How she embarrassed Valerie by making fun of her for not shopping. How she got drunk at the party and then used me to get back at Tony.

"Well?" Valerie says, trying to look at me but also trying not to. "What about you?"

Yeah, I like Valerie. She's amazing. She's smart; she's cute; she's funny. And I don't feel like I have to pretend to be someone else when we hang out. Which is totally cool. No wonder I was so protective of her in the bikini shop. And why I was so anxious to call her back to let her know I was okay.

I suddenly realize my mouth is hanging open. Not a very attractive look. I quickly shut it. I want to tell her how I feel. Except maybe I've waited too long. She'll probably think I'm lying. But the longer I wait, the worse it'll be.

"Yes," I say. "I do. I like you. A lot. Very much. Definitely. I do. Yes." Okay, bring it down a notch.

"Phew," she says, brushing a strand of hair from her face. "I thought when you didn't answer that maybe you didn't."

"No. I do. I just thought—"

Valerie leans in and kisses me. Her lips are soft and warm on mine. She smells even better up close.

I am suddenly light-headed.

This is nothing like I'd imagined it would be.

It's all so surreal.

And I don't want it to ever end.

But it has to.

Right when the number 87 pulls up and opens its doors.

We step up into the bus and find two seats together halfway down the aisle.

Valerie wastes no time in taking my sweaty hand in her dry one. It was so quick and unexpected that I didn't have time to rub my palm on my pant leg. "You're nervous." She smiles at me but doesn't let go of my hand.

"Yeah," I say. "A little."

She pats my leg reassuringly with her free hand. "Don't worry. I know *Always a Bridesmaid* sounds like a horror film, but really, it's just a romantic comedy."

After several stops, the bus is getting pretty full. The guy sitting across the aisle from me has some serious BO. I'm not sure if I should mention the smell to Valerie, because I don't want her to think it's me. But I also don't want her to think I'm mean by pointing it out. I wish I could just chill out and stop thinking so much, but all of a sudden it feels like everything is so important.

"I loved kindergarten," Valerie says. Somehow, while I've been stressing over some stranger's body odor, Val's gotten onto the subject of grade school. "That's when I started learning English. Before that I just knew French. That's all we spoke in my house. But my kindergarten teacher wanted to make sure we were bilingual, so she would teach us a new English word every day, and anytime you spoke English in class instead of French, you got a piece of candy. And I was all over that. I think I had, like, fifteen cavities before I got to first grade."

"Yeah," I say, breathing through my mouth. "I took Spanish until fifth grade, but all I can remember how to say is *Mi gato está en el árbol* and *Mi perro está en su casa.* Which, honestly, won't get you very far if you go to Spain."

Valerie laughs. "You want me to teach you some French?"

"Sure," I say. "But like I said, I'm not really good at remembering languages."

"Okay, wait." Valerie lets go of my hand and opens her purse. She takes out a small canister of Godiva Mint Chocolate Pearls. "Here. Every time you say something right, I'll give you a candy. And these are my favorites, so you know I'm serious." She rattles the little container for emphasis.

"Then I better focus."

"Okay," she says. "I'm only going to speak to you in French for the rest of the bus ride. You'll have to figure out what I'm saying and then repeat it. I'll give you clues, so don't worry. Ready?"

"Sure."

She places her hand on her chest. *"Je m'appelle Valerie."*

Well, at least she's starting easy. *"Je m'appelle Matt."*

"Très bon." Valerie nods and hands me a tiny ball of chocolate.

"Très bon," I say, popping the candy in my mouth. This is fun. I could see where this technique might work.

Valerie surreptitiously points to the guy across the aisle from me and whispers, *"Cet homme a une odeur terrible."* She pinches her nose and scrunches up her face.

I laugh and nod. *"Cet homme a une odeur terrible."*

Valerie picks up another chocolate pearl, but this time she places it in my mouth. Her finger lingers on my lips for a split second, which sends a shiver down my spine. If learning a language was this much fun in school, I would be multilingual by now.

The ride to the movie theater goes by much too fast. We laugh and speak French and eat candy the whole way. It's strange how easy it is to be around Valerie. It's like everything about her makes me feel good. The sound of her voice, her jokes, the feel of her hand in mine.

I still feel too embarrassed to use the coupon Mom gave me, especially now that this has turned into an actual date. So I buy the tickets with my own money and Valerie insists on buying the popcorn and soda, which is really cool because I was ready to pay for everything.

We make out through pretty much all of the previews. At first, I'm totally in my head wondering if I'm doing it right, if my mouth is opened enough, or too much, where I should put my hands, wondering if the chocolates have given me bad breath.

I finally have to tell my brain to shut the hell up. It gets better the more we kiss because I'm lost in all my senses. The salty taste of her lips, the clean smell of her skin, her hair, the chills all over my body. Mostly, I keep my eyes shut, but once in a while I open them and see that hers are closed.

If she wanted to, I'd kiss her through the entire movie. But I'm glad we decide to watch the film, because it's pretty funny and I like hearing Valerie's laugh. I don't know why, but it makes me like her even more.

CHAPTER FORTY-SEVEN

NO CIGAR

I'VE BEEN HAVING A BLAST this week with Valerie. She's shown me how to play chess, which is more fun than you'd think it would be, and I've shown her how you can play "Stairway to Heaven" on the guitar and make it sound like you're garroting chickens. Our French lessons have been coming along *très bon,* as well.

Valerie laughed when I told her that I'd heard she wasn't allowed to date until she was eighteen. She has no idea who started that rumor, but it made her feel better about having to pursue me so hard.

We're hanging out with Sean and Tianna in Valerie's basement. Valerie is letting me beat her at chess, while Tianna and Sean are curled up on the couch, watching one of Tianna's *anime* DVDs.

"You guys should give this a chance," Sean says. "Once you start watching, you get totally addicted."

"It's true," Tianna adds. "Sean was resistant at first, but now that's all he wants to do. Well, that and make out."

"You have to do *something* while you wait for the DVD to cue up," Sean laughs.

"I've tried watching," I say, studying the chessboard. "I just can't get into it." I move my castle three spaces forward.

Valerie clears her throat and shakes her head.

"What?" I say.

She widens her eyes like she's trying to send me the answer telepathically.

"Damn." I finally see that my queen is vulnerable, and Valerie lets me move my castle back, even though you're not really allowed to do that once you let go of your piece.

I'm examining the board for another move when I get a sudden jolt of panic.

"Oh, my God, what time is it?" I ask, grabbing my cell phone from my pocket and looking at the time. Crap. It's almost five. I'm going to be late for Ulf again. That's three times this week. Not to mention the day I skipped altogether. "I have to go."

I give Valerie a kiss, say, *"Au revoir,"* and bolt from her house.

Things always seem to conspire against you when you're late. And today is no different. Cars pull out of driveways right in front of me, lights turn red just as I approach them, and every person over eighty in Lower Rockville must be out for a walk this evening.

I pedal my bike like mad, dodging obstacles left, center, and right, because Ulf has already given me several warnings this week.

It's five twenty-three when I finally make it to the Elk Hills Country Club. I lock up my bike and tear through the front door. The lobby is choked with a throng of men in suits and women in gowns—another wedding, or retirement party, or cotillion. The club is always hosting some kind of reception.

Normally, I'm happy for the place to be busy, because it means nobody's looking at me, but today it's just another pain in the ass I have to navigate.

When I finally make it to the pool, I see Ulf sitting on the ledge with a pile of wet change beside him.

"Sorry, sorry, sorry," I say, scurrying over. "I lost track of time."

Ulf just sits there, staring into the water.

"It won't happen again. I promise."

Ulf sighs. "Yes. This is what you said last time. I am thinking that maybe you have bitten off more bullets than you can chew."

"I've just been busy lately."

Ulf stands and looks at me. "I would have more respect for you if you just quit rather than make me tell you that you are no longer welcome."

"What are you talking about?"

Ulf glares at me. "I am talking about that you do not want to be able to swim the one-hundred-yards butterfly!"

"Yes, I do."

"Why? To impress a girl? That is a very stupid reason."

"No. It's not that. Not anymore."

"Then why not quit? It is the easier way."

"Maybe I don't want the easier way."

Ulf frowns. "Most people want an easier way. You are not alone. Most people do not want to hang on when they can no longer hang on. That is why they come close and receive no cigar."

I shake my head and stare at the ground. "I don't even know what you're talking about. I told you. I just lost track of time. That's all."

"This is fine. You can continue to pretend that you have not given up. I am no longer going to live in the make-believe."

With that, Ulf turns and walks away, leaving me standing there, wondering what the hell just happened.

CHAPTER FORTY-EIGHT

COUNTDOWN

TWENTY-FOUR HOURS UNTIL CHAMPIONSHIPS. Twenty-four hours until I become the laughingstock of the Rockville Swimming Association.

I'm finishing up my fourth semi-continuous lap of clumsy butterfly, and I'm sucking air. Kelly's swimming in the lane right next to me, but I don't care what she thinks anymore.

It's the first time I've attempted the stroke at practice. I only had to stop and tread water twice, which for me is a huge accomplishment. Still, I'm pretty sure my form is so bad that even if I manage to complete all four laps in the actual race, I'll probably be disqualified.

Coop's hanging on the pool ledge when I arrive.

"Hey," I say, trying to find my breath.

He smirks at me. "I don't see why you're still killing yourself over this. I mean, Kelly's out of the picture now, and I'm sure Valerie doesn't give a crap one way or the other. Why don't you just drop out?"

"I don't know," I say, sliding my goggles up onto my forehead. "I guess I don't want to let the team down again."

"Oh." Coop nods. "I didn't realize you had such a sense of loyalty." Coop's been saying things like this all week at swim practice. It's like he's always in a bad mood.

"What the hell's that supposed to mean?"

"It doesn't mean anything." Coop spits into his goggle lenses, trying to defog them. "Unless you think it means something."

"What are you talking about?"

"Hey, look, I get it, okay? Whole nations have gone to war over the Wookiee's smile." Coop rinses his goggles out. "I'm not surprised you and Sean are bailing on me for it. I mean, I wouldn't do it, personally. But I can see how you guys would."

"We haven't bailed on you."

"Oh no? How many times have we hung out this week?"

"I don't know. I haven't been counting."

"Because there's nothing to *count.* We haven't hung out *once* this entire week."

I'm trying to remember, but everything's been such a whirlwind. "I guess . . . I've been busy."

"Yeah," Coop says. "Busy with Valerie's mouse house. I know."

"Hey. Don't talk about her like that."

Coop snorts. "Whatever, dude."

"Look, I'm sorry if I hurt your feelings."

"You didn't hurt my *feelings,* butt plug. Please. No. I'm just learning your true colors. That's all."

"Okaaay," I say. "Look, why don't we see if Sean wants to go check out a movie this afternoon?"

"You know what? I can't. I've got this funeral to go to. I'm mourning the death of our friendship."

Coop pulls his goggles on, pushes off the wall, and swims away.

I take a deep breath and let it out slowly. This really sucks.

I'm about to slide my goggles down and get back to my fly when I see Sean running over to a bench and grabbing his sister's light-blue towel. He flings it over his shoulder and carries it to Cathy, who's sitting beside the pool.

"Next time I want it quicker, Grunt," Cathy says, yanking the towel from Sean. All the girls nearby laugh.

The poor guy. Sean's really taking one for the team. So why can't Coop see *that*?

Sean scurries over to my lane and slips into the water next to me. "This has been the longest two weeks of my life. Thank God there's only one more week left."

"Sorry, dude."

"Don't sweat it. I'll get by. It's not the first time I've had to be her slave. Besides, it's totally worth it."

Someone clears their throat loud and long. "Are we having a nice, relaxing morning, ladies?"

I glance up to see Ms. Luntz towering over us, her hands on her wide hips, her flip-flop-clad dumpling feet right on the edge of the pool. It's very difficult to look at her. It's like she's walking around naked all the time now. On the bright side, I just can't take her that seriously anymore.

"Maybe if you actually *tried* a little, Gratton," Ms. Luntz jeers. "Maybe then you wouldn't be a complete embarrassment to the team. This is the first time I've even seen you swim butterfly at practice. A day before championships. Did you think all you had to do was just come in your Speedo and you'd magically be good at it?"

I feel Sean kick me under the water. I can see out of the corner of my eye that he's ready to crack up. I try to ignore him.

"I've been practicing, Ms. Luntz. It's just—"

"Excuses are like male nipples, Gratton." Ms. Luntz runs her tongue over her teeth. "They're completely useless."

Ms. Luntz suddenly looks up, a German shepherd catching a scent. "Hey! Wendy Stevenson! That's your fourth bathroom visit this morning!" She points toward the girls' restroom, where Wendy stands frozen, caught in Ms. Luntz's laser vision. "Did we drink a gallon of juice at breakfast this morning?"

Ms. Luntz marches off to deal with the serial-bathroom-goer.

Sean inspects his nipples curiously. "I guess they are kind of useless."

"Let's go," I say. "We better start swimming."

Sean suppresses a laugh. "Okay, but don't think you can just come in your Speedo and magically be good."

I smack the water, splashing Sean, who paddles away, chuckling.

I kick off the wall and start back in with the fly. It feels pretty good that I can start off so strong now. If only I could keep this pace up over four laps, I might actually finish the race without being completely humiliated.

I guess there's always a chance for a miracle.

Like if my appendix actually *did* burst.

CHAPTER FORTY-NINE

CHAMPIONSHIPS

IF YOU WANT TO BAIL, Gratton, it won't matter now."
Ms. Luntz sighs as she raps her clipboard with her pen.
"We can't win the meet unless you take first. You might
as well save yourself the embarrassment."

I'm standing at the fence, my fingers strangling
the chain links, watching the second-to-last race of
the Rockville Swimming Association's Thirty-Fourth
Annual Championships. Where the best of Rockville
meets the other best of Rockville. It's a carnival atmo-
sphere, like always. Everyone's here. Valerie. Mom. Peter
and Melissa. Grandpa Arlo and Mrs. Hoogenboom. Even
Sean's girlfriend, Tianna. There are strings of used-car-lot
flags strung from the diving boards. There are kids running around with balloons and sticky hands. The air is a
swirl of chlorine laced with Doritos and Fun Dip.

Once this race ends, our team, the Razorbacks, will
be tied with Tony Grillo's Dolphins. Which means that

when Tony the Gorilla takes first place in the butterfly, his team will win.

So Ms. Luntz is right. It doesn't matter if I swim or not. At least not as far as the team is concerned. It's a perfect out.

But I've been thinking. About this summer. About how I got myself into this whole mess in the first place. And about what Ulf said about hanging on.

"I'm going to swim," I say to Ms. Luntz.

"Fine." Another long sigh from her. Like I'd just blown her chance to go home early. "Suit yourself." She scratches a long diagonal line across her tally sheet with her ballpoint pen, then turns and walks away.

I stand there, staring through the fence, imagining what would happen if I actually *did* win. Our team would beat the Dowling Dolphins for the first time. Ever. In thirty-four years.

If this were a movie, like *Rocky III,* Tony and I would stare each other down, right until the starter's gun went off. We'd be in a neck-and-neck battle through all four laps. Him ahead, me ahead, him ahead again. Back and forth, back and forth. Until, at the very end, my two hands would smack the pool ledge a fraction of a second before Tony's and I would be lifted out of the water and hoisted onto the shoulders of my teammates.

I see Tony Grillo walking up to the pool gate, stretching out his Popeye arms, over his head. I look down at my own spaghetti noodles and the reality of things slams home.

Kelly skips over to Tony and snuggles up next to him. She's sucking on a Tootsie Pop, hugging his forged-from-steel body. They turn toward each other and they kiss. Obviously they've made up. I can't believe I was so crazed over her.

I turn and look up in the bleachers. Valerie's there, sitting with my family. She smiles and blows me a kiss. I wave back. She got dressed up for the occasion. A little white skirt. A purple blouse. She did her hair and put on makeup. I tried to tell her that she should skip this particular swim meet unless she wanted to witness a drowning.

But she was having none of it.

"You might need medical assistance after the race," she said to me, laughing. "And I give better mouth-to-mouth than Tony."

"Next up," the announcer calls over the PA. "Our final race of the day. The boys' fifteen-and-over one-hundred-yard butterfly. All swimmers up to the blocks."

Tony Grillo and Ernie Plingus, a short, round-bellied kid from the Barracudas, head up to the starting blocks.

I breathe deep and start to go, but someone grabs my shoulder.

"Dude." It's Coop.

"Hey," I say, facing him. "My race is starting."

"I know." Coop stares down at his feet. He looks up, giving me a closed-mouth smile. "I just wanted to wish you good luck."

"Thanks."

"And . . . to apologize. For being such a deer hoof about you and Valerie."

"Don't sweat it," I say. "Besides, I should be apologizing to you."

Coop screws up one eye. I can't tell if it's the glare of the sun or what. "Anyway, I've made it up to you."

"What do you mean?"

Coop looks around and then quickly flashes an X-Acto knife. "Let's just say I happen to know where a certain someone's mother does their wash."

"What?" I have no clue what he's talking about.

"You'll see." Coop claps me on the shoulder. "Now get going, dawg. Kick some Gorilla ass." He spins me around and gives me a little shove.

I step through the gate and join Tony and Ernie behind the starting blocks.

The starter is a man in his sixties with a handlebar mustache. He stands next to the diving boards and reloads his gun. Tony Grillo and Ernie Plingus shake out their arms and legs. I wish I could say that I was feeling confident. That just being true to myself and not giving up was all that really mattered.

But the only thing I feel is a cold-clam-chowder nauseousness. I didn't sleep five minutes last night. I must have swum this race in my mind a thousand times. And every race ended the same way. With five lifeguards diving into the pool to save me.

I glance over at Tony. He shoots me a quick, dismissive

sneer. But there's no stare-down. It's like he barely registers my existence. Tony rolls his head around his pro-wrestler neck. He looks straight ahead and slips his black Lycra cap over his thick, wavy hair. Slides his mirrored goggles over his eyes. The scar on his lip flutters a little.

"Go, Matt! Go, Matt!" I hear Valerie cheering from the stands. I turn and see her waving and leaping and smiling. This eases the grip in my stomach a little.

And then, standing right by the fence, I see Ulf. What the hell is he doing here? He doesn't smile, just gives me a little nod like he's proud I didn't bail out. I'd like to say that it bolsters my confidence to see him standing there, but it doesn't. It just amplifies my terror.

Two blocks down, Ernie Plingus pulls on his green swim cap.

I struggle to untangle my blue goggles. My hands are shaking. My fingers are cold, and they don't seem to want to obey what my brain is trying to tell them. Finally, I give up and just tug the goggles over my head. The twisted rubber strap yanks my hair and then snaps.

"Damn it," I mutter.

"Here. Take mine," Sean says, hurling his goggles over the fence. They land at my feet.

"Thanks," I say, picking them up and pulling them on.

The starter walks up to the side of the pool, with the loaded gun at his hip. "Swimmers, on your marks."

I step onto my starting block. The textured plastic prickles the soles of my feet.

"Get set." The starter raises his pistol.

I curl my toes over the edge of the block, knees bent, back straight, leaning forward, head down.

I'm ready. Waiting for the sound of the gunshot.

And that's when I hear a loud ripping noise. Like someone's just torn a T-shirt in half.

My first thought is that I've split my bathing suit. I barely have time to glance between my outstretched arms to check before I hear the loud BANG of the starter's pistol.

I spring off and into the air.

Right before I hit the water, I hear a cacophony of shrieks and laughter. I have no idea what's going on, but it'll have to wait until after the race.

When I surface, I find my sloppy rhythm. The first length goes by pretty fast. I spin off the far wall of the pool and start on my second lap. I glance to my left and see I'm keeping pace with Ernie. Tony is long gone. He's probably done and drying off already.

Each time my head lifts from the water, I can hear the cheers of the crowd over my breath. And then it's the *whoosh* of the water and the muted thump of my heart. I know the cheers aren't for me, but I pretend they are, anyway. I use them to keep me moving, even as my arms and legs quickly drain of usefulness.

On to the third lap now. I look over again and see that Ernie and me are still neck and neck. There's a chance I could actually take second. But I don't know. I'm starting to drag.

I lift my head, and a swell of water flushes up my nose and into my mouth.

The chlorine burns my throat. I start coughing. I'm tempted to break stride and start swimming freestyle.

But something keeps me going.

I hit the wall and turn into the final lap.

CHAPTER FIFTY

SWIM THE FLY

I CAN SEE THE END OF THE SWIM LANE. The starting block. The timer lady wearing a pink baseball cap, crouching down with her stopwatch. She glances to her right, and then she focuses back on me.

Everything burns. My muscles, my lungs, my eyes. I want to hang on. I do. But I just don't know if it's physically possible. My brain says go, but my body is quitting on me.

Then, out of nowhere, Valerie drops into my mind. Her laughter. Her sweet smell. Her cheers.

And the image of her moves me forward.

I trawl through the water.

I will my head, my arms, my shoulders up.

I force my legs to give one last kick.

And I slap my hands into the ledge.

Finished.

Thank God.

I turn my head and see Ernie Plingus floating into the wall like a dead sea lion pushed onto the beach by a wave.

Ernie looks over at me and shakes his head. He can't believe I beat him. And neither can I. I'd smile if I didn't feel like throwing up.

"Congratulations," the timer lady says.

"Thanks." I drag myself from the pool. My arms are dead.

The timer lady looks at her watch and laughs. "I think it's a new record."

"Oh, yeah?" She's making fun of me, but that's okay. I'm just happy I finished.

"Well, I can't imagine anyone else has ever come in first with a worse time. Three minutes, forty-six seconds."

"First?" As I say this, I see my entire team surging through the gate. They're all headed toward me, whooping and shrieking.

Mom and Grandpa Arlo and Peter and Valerie are caught up in the pack, but they are leaping and smiling and waving.

"How is that possible?" I say.

"Tony Grillo was disqualified." The timer lady smiles at me. She steps aside as all the Razorbacks swarm around me.

There's a chorus of screams. "You did it! You did it! We won! First time in thirty-four years! Holy crap!"

Coop and Sean are right beside me, slapping me on the back.

"Tony breached his Speedo." Sean laughs.

"You should have seen it, dude," Coop yells over the crowd. "He flashed his saddle bags to all of Rockville. It was friggin' awesome."

"He leaped from the starting block and ran into the bathroom," Sean says.

I narrow my eyes at Coop, who smothers a laugh. "It's amazing what a few light strokes with a sharp blade will do to Lycra."

"You're insane." I crack up and fling my arms around my two best friends.

We walk through the crush of our cheering teammates. Three of the most out-of-shape champions you'll ever meet.

I glance over to the fence and see Ulf walking toward the parking lot. It's strange. I was wishing he hadn't come, but now I'm glad he was here.

"So," Sean says as we approach Valerie and my family, "this has been a totally kick-ass summer. The only thing is, how are we supposed to top it next year?"

"Oh, I don't know." Coop smiles big, looking over at a busty lifeguard in her *Baywatch* Speedo. "I'm sure we can come up with something."

"All right!" Ms. Luntz screams. "All Razorbacks on the bleachers for the team photo." She blows the hell out of her ear-piercing whistle. "Let's go, people! Move it! Before the Tricentennial."

As I pass Mom and Grandpa and Peter, Mom gives me a confused glance.

"I thought you guys took your team photo weeks ago," she says. "With the shirt and tie and towel?"

"Uh, yeah," I say, my eyes sliding sideways. "I'll explain later."

Valerie comes running up and wraps me in a hug. *"Très magnifique!"* She plants a big kiss on my lips right in front of the entire Rockville Swimming Association.

"Merci," I say, which gets me another kiss because we've found kisses work even better than candy with the French lessons.

Shannon Motts starts singing "We Are the Champions," and even though a few people grumble, Coop, Sean, and me join right in, and soon the whole team is belting it out as we make our way up onto the bleachers for our first team photo as gold-medalists.

Ms. Luntz does her best to arrange us roughly by height, with the taller swimmers at the back, but Sean pretends not to know what's going on and sits right next to Coop and me, even though his face will probably be hidden by Gregg Zuzzansky's big head.

The photographer adjusts his camera. He points the

lens at us and says to smile. As if he really needs to tell us this.

"One, two, three," he says.

The shutter snaps and the flash pops, freezing us all in time.

And with that, the summer is officially over.

ACKNOWLEDGMENTS

I am indebted to many people for helping make this book what it is. My deepest gratitude and thanks to: Kaylan Adair, for plucking my manuscript from the slush pile, for her tireless and exceptional effort in editing this manuscript, and for putting up with my countless e-mails and questions about everything from em dashes to Jolly Ranchers; Liz Bicknell, for her comments and suggestions and for being the mysterious and encouraging "editor behind the scenes"; Jodi Reamer at Writers House for her guidance, wisdom, and direction; Ken Freeman and James Fant, my writing-group cohorts, for their brilliant, writerly advice; Christianne Hayward and her Lyceum Book Clubs for their enthusiasm and recommendations; Caroline Lawrence, Kate Cunningham, and James Weinberg for all their hard work on the design of this book, inside and out; Hannah Mahoney and Karen Weller-Watson for their eagle eyes in copy editing; Sharon Hancock for championing this book to schools and libraries; and everyone at Candlewick—people whose names I may never know (though I'd like to)—for all their hard work in getting this book into shape and getting the word out.

Most of all I want to thank my wife for just about everything, including seeing a novel in a couple of short stories I wrote, and for not leaving me alone until I wrote it.